Theo Tomasis met Liz Cassidy

at a party at his home in the south of France. It was a party where the beautiful people swam, drank and glittered. Theo's wife was hostess, and his star-actress mistress was there too, as well as other women he had wanted for a time—and had had. But Theo had eyes only for Liz. In fact, he was so interested in keeping her near that he summoned an ex-head-of-state to come and keep Liz's ambitious senator husband occupied.

Theo Tomasis, the Greek tycoon,

could arrange almost anything if he wanted it enough—and now he wanted the wife of the man who would someday be President of the United States.

Allen Klein

presents

Anthony Quinn   Jacqueline Bisset

in

THE GREEK TYCOON

starring

Raf Vallone

Edward Albert

Charles Durning

Luciana Paluzzi

Camilla Sparv

Marilu Tolo

Roland   &   Robin
Culver   Clarke

and

James Franciscus

as

President James Cassidy

Co-Producers

Nico   Laurence
Mastorakis   Myers

Story By Nico Mastorakis & Win Wells and Mort Fine

Screenplay By Mort Fine

Produced By Allen Klein and Ely Landau

Directed By J. Lee Thompson

AN ▚▚▚ FILMS PRODUCTION

A Universal Release

THE GREEK TYCOON

A novel by Eileen Lottman

Based on a screenplay by Mort Fine
from a story by Nico Mastorakis & Win Wells
and Mort Fine

WARNER BOOKS

A Warner Communications Company

WARNER BOOKS EDITION

ISBN 0-446-82712-6

Warner Books, Inc., 75 Rockefeller Plaza, New York, N.Y. 10019

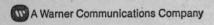 A Warner Communications Company

Printed in the United States of America

Not associated with Warner Press, Inc. of Anderson, Indiana

First Printing: May, 1978

10   9   8   7   6

CHAPTER ONE

Rough seas and very high stakes were his elements, a raunchy ship and a lusty woman his
pleasures. When the cutthroats or the authorities
were at his back, and the gamble was for millions, Theo Tomasis felt the blood roaring through
his body like an adolescent boy's, energy building
inside him until it burst forth in a satisfying spew
of conquest. And he was always the winner. No
one had his energy, his power, his daring; there
was no match for him in the world of men hedging
their bets, governments protecting their borders,
women accustomed to having their own way. It
was Theo's way that won the game, any game,
because he was intimidated by no one on earth.
His joy in winning never paled; life was a riotous,

rough-and-tumble game, and his secret weapon was his love of the contest itself.

He climbed up the hatchway from the radio room to join the captain on the bridge of the *Hellas* with a grin on his weathered face, brimming with the excitement of a new, secret victory. In his early sixties, Theo was still a handsome man, with craggy features and eyes that were bold and laughing.

"Are they still on our tail?" he shouted off the wind to the captain, who huddled deep inside his oiled sweater and souwester against the brutal North Atlantic gale.

"Yes, sir!" the captain responded. "Two patrols, about a mile astern."

"Keep 'em that way for a while," Theo ordered. The sea was high and there was a heavy chop as the waves crashed in irregular rhythm against the hull of the old tanker. She surged upward and dashed down again, making no forward speed, riding the rough weather like a giant ox. Her bow was pointed, her engines set low ahead; she creaked in protest but she would stay afloat. Rust-rimmed, in need of paint, the *Hellas* rose and dropped again through the icy waves and mist-fogged morning, screeching as her screws lifted above the waves, sighing with resignation as she dipped again and the heavy spray washed over her decks. His wool cap pulled down over his ears, Theo Tomasis let the icy saltwater redden his cheeks and fall away as he peered into the gray sky, listening.

Below decks, the tanker had been converted into a modern factory, with neatly arranged rows of Sven Foyn harpoon guns and stainless steel equipment for flensing, peeling, and boiling down the illegal catch. Huge vats of rendered whale blubber were stored in the hold, a valuable source of oil that most countries had agreed not to pillage. Not all countries, but most—including his own.

Theo's eyes danced with anticipation as he surveyed the overcast sky, and a great burst of laughter escaped his throat as he caught sight of a tiny whirring insect through the mist. It swooped down, a helicopter, circling low over the tanker and then following its wake to the two patrol boats.

"Hey, Karayannis!" he shouted to the captain. "They want to declare war on me! Let's give 'em a war, Captain, what do you say?" He grinned, savoring the battle. "Go! Invade Norway! Let's go!"

The captain gave the order, and the *Hellas* turned her nose toward the shoreline, twelve miles off in the enshrouding fog. The helicopter hovered, then yawed sharply as one of the patrol boats reverberated with a fiery explosion. A burst of flames and an eerily muffled roar cut through the cold wet mist, and the tanker bobbed on a downcresting wave just as the cannon's shell shrieked across her starboard bow. It landed in the sea, swallowed in the maw of a twenty-foot surge. Silence followed, except for the revved-up engines of the *Hellas* as she plowed her way toward land.

Now the patrol boats began to move in, flanking the tanker. The *Hellas* had crossed the international limit and was in Norwegian waters.

The helicopter circled the superstructure once and set down on the aft deck. Three men got out as Theo and the captain strode down the deck, clinging to the life ropes, to greet them. They shook

7

hands quickly, formally, and some papers were exchanged.

The Norwegian Navy tender pulled alongside and the commander boarded, with an entourage of sailors carrying sidearms scrambling up the ladder behind him. In an orderly military march, they made their way aft. Theo, Captain Karayannis, and the new arrivals stood waiting for them. The blades of the helicopter still rotated in the gale-force wind.

The commander wasted no time in calling off the charges, addressing himself to the vibrant presence of the man who was clearly in control. There was something about Theo Tomasis that immediately signaled to anyone in his vicinity that he was in charge. At the opera, on board a grungy tanker, on his own magnificent yacht, at any dinner party or in any dictator's palace, it was Theo Tomasis who drew the eyes of all, and the attention and respect.

". . . hunting whales out of season under the flag of Greece," the commander was saying, ". . . Greece being a signatory to the International Convention . . . and now, in Norwegian waters. Mr. Tomasis, your cargo and your ship are impounded."

Theo smiled with the utmost civility and warmth. "Ah, but there is a mistake, my friend," he said. "I am a guest. On this ship I am simply a guest. For the ride."

". . . and you are under naval arrest. You and the captain. Karayannis?" The commander turned to the captain, who followed Theo's lead by smiling as genially as he could under the circumstances.

The men who had alighted from the helicopter

8

were silent, watching and listening and waiting. They also smiled pleasantly.

"But the captain of this vessel is not Karayannis," Theo said. "The captain is Ishawara. Not Karayannis." He nodded toward the three men who stood slightly apart from them. They were Japanese. Two were dressed in dark business suits and overcoats; they clung to their hats with stiff gloved hands. The other wore the uniform of a Japanese merchant sea captain. Theo addressed the latter in his own language. "Captain Ishawara, say hello to the Norwegian Navy," he said.

The new captain smiled and bowed low, an admirable feat of balance in the face of a gust that pounded over the rail and washed at their feet.

"What the hell is going on?" the commander shouted into the wind.

"You should return his bow, Commander," Theo admonished the tall, broad-shouldered Norwegian. "After all, Ishawara's got a new ship, he is to be congratulated. Do it, Commander. Give him a nice bow." Theo didn't bother to hide his delight at the commander's discomfort. The Japanese waited.

The commander managed a small, quick bow in the general direction of the three men, who returned the gesture gracefully. He turned to Theo again. The bewilderment on his wind-reddened face was slowly giving way to anger.

"I see," he said. "He came on that 'copter." His blue eyes squinted against the wind and peered at Theo for an answer.

Theo nodded. He put his arm around the commander's shoulders and walked with him to the rail, out of the lee shelter behind the superstructure. The gusts of wind and water forced them

9

both to grip the rope with all their strength. But Theo seemed to enjoy the ferocity of the weather and the need to shout above it.

"I have to admit, Commander, you've been a very big problem to me," he said. "Two months we've been chasing whales through forty-foot seas, twelve thousand miles from the tail-end of the world . . . and you won't let us make port."

He pointed off toward the coastline. "Less than twelve miles, and we're running out of fuel, and you bring your Navy to greet us." He shook his head, admonishing the commander for his inhospitality.

"Let me tell you something," Theo went on, as if in chatty conversation at a dinner party, but still shouting to be heard. "Life is a progress. It is not a station. Everything moves, constantly; one cannot sit back and say—ah, now I may rest, allow myself to be carried along as a ship at sea . . . ah, no, one must never rest. To rest is to die. So if I must sit on a ship going nowhere off the coast of Norway, I must think of a way to make this a progress, too. So . . ." He stopped and grinned, tightened his arm around the commander's shoulder, and took a dash of brine in his face before continuing in the same even tone. "So I did a little business. I wired London, and I did a little business."

He turned from the rail and pointed forward to the ship's bow. The commander followed Theo's gaze. The Greek flag was being lowered from the staff, flapping wildly against the wind.

The tall, fair Norseman scowled, briefly puzzled, and then grunted with understanding and frustration as the new flag slowly climbed the line. Now the ship flew the Japanese colors. The realization

10

of what had happened, under his very nose, hit him with a strong mix of admiration and fury. He turned to the laughing man at his side. Theo raised his hands in a simple, internationally understood gesture.

"Maybe you can interest the Japanese in signing the whale-hunting convention," he said helpfully. "It is between you and them now."

"You sold the ship," the commander muttered in amazement.

"Every day is a small life, Commander," Theo said. "A modest enterprise. One makes of it what one can."

"You son of a bitch." The commander was really more impressed than angry as he paid his dubious tribute to the sheer guts of the maneuver. "You sold the ship. In the middle of the ocean . . ."

"Oh, yes, and the cargo, too." Theo admitted.

The commander stared at him, shook his head and moved away from the rail toward the three Japanese, who were standing more or less at attention as their flag ascended the bowstaff. As it finally snapped into place at the top of the line, the men relaxed visibly, smiled at each other and shook hands all around. Then they looked toward the commander and Theo and bowed with a quick nod to each, clearly eager now to take over and at least get inside out of the weather.

"They own a tanker and a whole lot of whale oil now," Theo said. "Eight million dollars worth. I think we ought to give 'em a bow, what do you say, Commander?" He bowed, and so did the furious, frustrated Norseman.

The sailors, still clutching their sidearms, followed the commander in quick march down the

11

deck, and in a moment the tender was roaring away. The second patrol boat circled the *Hellas*'s bow and followed its leader to disappear in the fog.

Theo and Karayannis climbed aboard the helicopter and the pilot lifted off. In a few moments, they set down at the little airfield in Tromso, where Theo's Lear jet was standing by.

In the jet, settling back in the huge tan leather recliner, Theo picked up the telephone transmitter and made several calls, while the captain sipped his brandy and gazed down at the quickly passing terrain below. The fog cover lifted as they headed south: along the magnificent fjords of the Norway coast, over Bergen and Stavenger, across the Skagerrak Straits, back into the clouds over the lower North Sea, and then Amsterdam, Brussels, the Somme Valley, the narrow tracing of the Oise River, and Paris.

"I want a hot bath first, and then some lunch," Theo told his Paris secretary over the plane's phone. "Order the oysters, they do them so well. Lots of them, dozens. And . . . send over to Chez Laurence for a bit of their paté, just a bite or two. I'm in the mood for some of that. And . . . oh, whatever else. I don't care. And place the following calls for me . . ." He listed a score of names, in cities that spanned the globe. "Have 'em on the line in the bathroom, I'll talk to them while I soak some of this salt out of my hide. Get the tailors up there by two-thirty, no later. I can't spend all day on fittings, you know how antsy that makes me. I want to be home for a party this afternoon. No, I won't be staying overnight. Well, tell the ambassador I can't make it. Invite him down to the house instead if he wants to talk to me. I'll see you in an hour or so. How's the traffic? Make sure the bathwater's good and hot. . . ."

The limousine he kept in Paris met him at the airport, and the skillful driver managed to avoid the perennial congestion of the approaches to the city by maneuvering through back streets. Theo strode into the lobby of the Georges V, not unaware of the stares and whispers. In his rubber boots, thermal trousers and patched wool sweater, with the watch cap still settled on his thick graying hair, he was a startling sight to the quietly elegant crowd that murmured among the velvet furnishings and crystal accoutrements of the hotel. But the manager greeted him with warm delight.

"Ah, Monsieur Tomasis, such a long time we have not seen you! Welcome home, may I say?"

"*Merci*, Jacques. Everything goes well for you?"

"Oh, yes, yes. You will find your apartment ready, as always."

"Thank you," Theo said, clasping the well-tailored shoulders. He strode to the elevator with the manager stepping briskly alongside. "How is your fine young son, who had the skiing accident?" Theo asked.

"It is kind of you to remember. He is well, completely recovered. He will not limp."

"Good, thank God, hah, Jacques? Give him my regards. A fine boy."

"*Merci*, Monsieur Tomasis. I will, surely. If everything is not exactly to your satisfaction, you will let me know at once?"

Theo stepped into the elevator and nodded, with a warm smile, just before the doors closed between them.

A man's son is his universe, Theo thought as the silent rococo car whisked him to the top floor of the hotel. When you ask a man about his son, he knows you truly care for him, for his hopes and dreams.

The longing to see Nico hit him forcefully, almost like a physical blow as the elevator glided to a stop. Two months away from home, it was too long. The boy was twenty-one already; grown almost to a man behind his father's back. He was away too much.

Delightful Anne-Claire. She had his bath ready, steaming and filled to the brim, and his calls lined up, his appointments scheduled, his lunch waiting in heavy silver tureens on the terrace. Within four hours, he was finished with Paris and on his way south again.

He took the controls himself, to dip low over the châteaus of the Loire Valley in tribute to the extravagances of another century, and then headed for the Riviera. He flew close to the rocky promontory that traced the shoreline, in a heady race against the uncertain winds that darted around the Corniche, those rocky cliffs high above the sea. He loved the feeling of freedom as the jet skirted the little villages clinging to the hillsides along the water, and the vast blue of the sky all around him and the Mediterranean spread below. Sighting the little harbor at Monte Carlo, he circled low over the pink palace and the nearby Casino, which he owned. In the harbor, he surveyed the array of trim sailing yachts, motor launches, and speedboats. There was his brother Spyros' three-masted schooner, black and sleek and the second-largest private vessel in the world. And there was

La Belle Simone—bigger, more beautiful, world-famous—his own. She dominated the little port, sitting proudly on the water like the queen she was.

Theo headed the Lear high again into the clear cloudless sky, up from the seductive panorama of white sails and azure sun-sparkled water, toward home. He thought briefly of Tragos, his own island, as much home to him as any place in the world. But he was at home here too, in the sky, and on the wildest seas, afloat on *La Belle Simone* or in any important city on earth. Wherever he turned his head, there was a home waiting for him, just for him, finely decorated and well-staffed with servants and cars and a closetful of his shoes and clothes, ready for his impromptu appearance at any moment. Tragos was his special island, and it was Greece. The slums of Athens where he had grown up no longer existed for him. The island he had bought and made fertile, where water was brought in daily on three great tankers, where he reigned as sole monarch . . . but that was not where he was heading today. His fine, beautiful wife waited in their villa on the mountaintop he circled now, on the Riviera near Antibes. And his son.

CHAPTER TWO

"Nico," the young girl sighed, nuzzling with her lips against his neck, "you're not really concentrating."

The young man sighed and pulled away slightly from the naked flesh pressing against him. The float bobbed on the surface of the pool with the weight of their two firm slim bodies. It was hot, the sun was baking his head, it began to ache. He thought of rolling over, tipping them together into the cool water. How nice it would be to sink, sink, sink into the silent, undemanding cleanness of the depths. But this was his father's pool, and someone would find them. The girl would be hurt and rejected if he tipped them over, even as a joke. He lay quietly with his arms around her, his eyes closed against the beating sun.

"Nico? What's the matter?" she asked.

"Nothing, nothing," he answered. "I'm sorry. Nothing's wrong. I guess it's just the sun. Too hot."

"Too hot for loving? Anyway, how can the sun bother you, it never did before. You love the sun. You're Greek!"

"I said I'm sorry, Leila. Is it so important, making love, right this minute?"

The girl sat up, tipping the float dangerously. Nico fought the impulse to slide off into the inviting water. He guarded his eyes from the glare with one hand and peered at her. A lovely, slim wisp of a girl, her smooth skin brown from endless days of sun, small round breasts no whiter than the rest of her, across her bottom a minute strip of cloth that was no more than a crocheted piece of narrow string. She was lovely—and eager.

"You don't want to make love with me. You don't care for me any more?"

"Oh, come on, Leila. Don't make an international incident out of it."

"You're too young to be tired of love, Nico. Twenty-one is too young not to care about making love. It's all right, I understand." She leaned over suddenly, and slithered headfirst into the water, making hardly a ripple as she dove straight down. Relieved, he rolled in after her, but let his weightless body float in the opposite direction from her deft strokes that headed toward the fountain at the far end of the pool. He lazed to the surface and shook the water from his hair, breathing deeply, and then dove again with the delicious sensation of being suspended, with no demands on him, no sounds, no world.

When he rose to the surface again, she was

17

there treading water and waiting for him with a questioning look on her shining wet face.

"It's all right, but tell me true, Nico. You don't care for me any more?"

"It's not that, Leila," he said slowly, between gasps for air. "I . . . I'm just preoccupied. Thinking about things. It's time I started thinking about . . . well, business. Things."

"Oho! I see now! Your poppa is coming home today! You are scared of your poppa, that's what."

She flicked her open palm across the surface of the water, splashing his face, and broke away from him with long, smooth strokes. She reached the side of the pool and climbed out, looking around the lounges and tables in search of her discarded bra top.

Nico treaded water, watching her.

"I'm not afraid of him, Leila. You don't understand at all, do you?"

"You want to tell me?"

"I told you. I've decided to start in the business, that's all. It's a big decision."

"Also, you don't want to be like your father, I know. When you think of poppa, you think it is wrong to make love. Because he does, so you cannot. I understand more than you think, Nico."

"Yeah, I know. All those psychology courses at the Sorbonne."

"Nico." Leila squatted at the edge of the pool to look closely into his face. He held onto the tiled edge with one hand, as if prepared to sprint away. "Nico . . . your father is a good man. He loves you. I know that. You know that too. Why are you so intolerant of him?"

"I'm not! You really don't understand a damned

thing, Leila. Stay out of the psychology business, will you? Jesus!"

"You are afraid you are too much like him, that's what I think. When you make love to me, you are thinking, 'am I as good a lover as he?' Am I right, Nico? That's right, isn't it. You told me so."

"You're terrific, you know that? I tell you something personal, something so private I can hardly even think about it, I tell you in a moment of tenderness . . . and you throw it in my face now. That's rotten, Leila, really rotten. Go to hell."

"Yes. All right." She stood up slowly and walked away from the dark eyes that glared after her from the sun-sparked pool. She waited for him to call her back, but he did not. As she rounded the far end of the circular tiled courtyard near the fountain, she looked back. Nico was nowhere to be seen; he had ducked beneath the water. Leila sighed and headed toward the dressing rooms.

"Leila?" he called out.

She turned. Only his head was visible from this distance, a solitary dark floater in the enormous expanse of water.

She didn't answer him. She was crying when she entered the loggia. The maid who offered her a huge white fluffy towel and escorted her to one of the dressing rooms didn't notice. It wasn't her job to notice anything.

Theo let the pilot bring the plane down at Mandelieu. The Rolls was waiting for him, the driver standing at attention with the door open as Theo alighted from the plane.

He made only one phone call from the car, to Simi. Then he settled back to relax, with the same

19

compressed concentration of energy that he brought to every moment of his life. He relished the vista of sparkling blue sea below the road, and the pale beaches where one could glimpse the oiled sleek bodies of nubile sun-worshipers dotting the sand like toasted almonds on a cake. One or two wore narrow bikinis across their bottoms, delectable ornaments to catch the eye. The road curved upward along the mountain, and he marveled at the beauty all around him, thinking of Simi who waited at the top.

She would be dressing for him now, in something long and white and simple, with a subtle Greek motif to emphasize her classic blonde beauty. He had chosen well. His wife was a true Grecian treasure, outwardly cool as marble and eternal as the finest works of antiquity, and underneath as torrid as the beating sun of Greece itself. A fine woman, an aristocrat. Over twenty-three years married to the same woman, and still he felt an urgency when he approached her.

The car rounded the crest of his mountain and passed the only other villa, just below his own, hidden by high walls and fourteen acres of trees between the road and the house. Suddenly he tapped on the glass and motioned the driver to pull in through the gate, which opened at their approach. The gatekeeper raised his hand to his cap in a semi-salute as the driver began the series of turns that brought them to the front entrance of the villa.

Theo leaped out of the car before it had quite come to a full stop, and threw open the door of the house.

"Sophia!" he bellowed.

"She is resting, sir," whispered the little maid who came running from another room.

"Good," Theo nodded. He took the steps three at a time and burst into the bedroom at the top of the wide landing.

She was brushing her long black hair at the dressing table, and admiring herself shamelessly in the mirrors. Her eyes never left her own image, but she laughed her low throaty laugh when he entered the room.

"Sophia. Sophia."

"Welcome home," she said. She put the brush down and turned to receive his kiss.

"How was the voyage, Theo. Did you manage to find someone to fuck? An Eskimo, perhaps?"

He grinned. "What Eskimos?" He shrugged and lifted her to her feet, holding her closely. She was wearing a diaphanous nightgown, soft to the touch and transparent enough to be maddening. "In the Antarctic, nothing but penguins!"

They embraced and their hands clutched at each other, holding and caressing hungrily. In a moment they were on the wide bed, and rolling with laughter and loving murmurs in each other's arms.

"It was quick," she commented lazily in her heavy Italian accent. "You are going somewhere?"

He sat up. "Home," he said. "I haven't been home yet. Simi's expecting me."

"Ah, yes." She got up from the rumpled bed, pulling aside the silk drapes that hung from the ceiling track fifteen feet overhead. She pirouetted around the room slowly, draping her nightgown's folds to one side and then the other, studying the effect in all the mirrors that lined the room. He peered at her with wry amusement as he reached down for his shoes.

"You like my nightgown, Theo?"

"Very much. Very, very much."

"That's good. Because it cost you quite a lot of money. Um . . . about twenty-eight thousand dollars, I think."

"For a nightgown?" This woman could always surprise him; no one else could. He laughed out loud. Theo knew the value of women's clothes, he knew the value of everything that could be bought, and yet Sophia never lied. It was a game. He entered into it with the same zest he brought to every game. "For a nightgown, twenty-eight thousand dollars?"

"Well, you see, I saw a girl, an American, skinny little thing, no tits at all . . . but she was wearing a sweet T-shirt, on the quay at Cannes. A simple little nothing, but cut so well, it would have looked wonderful on me, so much better. I asked where she bought it, and she said at a little boutique on Madison Avenue."

"In New York," Theo finished, beginning to see the light.

"Yes, of course. Well, there you were somewhere on the high seas and God knew when you were coming back. I was a bit bored, and ah, it was such a nice little T-shirt. It cried out for breasts, real breasts . . . round, like this."

Theo nodded. He was knotting his tie.

"I suddenly had a terrible urge to stroll through all the little charming boutiques along Madison Avenue, up and down."

"But twenty-eight thousand dollars, Sophia. How did you manage to spend that much, even on the airfare and the T-shirt and the nightgown. How many boutiques did you visit?" His grin was wide, indulgent, as if he were being told a delicious, complex, slowly-unraveling joke on some-one else.

"Well, you understand . . . an impulse, my darling. I had to do it—zip, like that, at once."

"Oh, yes, I understand. So?"

"So. I am loyal, as you know, I would take no other airline but yours, of course. But—oh, Theo, they said there were no seats that evening. All sold out."

"Good," he said. He sat down on the wide blue satin chair. The story would not be completely amusing, there might be a catch somewhere. It began to seem like there would be. There usually was, with Sophia.

"So . . . I had to use a little push. As I have learned from you, my darling."

"You had everybody bumped. The tickets had to be refunded."

"Yes."

"Bitch."

"But Theo, you love the nightie, yes?"

"What else did you do? A planeload of passengers, even with the first-class section sold out, comes to $16,597.33 only. The nightgown cost $11,408.67?"

"And the T-shirt. And a few other things I picked up, you know. I strolled the entire length of the Avenue. It was sweet there, so cool in New York. One needs a coat this time of year."

"A mink?"

"A sable. It's really very cool there, in September."

"Sophia—"

"Yes, my generous lover?"

"How much did the nightgown cost?"

"I told you. Twenty-eight thousand dollars. And some odd change."

"For tips, no doubt."

"No, Theo. That I absolutely saved money on. I didn't even stay overnight, no tipping bellboys, room clerks, nothing like that. Not even a taxi. Well, I did hire a car, of course, with a most handsome driver. Nice, too, but what I gave him was only his fee, plus a little something extra for being so nice. But not a single extra lira Sophia, I said, one must draw the line somewhere."

"Clever girl."

"I knew you'd be pleased."

"You should be spanked."

"Peasant."

"Trollop."

"Beast."

"Whore."

"Let me see you smile, Theo."

"Let me see the coat."

"It's not here. It's in cold storage in Paris. Too warm here, the poor little thing might catch the mange in this sordid heat."

"And the T-shirt?"

"It didn't look so good on me as it did on the poor little titless girl, after all."

"Come here, Sophia."

"You're not angry?"

"No. I have something to tell you."

She curled up in his lap, letting the soft silk of the gown brush against his face. She nestled herself close to him and found the easy fit of her body

24

with his that had become familiar to them both. His hand caressed her thigh beneath the fabric as he talked.

"Simi has given me an ultimatum."

"Pooh. It's not the first. She'll get over it."

"No. This time she meant it."

Sophia's anger was as quick as his. She pulled away from him. Rage made her large eyes flash and her breath rose in a pulsating danger signal. Theo knew it well, but he held her firmly at arm's length and kept his voice calm.

"I have agreed that you will not come to my welcoming party tonight."

Sophia looked as if she would spit; instead she laughed. Her laugh was slow and deep, rising with the power of her dramatic training—a performance. Theo's relief at the unexpected reaction was a bit uneasy.

"So I am not welcome on *La Belle Simone* tonight, to welcome you home with the others?" she roared. "I am not good enough to mingle with your fine guests any more? I am to creep quietly around, in the alleys, waiting for your pleasure, hidden away? Not my style, Theo, not my style!"

"But you will, Sophia. You'll do exactly that. For a little while."

"Hah!"

"Or I will not see you again."

"You forget that I am not a nobody, Theo. It is too late for me to assume the role of a shy little flower, waiting for my master's command. I am Matalas!"

"Yes, and I made you."

She stood up, furious, and turned on him with

clenched fists raised in the air as if to bring them down on his head.

"I am Matalas!" she screamed.

"Bravo," he said wryly, and clapped his hands as if in bored applause. "Now shut up and sit down, and show me your famous smile."

"Go fuck yourself, Tomasis! I don't need you!"

He stood up slowly. "*Ciao*, Sophia," he said. He started to leave the room, expecting her to throw herself in his way, but she stood alone and magnificent in her rage, reflected thirty times over in all the mirrors, as if waiting for the curtain to descend on the second act. Theo went to the door. He turned back briefly.

"I'll see you tonight, after the party," he said. "I'll come to you, and you'll throw yourself at my feet and cry with those great big glycerin tears and ask to be spanked as you deserve. But I'll be tender with you, little Sophia. It will be good, very, very good. Until then."

He walked out, slamming the door a split second before the actress, in the finest tradition of melodramatic frustration and rage, hurled a Tiffany china box to shatter loudly against the mahogany paneling.

The Rolls was waiting for him, purring, and he motioned the driver to take the back exit from the property that led through the forest out onto his private road again. Within five minutes, the car was entering the grounds of his villa. Here the trees had been placed to enhance rather than hide the view. Sweeping down on all sides from the main house, the grounds overlooked the sea in three directions and the jagged mountains to the north. There was something absolute about the villa and its grounds and its view from the mountaintop. Something absolute about the sprawling house and the winding road lined with sculptures and fountains that approached it, something that said: Theo Tomasis is the owner here, absolute monarch. A benevolent man, friendly, happy, generous to a fault and perhaps loving to a fault as well, eh? But make no mistake, Theo Tomasis owns it all.

When the car pulled up at the entrance, Theo didn't wait for the driver to open the door, but leaped out and strode into the house.

"Simi!" he called. His voice echoed in the huge marble hallway, sent tinkling chords along the great chandelier hanging thirty feet above his head. The tapestries along the walls could not soften the sound of the owner's voice. They had been purchased at a huge price from the government of Spain, illegally brought out of that country through the generous auspices of a dictator who found the green of Theo's drachmas and pesetas more alluring than the delicate colors still living in these museum pieces. But it had been worth the price. Other tapestries all over the world had faded into monochromatic memories of what they had originally been; in El Escorial Palace, the dry cold of the mountains outside Madrid had kept the colors intact, and now the best of them belonged to Theo Tomasis. On another wall in the entrance hall hung other masterpieces—Utrillos, Van Goghs, a Matisse, a Renoir. Their bold splashes of color and experimental forms made a satisfying contrast to the delicate, subtle stitching of the Renaissance artists.

Theo waited for his wife's entrance with relish,

savoring the magnificence of his possessions in a mood that reached as close to tranquillity as was ever possible for him.

"Welcome home, Theo."

He looked up the high, curving staircase.

She moved down the wide steps with a grace and nobility that was inborn. Daughter of the wealthiest shipbuilder in Greece, married to the man who had supplanted him in power and money and ambition, she fit her role perfectly. Simi Tomasis was slender, full-bosomed, beautiful. Twenty years younger than her husband, she pretended not to love him as desperately as she did, because the passion he aroused in her threatened the calm and serenity she knew was necessary to keep him. She would never age, never allow herself to crack or crumble. As she descended the stairs, she performed the entrance as she knew he wished her to, and he stood below admiring her elegance, her elusiveness, her impeccable classic style. He had guessed correctly; her gown was white, long, and simple, with geometric Grecian-key embroidery along the hem. A silver belt, a single diamond on her hand, and around her neck the heavy silver necklace he had given her for their anniversary—five years ago? Ten? He couldn't remember.

"Beautiful," he murmured as she reached the lower steps.

She smiled. "How was your voyage, Theo? Successful?"

"Very successful, my love. As always. Almost." He grinned and reached out his arms to her. She went easily into his embrace, holding him closely.

"Simi . . . ah, Seeemi . . ." he sighed against her

sweet-scented hair. It was gold and shining, caught in a smooth knot against her patrician neck.

"You were missed," she whispered, as if afraid he might hear her and sense the real emotion behind the words. She lifted her head from his shoulder, and looked into his face. "Welcome home, Theo."

For an instant, it seemed to them both that he might sweep into his arms and carry her up the stairs. But her serene elegance—the thing he loved most about her, the thing he feared and worshiped, the quality that attracted and excited and terrified him into feeling like a peasant again—made him step back from her.

"Where's Nico?" he asked.

No one could have seen the touch of disappointment that shadowed Simi Tomasis' eyes for the briefest flicker; instantly, it was gone.

"Your son is with your guests," she replied. "Enjoying the sunshine."

He took her hand and led her through the echoing empty salon to the wide french doors opening out onto the lawn. They followed the rose-lined pathway down the long slope, past the tennis courts and the fruit arbors to the pool.

The Olympian pool was perched on a terrace that jutted out over the private beach and boat docks. One leg of the pool was nearly a hundred feet long, for serious swimmers; Theo himself swam four laps each morning when he was in residence here. The pool curved then, and in the center of the circular end was a marble fountain depicting a small boy holding two fish in his arms. Fresh water sprang in an arc from each fish's mouth and in jets around the boy's chubby feet to splash against his laughing marble face. The circular part of the pool was ringed with guests now, who milled about in costumes ranging from the barest bikinis to full-length flowing djellabahs. The rich sounds of conversation punctuated with laughter mingled with the playful splashing of a Scandinavian starlet and her portly, aging companion in the shallow end of the pool. She was tan, but he was tanner. White-coated waiters circulated among the guests with trays of chilled champagne and warm hors d'oeuvres. Diplomats, oil sheiks, rivals in the shipping trade, famous artists and spies from every major power in the world mingled with the most beautiful women on the continent. These were the movers of the world, the usual relatives, friends, business consorts and rivals who did business with Theo, or wished to.

"Ah, Theo! Welcome home!"

Theo greeted them all, genuinely delighted to play the genial host. He loved people; they were part of the mystery of life which he found ever-lastingly fascinating and freshly challenging. His warm, firm handclasp and the brief moment when he turned his full attention to each of his guests left them with the feeling that they had been touched for the moment by something special. Whether it was simply his aliveness, or his Midas touch, they felt quickened by the encounter and sincerely happy to be in his presence.

He circled the pool, greeting each guest, bolting back a glass of champagne, laughing, touching, pounding his male friends on the back, kissing the women's cheeks. He reached the prone form of a lovely girl, stretched out alone on a beached rubber raft, sunning herself with only the briefest string across her slim derriere. Lying on her stomach, she turned her face to him as his shadow fell across her.

"Hey, Leila!"

"Hello. Welcome home." She smiled, a bit shyly. "Where's Nico?"

"Oh, Nico. He's waterskiing, I think," she said.

"Not with you? I thought . . . you and Nico . . ." He smiled at her with the full thrust of his concern. Leila reacted with a blush.

"Theo!" Someone called, a low, throaty woman's voice. He turned from the girl to greet his wife's closest friend.

"Penny, hello. How lovely you look today."

She was a stunning woman of thirty, just at the peak of her ripening beauty, full-bodied and sensuous. She was dressed in a dark satiny cotton frock with bare string straps, cut to skim her body like a promise. Her long tan legs were shown to exquisite advantage in jeweled sandals. Her hair lay shining, soft and warm against her sleek bare shoulders.

She put her arm through Theo's with the authority of a close family friend, and led him a few steps away from the others, under the wide awning that fronted the loggia outside the dressing rooms.

"What happened in Zurich, Theo?" she murmured softly. "I waited a whole week for you in Zurich."

"I was chasing a great white whale, Penny," he answered. Their smiles as they chatted betrayed nothing more than a friendly interchange of small talk to anyone who might observe them. "Call me Ishmael," he went on, referring to *Moby Dick* and to a more private matter as well, "or call me what-

31

ever. We'll do something soon," he promised casually.

Penny kept her voice low, seductive and undismayed. "Yes, arrange it, will you do that? Paris would be lovely."

"Paris?"

Simi Tomasis came up to them, catching the last word, and echoing it pleasantly. "When are you going to Paris, Penny?" She kissed her friend's cheek. Penny, her arm still through Theo's, widened her smile to include his wife.

"Soon, maybe," she said. "I was just telling Theo . . . very soon, I hope."

"Can you wait a few weeks?" Simi asked. "And I'll go with you. But first, Theo and Nico and I are going sailing, just the three of us. Remember, Theo? You promised, before you went whaling. When you came back?"

He remembered. If he came back, they had said. If. She had left it up to him, as if she really believed that he might decide to go to Matalas instead. Had she really thought that he might choose between them? Of course he had come home to her, as he always did. She had taken this as a sign that all was well, that the earlier promise of a family holiday would seal the "bargain." Well, why not? It would be good to get away with just Simi and Nico, to spend time with his son again.

Theo's attention wandered as his wife and sometime-mistress chatted about their plans. He loved the richly variegated mix of people who always gathered to enjoy his hospitality. The world's most elegant women, the most powerful men, their conversation like music and their company a tribute to his own achievement. He needed people around him; he drew special pleasure from the new faces that graced his parties, people he didn't know yet, always the cream of the social and economic and political crop—people drawn to him because of his reputation, people whom he could conquer with his civility and wit and intelligence. Everything, everybody was a challenge to Theo, and his blood quickened easily at the prospect of winning the respect, the friendship, and—yes—even the love of the whole world.

He glanced over the familiar faces, nodding genially as eyes sought his . . . his brother and rival in business, Spyros; his sister-in-law Helena, drinking too much again; other relatives, old friends, recent friends, faces that smiled back eagerly at him. A chubby Iranian in full turban and robes raised his wineglass to Theo from the other side of the pool. The backsides of two slim young women wiggled as their heads craned to peek at him from their floating lounges. Down the slope on the wide green lawn, Theo's eyes followed a waiter who was bringing food and drinks to someone at one of the umbrella-shaded tables.

One of the men at the table was known to him from the newspapers: a young United States senator. Theo's memory raced through his mental computer and came up with the name: Cassidy. Senator James Cassidy. Bright, liberal, charismatic, with growing influence in the government. Also known for the grace and beauty of his trend-setting wife, Elizabeth, known to intimates and to gossip columns as Liz, or even Lizzie.

Theo stared at her across the forty-foot width of the pool and knew she felt his attention focused on her. She did not look at him, but moved a bit in her chair, as if his gaze had telekinetic powers. She was in her early thirties, about ten years younger than her husband. They were an extraordinarily attractive couple, tanned and healthy, lithe and smiling with the unassuming aura of two who have inherited the best the earth has to offer. There was a subtle imperiousness to the tilt of her chin, her straight back and nonchalantly crossed tan legs. She wore a simple one-piece maillot swimsuit.

". . . and we do want to spend about a week on Tragos," Simi was saying to Penny. "We haven't been on Tragos for so long."

"I don't know how you keep from being bored there," Penny answered. She pretended not to notice when Theo slipped his arm away from hers. "That whole island with nobody on it except servants . . ."

"How was Zurich, Penny? You haven't told me about your trip. What on earth did you go to Zurich for?" Simi's question was neither suspicious nor probing, just making amiable conversation. Theo moved away from them and the two friends went on talking, accustomed to his casual abandonment.

Making his way around the party, he was stopped by every guest to be wished a hearty welcome home, and almost everyone wanted to know about the famous whaling expedition. He smiled, and touched, and kissed, and moved through the sunny groups with ease until he fell afoul of his sister-in-law.

Helena Tomasis was a few years younger than Simi, and might have had the same classic Greek beauty, except that her taste ran to the unrestrained in too many areas. Her version of the Greek theme in dress was a Givenchy toga, wrapped and draped dramatically, overplayed with huge hooped earrings and upswept hair that fell about her flushed face in carefully untidy ringlets. Her wide-set dark eyes were outlined in makeup to exploit the natural slant, and her mouth was a slash of sweet thick paint. She planted a sticky, open-mouthed kiss on Theo's lips, and her arms went around his neck in a clinging embrace.

Behind her, Helena's husband Spyros shrugged his shoulders and spread his open hands as if to say "what can you do?" There was a wide grin on his face.

Spyros Tomasis was a formidable competitor for Theo, tough and smart, as willing to gamble as Theo himself, and no more fastidious about other men's rules. He was a stocky, powerfully built man in his late fifties. Always rivals, the two brothers had married the two most beautiful and wealthiest women in Greece—daughters of a rich shipbuilder. The brothers had proved to be not only rivals between themselves, but competition for their wives' father. There were three indomitable forces in the world's shipping industry now, all closely related through marriage, as loving and genial in business among themselves as sharks feeding on fresh meat. Fortunately, there was enough meat to go around. But each wanted it all, and there was no honor among sharks. It kept the blood racing, it kept the family ties taut, and though neither Theo nor Spyros would admit it, they wouldn't have it any other way.

Gently, Theo separated himself from his sister-in-law's grasp. He held her at arm's length. "Let me look at you, Helena. Let me look. What a beautiful thing, to look at you."

"You love me, Theo?" she asked, her words slurring from an overage of champagne, probably laced with vodka.

Theo grinned expansively. "What a thing to ask. Why do you have to ask?"

"Who doesn't she ask?" Spyros muttered from behind his wife, with a guttural stab at a laugh. He came up to them.

"Why didn't you wait for me, Theo?" Helena was pouting, almost whining, trying to nuzzle up close to Theo again.

"Because Theo is a robber, but not the cradle, eh, Theo?" Spyros took the empty wineglass from his wife's hand and replaced it with another, filled. He wound her fingers carefully around its bowl. She raised it to her lips without looking away from her brother-in-law's eyes.

"You should have waited for me," she said, nodding and taking a long gulp of the champagne.

But Theo was looking elsewhere now. The Cassidy table was empty. Spyros put his hand on Theo's shoulder and led him toward his own table, where they sat down together. Abandoned, Helena frowned and finished off the wine in one gulp. The glass dangled from her hand and she moved toward a group of three men who stood talking earnestly. She almost stumbled, but caught herself, smiled brightly, and interrupted them with a huge smile and kisses for all.

"Hunting whales," Spyros was saying, "For Christsake, what for . . . what's the sense to it?"

"You should try it some time, Spyros . . . get

away from all this. A little fresh air in your lungs. Do you good."

"Skata . . ." Spyros spat in disgust. "Bullshit, my friend," he went on, chuckling low. "To the South Pole for a little fresh air? Jesus!"

He leaned toward Theo, smiling. "My Helena says you got on a tanker because you needed time to make a decision. She says your wife gave you a choice: her or the actress. Is that right, friend? What's it going to be, you going to divorce Simi, or you going to give up Matalas?"

"Hah? What?" Theo's attention had wandered. His head half-turned in one direction and then another as he glanced casually over the guests. Then he turned back to Spyros. "Your wife drinks too much," he said. "She talks—it's a pity." He started to get up from the table. Spyros put out a firm hand and stayed him.

"Wait, wait, wait. Sit down, Theo. I have something to tell you. Sit."

Theo sat down. "You want to talk crap, or have you got something to say, Spyros?"

Spyros sat back, enjoying the moment. "You remember the *Selena?* The tanker, the big tanker?"

Theo knew the *Selena* very well, and his interest went on red alert instantly. But his face revealed nothing. He too leaned back, as if resigned and impatient for his brother to be finished with the small talk. His glance wavered deliberately from Spyros's eager face, off toward the sweeping vista of the pool and his guests clustered around it, down the slope to the beach, and back to Spyros, then off to the side where Helena Tomasis was laughing loudly, her arms draped around a man in brief swimming trunks.

37

"Forget it," Spyros said, hard put to contain his glee. "Forget the *Selena*. It's mine. It belongs to me now."

"Oh?" Theo responded, apparently unconcerned, even bored.

"Your friend, Christopoulos . . . Christopoulos got a little bit squeezed. He needed a million five to cover the banks, Theo—and where were you? With the whales!" He couldn't hide his delight, and Theo's casual disinterest didn't fool him for a minute. "With the icebergs and the whales!" He laughed loudly, pounded the table once with his fist. "A beautiful ship, the *Selena*. You always wanted her," he said, nodding.

"True," Theo admitted. He showed no emotion, but looked at his brother now, waiting for him to go on.

"The papers come from Athens tomorrow. I sign them . . . we'll go to Piraeus. I'll give you a ride," he offered, expansive in his victory. "What do you say, Theo?"

Theo grinned suddenly, leaned over to slap Spyros's knee, and stood up. He gestured toward Helena.

"Go to her, take care of your wife," he said.

Spyros sighed. "I wish I could lend her to somebody."

"So you can rent that black girl again?" Theo said quietly, shrugging his shoulder in the direction of a slim black woman who lay motionless on the diving board. "She tells people that you scream obscene things in bed. Ah, Spyros!"

He walked away from the table, scanning the guests to find the Cassidys again.

"Theo?"

It was Simi, calling to him from a few feet away. He turned and saw her approaching him with the American senator and his wife. How magnificent they were, really! Simi was a fine match for them, with the breeding and style that only money can buy. A lifetime of the right food and expensive exercise, the best air and the finest wines, milk and orange juice and the heady company of world leaders at the family dinner table. Simi growing up in her father's mansion overlooking Mount Parnassus was as beautiful in the blood and flesh as Elizabeth and James Cassidy were with their heritage of the bounties of the New World. His heart swelled and pounded in his chest as he held out his hand to the senator.

"You haven't met Senator Cassidy yet, Theo," Simi said, "and Mrs. Cassidy."

"Mr. Tomasis," the handsome young man said warmly. "Thank you so much for the afternoon." His grip was firm and sincere.

"Getting ready to leave?" Theo exclaimed with genuine dismay. "Why do you have to leave? Why?"

"We must," Liz Cassidy murmured.

Theo turned to look at her. Her voice was gentle and soft. She was a delicate kind of beauty, despite her generous mouth and huge wide dark eyes. Something vulnerable, almost frail about her aristocratic bearing, something possibly hot and boiling beneath the cool unruffled surface. In an instant he knew that he would have her someday. Some day. He could wait, the prize would be worth the waiting. This was a woman unlike any other he had ever known. Their eyes met for the merest instant, and Theo turned back to her husband.

"Stay for a while, Senator," he urged. "We can get acquainted. Why not?" His famous smile and eager warmth extended to both of them. He turned back to her. "Stay," he said quietly.

"I'm afraid we can't," the senator responded. "Maybe another day, before we leave Antibes."

"James, I'm getting rather chilly," his wife said. The sheer flowing wrap that matched the sea-green of her bathing suit offered no protection against the afternoon breeze. The transparent fabric danced softly against her body, emphasizing rather than concealing her almost too-thin figure. But the breeze was warm and caressing, the sun still burned from high in the cloudless sky, and Theo understood her complaint as a signal—not yet a conscious one—that the chill she felt was not caused by the weather.

"How long will you be here?" he asked the senator.

"I really don't know. It depends."

"But we're making a party tonight! Aboard the *La Belle Simone*. Lovely people! Everybody!" Theo's enthusiasm was hard to resist. But the charm was not working on the senator's wife.

She was accustomed to having her own way. Theo recognized that quality and admired it. But he, too, had his habits, and winning was the one he cherished most. The senator's wife was rich and beautiful—was she also ambitious? There had been rumors that the senator was moving up quickly, an election was coming. Liz Cassidy would not let her whim, or even a little warning chill, step in the way of that.

Making a shrewd guess, Theo spoke quickly to the senator. "Robert will be disappointed. He wanted to meet you. He asked." He had the senator's attention now; the intelligent dark eyes sparked with curiosity. "Robert Keith," Theo finished.

"The prime minister asked to meet me?" The senator was not flattered, but definitely interested.

"Yes. Fantastic man, a close friend," Theo said.

"James, we've made other arrangements." Liz Cassidy spoke quietly, her husky voice belying the bland finishing-school accent. There was passion here, controlled, but deep and rich.

"I'm sure they'll understand, Liz," the senator said.

"Wonderful! Any time after dark, hah, Senator? Mrs. Cassidy?"

Theo was rewarded with a polite smile, the subtle salute of the vanquished in a private jousting match. Neither Simi nor James Cassidy was aware that the contest had been waged, but Theo felt the pulsing in his veins and would have bet a million U.S. dollars that the lady felt it, too.

"A boat will pick you up after dark," he said, smiling warmly.

"We'll look forward to it. Thank you." The senator shook his hand again. They murmured their thanks to Simi and turned toward the water.

Theo watched them descending the rock steps to the boat dock. The senator put his arm around his wife's shoulders and said something which she answered with a nod. Theo thought he could guess what they were saying.

"Robert Keith wants to meet me . . . a man who helped to change the world. I wonder why he wants to meet me?"

And Liz Cassidy probably answered, "Yes, that

is a thought, isn't it?" But nothing more. She was clever and contained. And she loved her husband.

Theo and Simi stood at the top of the slope, watching the Cassidys walk out onto the pier and step down into their small motor launch. The beach below was a wide, curved, white-sand bathing area, framed by the rock jetties where the boats were tied up. High masts of sailing yachts and tenders bobbed in the water alongside the piers, and now and then a speedboat would maneuver in or out of the marina, carrying the vibrant voices of the guests across the water as they called to one another.

"Theo?" Simi was holding him lightly about the waist, and her eyes were on him instead of on the pleasant view below.

He turned to look at her.

"Robert didn't ask to meet Senator Cassidy. You haven't even spoken to Robert since you've been back."

He grinned. "No, but I will."

A boat with a water-skier behind was rounding the outermost edge of the harbor. A beautiful sight, a graceful male body, holding taut to the lifeline and skimming over the water like a god. Theo sighed for his own youth, a time when he might have become an athlete, felt the pure thrill of physical challenge, grown hard muscle and worn the laurels that belong only to the young and fleet. He had spent those years meeting other physical challenges—how much weight he could carry on his back, how long he could stand at an anvil, how fast he could run with other men's messages—no time then for games other than survival.

"Is the senator such an important man?" Simi was asking him.

"Oh, yes," Theo answered. The graceful young man on waterskis leaped the wash of an outgoing motor launch and soared over the granite rock that marked the rim of the jetty, clearing it by inches and landing with ease on the calm inside waters of the marina. "Very, very important . . ." Theo saw the young man let go of the lifeline as the boat careened to avoid crashing onto the rocks. He skiied the water alone now, momentum and balance carrying him in toward shore.

Theo ran a few steps down the slope, leaving Simi alone. "Hey, Nico . . . Nico! Hey, Nico!" he called out.

Nico glided onto the sandy shore, stepped out of the skis, and fell into the embrace of a lovely girl in a flesh-colored bikini who waited for him on the beach. He didn't hear his father calling at first; when he did, he stepped back from the young woman quickly.

"Poppa!" he shouted. He threw back his head and sparkles of water flew from his sleek brown hair. Nico was a fine-boned replica of his mother, as if he had inherited none of Theo's sturdy peasant genes. His body was slender, coltish; his eyelashes long and dark and his olive skin translucent. As if to make up for what might be interpreted as frailty, Nico took chances.

It was time to train him for responsibility, for business. Theo had spoken to him about this once or twice, but Nico had shied away, dashing out to prove that he was a man by flying his plane, taking chances on the water, riding wild horses, pushing himself in the kind of risks Theo didn't understand.

43

Together, Theo knew, they would make one hell of a team. It was time. But now, how handsome he looked in the sun, his wet body graceful and glistening like a statue carved by the hand of the ancients. Theo hugged the boy close to him, wetness and all.

"Nico . . . Nico . . ."

"Welcome home, Poppa."

"I saw you skiing. I didn't even know it was you out there. Now there's a fine young man, I said to myself, strong and daring, beautiful."

Nico stepped back from his father, embarrassed. "How are you, Poppa? How were the whales?"

"Fine, fine, the whales were fine. It's a good story, I'll tell you all about it. Put one over on them, sold the ship in international waters, made a nice profit too."

"Well, welcome home," Nico said.

"How are you, Nico? How does it go?"

"Okay."

Theo put his arm around the boy's shoulders again, as if he hadn't noticed the slight rebuff. "Okay, hah? Everything's okay!" He leaned his head close to Nico's and boomed out in a man-to-man chuckle, "The girls treat you good, hah?"

He gestured toward the girl who waited a few yards down the beach. His son grinned and shrugged. The girl watched them, her eyes shaded by one raised hand. Above, on the stone steps, Simi watched them too.

"Ah, it's good to see you, son," Theo said. Impulsively, he hugged his son closer to him. It was hard, sometimes, to find the words with Nico. It was curious. Theo Tomasis always had the right word for everyone, in business or love or politics.

44

But with his son, who meant more to him than all the world, sometimes lately there was a certain awkwardness. The boy was growing up, almost a man. Hell, he was twenty-one, a man already! At his age, Theo had made and lost his first million dollars.

He drew the boy a few steps down the beach, away from the women. "It goes well, Nico?" he asked. "The girls, the skiing, you have a good life, hah?"

"Sure, Poppa. But . . . it's time I started to work. My own life . . ."

"Hah! Exactly what I wanted to talk to you about. I have been thinking about exactly that. Listen . . ." In his enthusiasm for the plan that was shaping in his head, he dropped his hand from his son's shoulder and began to gesture with sharp, jagged, open-handed thrusts in the air. "That uncle of yours, Spyros, says he's buying the *Selena*."

Nico was silent, listening with more respect than interest.

"Fuck him," Theo boomed with a single finger jabbing the air. "We'll buy it right out from under him. What do you say? You like that?" He looked for response in his son's eyes, which were downcast, staring at the white sparkling sand.

"It's between you and Uncle Spyros, Poppa," the boy said.

"No, no, no! Listen . . . it's for you, Nico. I'm going to buy the *Selena* for you. What do you think, hah?"

"Why, Poppa?" Nico's eyes met his father's now.

The boy had a mind of his own, but Theo was damned if he could read it. What kind of a question was that? Ah, well, it had been a long time

45

since Theo himself had been so young, it was hard to remember. But surely at his age, Theo would have known right away "why" if someone had offered him a tanker. He thought briefly of the difference between his hunger at that age and his son's comfortable life. It wasn't the boy's fault. He had to be patient with him, to explain, that was what a father was for. To educate him, to bring him along. His heir.

"So you'll own a beautiful tanker!" he said. "So my son will start his own fleet, get into business. Like his poppa."

Nico startled him with a quiet, humorless laugh.

"What's the matter?" Theo exploded, his patience at an end. "What's the matter with starting out by buying a tanker?"

"Nothing," Nico answered. His laugh had frozen into a resigned expression, almost as if he were the one being patient. "Nothing at all, Poppa. It's very generous of you. You give me everything, Poppa. Now a tanker, to start my own business. My own?"

"What do you want to do, bust your ass on the docks, like me? Roll cigars with your spit? Like me? I did it all, Nico! Enough for both of us."

"Okay, okay," Nico said. His eyes, so like his mother's, flashed now with the fire that was more like Theo's own. "Let me start my own business my way, Poppa. Let me do it myself," he said quietly.

Theo didn't understand. "So?"

What the hell was the big difference between what he offered and what the boy seemed to think so important? Of course it would be his own business, hadn't he said so? The boy could do it in his own way, of course he could. His father was only trying to help him. The *Selena* was a beauty, and an important way to start. And screwing Spyros was the best part of all, the spice that made the feast worth having. Why was the boy so slow in understanding that? A little help from his father, what was so wrong about that?

"Let me buy the tanker," Nico said. "Not you. Let me prove that I can do it without you. Let me do the negotiating. I want to deal, okay? To bargain. All of it. Me, Poppa. Not you. Me. Okay?"

"Fine, fine. Sure, Nico. That's what I want for you."

"Otherwise, Poppa . . ."

The passionate nature he had inherited from Theo was tempered and made into steel by that cool aristocratic control; the boy would go far, farther even than his father, Theo thought. One more generation and there would be no Spyros, his son would have it all.

"Otherwise," the boy concluded, "if you want to screw Uncle Spyros, do it yourself."

He turned to go back to the girl who waited for him on the beach.

"Wait, Nico."

The boy turned around, waiting. "Buy the *Selena*," Theo said. "Go ahead, do it yourself, all by yourself. I want you to. By yourself, okay?"

Nico stared at him. The sun glared into his eyes, but his gaze was steady. "Without you on my back, Poppa," he said. "Either I make it happen myself or I fall on my ass. Myself."

"Buy the tanker," Theo said. His hands reached out expansively in a gesture that said he was out of it, handing it all over to his son. He was rewarded with a grin from the boy. What a hand-

47

some lad, bright too, and with a fierce streak of independence. Good. With Theo's power and wealth and guidance, the boy would finish all his father's dreams. Wasn't that what Theo had worked so hard for, for his son?

"Thanks, Poppa," Nico said.

Theo nodded, smiling. "But a little advice from the old man is okay?" he asked, and without waiting for Nico's reply, he went on. "This much advice. Call Christopoulos in Athens. Whatever his deal with Spyros, tell him to cancel. Bargain with him, set a fair price. Then, if he says no . . . then tell him that the government will see the papers in my safe."

Nico stared at him. "That's blackmail," he said.

"Blackmail, shit." Theo exploded. "It's commerce." He calmed his voice. "Go. Buy the tanker, Nico. Okay?"

Nico stared, and finally nodded.

"And listen, Nico, be sweet. Christopoulos is an old friend. Let him have no doubt about the papers in the safe . . . but be sweet. All right?"

He stepped forward to close the gap between him and his son, and touched Nico's shoulder again. It was warm now and dry from the sun. Nico did not pull away. Theo's pat was like a dismissal, and the boy turned to rejoin his waiting companion.

Simi was watching a boat that had pulled out of the little harbor and was now revving up in a wide sweeping arc around the jetty. Theo followed her gaze.

James Cassidy was at the wheel, and behind him a slim tan body rose from the sea like the graceful Aphrodite born of the foam. Liz Cassidy in her pale green swimsuit skimmed the water with her dark hair flying and her body taut with fine control over her skis.

"She's lovely," Simi murmured, "isn't she, Theo?"

"Too thin," Theo commented. He let his hand slide down his wife's back to caress her hip. She smiled and turned to go up the steps, back to their guests. But she didn't remove his hand, even though their son and his girl were watching from below.

CHAPTER THREE

La Belle Simone was berthed in the harbor at Monte Carlo, the only marina deep enough for her on the whole Riviera coast. He could have dredged his own cove to make a more convenient resting place for her, but then who would see her, who would admire her great sleek lines, her proud bearing, her sheer size and stability and unmatchable regalness? Theo was honest with himself. He knew his own need to be admired, to see reflected in other people's eyes the measure of his success. He had run a long way, still ran with the breath and fortitude of the toughest and fastest in the race, and he wanted the laurels that came with winning. He knew it, he admitted it; he used what in other men might be considered weakness as part of his strength. It was needing other people's praise that spurred him onward, in part. *La Belle Simone* was world famous, and rightly so. She had cost nearly ten million dollars to build and outfit.

She was anchored offshore, and in the velvety Riviera night her rigging lights were strung like diamonds against the dark. Her guiding light shone across the water to Monte Carlo, and all the smaller boats were caught in her blaze as she bobbed on the low offshore tide. The guests were arriving. The launches hove to her boarding stairs, and an almost constant stream of splendidly dressed men and women ascended to her deck to be greeted by by their suavely beautiful hostess.

On the aft deck, the helicopter and the small seaplane were secured for the night. The beach buggies, sports roadster, and a Rolls Royce were battened down with canvas against the salt air. A few steps forward and down, the mosaic-tiled pool shimmered quietly in the reflection of the lights overhead. Beneath the clear blue water, Poseidon raged, brandishing his trident in a mood as violent as the sea itself. His long curling hair and dark beard seemed to flow with the motion of the water that covered him. All around were the symbols of the sea-god's kingdom: a dolphin as playful as the god was fierce, a tuna cavorting between the raised forefeet of a shining black stallion, and a bull about to attack the shimmering pine tree from which flowed the constantly renewing fresh water of the pool. The nude Poseidon had caused many comments over the years, particularly among the female guests aboard *La Belle Simone*, who found his enormous specifications either an embarrassment or a challenge. Theo enjoyed his women guests' reactions, whatever they were. And below the water, the god Poseidon prepared for his battle with Athena for the conquest of Athens, the center of the universe. He would lose, as fate had decreed. For Theo, the legend was a private, personal caution; Poseidon had reached too far and had been defeated, yet he still reigned supreme on the sea.

"Still jealous of the gods, Theo?" taunted a cheerful female voice behind him.

He turned with a smile to the lovely woman who had sought him out here in his brief moment away from the evening's crowd. "Now, Penny, you should know that Tomasis has nothing to be jealous of. Why, the frieze was modeled after me, didn't you know?"

She laughed and put her hand on his white-jacketed arm. "Yes, it did cross my mind, once or twice. But it's been so long, I've nearly forgotten."

"Soon, Penny, soon," he said.

They walked back along the pool deck to the wide steps leading to the sun promenade, and past the dressing rooms and day bar, now shuttered but brightly outlined with strings of sparkling lights. Farther forward, they encountered some of the other guests—a starlet in a dress calculated to remind everyone of her sole claim to fame, a nude scene in a Fellini film; two women of a certain age and sexual persuasion who seemed to be having a quiet argument near the library deck; many of the same faces which had spent the long afternoon at the villa, now dressed and coiffed and jeweled to rival the glitter of the bobbing lights of the harbor and *La Belle Simone* herself.

Theo greeted everyone with buoyant pleasure in their company, and gently disengaged Penny

Scott from his arm as he began a conversation with a banker from Geneva. She took the hint and moved off toward the grand salon where the orchestra was summoning dancers to the floor. In a few minutes, Theo joined Simi on the forward deck and played the genial host, greeting a launch-full of new arrivals, kissing the hand of the French ambassador's wife, sharing a joke with a Libyan politician in his own language.

The party was amply oiled and fueled with champagne, fine wines, ouzo and brandy, and a lavish supper set out for a buffet in the dining salon. Everyone seemed to be enjoying the little gathering; there were even one or two guests admiring the paintings and sculptures here and there as Theo sauntered through the yacht, greeting and joking and never letting on that he was looking for a particular couple.

He had welcomed them aboard a half-hour earlier, and had introduced the young senator to the prime minister, who took up his cue with the instant diplomacy Theo had counted on.

"And here, as I promised you, Robert, is the young senator whom you've been wanting to meet, James Cassidy. And his wife, Liz Cassidy. You will have much to talk about, I am sure, hah?"

Robert Keith was, in fact, pleased to meet Cassidy, and mildly amused at Theo's maneuver, wondering what the lively old curmudgeon had up his sleeve this time. Keith was also interested in chatting a bit with the man who had been rumored as a possible candidate for the United States presidency. And his wife was as lovely as her newspaper pictures had hinted. Count on Theo Tomasis to make life interesting.

"I'm very glad to meet you at last, Senator Cassidy. And Mrs. Cassidy, what a pleasure," Keith said with obvious sincerity.

"Perhaps there is a place where we can talk?" Cassidy asked him, and Theo showed them to the library. He had been pleased to note Liz Cassidy's glance around the walls, at the thousands of books and the collection of Picassos. Quality knew quality when she saw it. He had left them alone and gone to the aft deck to muse for a moment by the pool. Now he found the two men in animated conversation, and the lovely Liz, too well-bred to look bored, feigning interest in their rehash of recent history.

". . . and that was our policy at Potsdam," the prime minister said as Theo came quietly into the room. "Churchill insisted on it. He kept insisting, over and over."

Theo stood watching Liz Cassidy intently in the moment before they noticed his presence. She sipped at her wine, her wide doe's eyes never leaving the two men who leaned toward each other, momentarily oblivious to her presence.

"It was your president, your Mr. Truman," Keith said to the senator, "he would think one thing one day, another the next morning."

Cassidy smiled ruefully. "Mr. Truman told me . . . oh, it was years later . . . that at Potsdam, his one experience with Stalin, he wanted to feel him out, to learn Stalin's attitude."

"My boy," Keith cut in, "Mr. Truman knew that Stalin had broken forty-seven treaties since he came into power."

"Why point to Truman?" Theo put in from the doorway. The three turned, startled. "At Potsdam,

54

you all fucked up!" he commented, striding across the deep carpet toward them, relishing their attention, conscious of her eyes on him.

"Fucked up?" Keith echoed in his perfect Oxford accent.

"Fucked up," Theo repeated.

James and Liz Cassidy said nothing, but stared at him curiously as he approached the deep leather couch where they sat.

"Rather graphic," the prime minister commented sourly. "I've never heard it put quite that way before. Fucked up," he repeated again, as if musing on the quaint expression and trying to determine how to deal with it.

There was a moment of dead silence, and then Robert Keith put down his brandy glass, puffed on his cigar, and stood up.

"Would you excuse me for a moment?" he said politely, nodding to the Cassidys. They responded with automatic good manners, avoiding Theo's suddenly distressed eyes. "I'll be back," Keith said, and walked past Theo to the door.

I've gone too far, Theo thought desperately. She thinks . . . they all think . . . they're right, too . . . that I'm a boor, a grotesque, a peasant. I've done it, put my big foot in my big mouth, goddamn it . . . now Keith is off me, and the Americans, too. What a goat I am . . . what a goat after all. . . .

With a glance at the silent couple on the couch, he turned to follow Keith out of the room.

"Theo! Darling! Where've you been all evening, your guests hardly get a look at you!"

"How about a dance, Theo? Won't you dance with me?"

"Say, Tomasis, I've been wanting to talk to you about—"

"Opa! Opa! Hey, Theo, good party, wonderful. . . ."

He made his way past the guests, along the deck until he found Robert Keith, alone. His cigar was a solitary glow against the dark water below as he leaned over the polished mahogany rail.

"Robert . . . Robert!"

Keith turned toward him.

"I'm sorry. I apologize," Theo blurted out. "I'm a peasant, a vulgar peasant, uneducated . . . I shouldn't have said that."

Keith stared at him. Away from the lights, it was impossible for Theo to see what was on his face.

Theo's deep despair was as passionate as his ebullience and came over him as quickly and as completely. Now he felt sunk into a hideous morass of his own making; the thing he most feared was his undoing. All the money and power in the world couldn't change a goat into a god. How had he ever thought he could exist on an equal level with men of education, with women of breeding. . . .

"Oh, God, I'm sorry," he whispered, as much to himself as to the man who stood witness to his shame.

"Theo, you are not a peasant," Keith said quietly. "You are not uneducated. You are a very intelligent man. Your education comes from life, from your incredible understanding of people, of the world as it is. I'm not angry at you, Theo. I'm angry at myself."

"At yourself?" Theo asked, not understanding.

56

Was he to be the recipient of patronizing, charitable pity now? That he would never stand for. He felt the ego rising in him again, as uncrushable as the life force itself.

Keith went on, and as he spoke Theo knew that he was speaking honestly, and that it was not easy for him. Education, formal education, made frankness difficult; Theo had observed that in many men. For him, it was a curse, the instinct for honesty; he had to curb it so often in his dealings with educated politicians, businessmen. And women . . .

"Because what you said is the truth," Keith said. "We did indeed fuck up at Potsdam."

"Hey, Robert . . ." Theo murmured.

"No, don't try to dissemble now, Theo. I am grateful to you for pointing it out so plainly, so exactly. A friend like you is a rare and priceless asset. Now, where's the toilet on this scow?"

Roaring with relieved laughter, Theo hugged his old friend and led him to the doorway of the grand staircase. He pointed toward the long corridor lined with deep red carpeting and said, "Take your pick, Robert, any suite you like. Sitting room, bedrooms, bathrooms, have a sauna, have a massage, stay the night . . ."

Keith laughed too and grasped the velvet rope to start down the steps. "That won't be necessary, Theo, and I don't need your help, either. My lord, what's that racket?"

He shook his head and went on downstairs, while Theo returned to the rail to investigate. Many of the guests had crowded the rail along the port side, looking back toward the source of the noise and excitement. Several motorboats were heading toward *La Belle Simone* full speed, and camera bulbs were flashing. Shouts could be heard above the roaring engines of the outboards and inboards. It was a triumphal parade. All the boats were trailing and trying to surround *La Belle Simone*'s own launch, which bore the solitary figure of a laughing, waving woman in white, with flowing gown and scarf that soared in the wind like living adornments for the proud figurehead.

Center stage on the wide dark waters, against the backdrop of all the lights of Monaco, Sophia Matalas was in her element. The lights all played on her, the entourage of photographers and reporters yammered and contorted to get her attention, the guiding light from *La Belle Simone* was a spotlight for her alone, and the guests lined up to watch her, captivated by her entrance as any paying audience at the theater.

"Hey, Miss Matalas, are you going on a cruise? Or just a party?"

"Hey, Sophia, blow us a kiss!"

The papparazzi flashed their cameras and the reporters shouted their questions as Matalas laughed and waved and posed for them. Theo leaned against the rail in alternate spasms of rage and undeniable amusement. By God, that woman had gall!

"Sophia! Hey, *prego* . . . Sophia!" the reporters pleaded for her attention.

"Hey, Sophia, wave to the yacht and blow a kiss!" a photographer shouted in Italian.

"How long are you staying aboard, Sophia?"

She answered with a full-throated shout, in lusty Italian, with gestures. "I don't know . . . it depends . . . *que sera, sera!*"

They laughed, and the flashbulbs went off like firecrackers at the Feast of St. Anthony. The launch slowed and pulled up alongside the boarding stairs. Sophia stepped onto the platform, pausing to turn back to her admirers and wave as the final explosion of flashbulbs and shouts punctuated her salute like applause. The chief steward handed her up the steps, and she was engulfed by the little knot of guests who had gathered under the flowers that arched the gangway. But not her hostess. Simi had left her post in the greeting area and was nowhere to be seen.

"Hell!" Theo muttered under his breath. But he couldn't keep back the smile that played on his lips. She was something, that one, and a peasant like himself too. He strode down the deck to greet her.

"Theo! How lovely! I'm so happy I could make it, after all!" she exclaimed loudly as he made his way through the people. She would have thrown her arms around him, but he took her hand firmly and led her toward the salon.

"Get your ass in here," he breathed in her ear, "and stop making so much noise!"

She turned her face up to his with a low laugh as intimate as a kiss. He held her arm in a grip that must have hurt, but she only laughed more.

"A drink?" he offered through clenched teeth.

"How nice," she replied, nodding to everyone as they moved toward the bar. Conscious of the stares, she smiled and greeted people as if the party were in her honor. The waiter offered them a tray, and Sophia raised her glass to him before taking a sip. A finger in the air to you, my darling, the gesture said.

The orchestra began to play with a lively, sensuous beat, and Sophia set her glass down on the tray of another passing waiter. Theo shook his head imperceptibly and leaned toward a diplomat who had been trying to get his attention all evening.

"You've been whaling, they say, Mr. Tomasis? But it is illegal, is it not, this time of year?"

"I was a guest on a Japanese ship," Theo answered, turning his full attention to the elderly statesman. "I went along for the ride. Very healthy, nothing like the bite of the North Atlantic for one's health."

"But it was your own ship, surely?"

"Only when we started the voyage," Theo said.

He put his arm around the man's shoulder and began to tell his story. Sophia Matalas's head, too, was close to his great dark mane, and the effect from outside the tight little circle was almost conspiratorial, with the famous actress and the proper statesman listening to the bold and amusing tale. Theo was a famed raconteur. His stories were always wonderful and true and boisterously told, and when he had finished there was a burst of laughter. Sophia's trained tones rang out louder and clearer than the trumpets taking riffs off the rock ballad they were blaring out.

"It doesn't mean anything, Mother. He didn't invite her. I'm sure of that."

"Are you, Nico? Yes, of course, you're right. She has nerve, that one. But he seems pleased enough to see her." Simi's public smile was gracious, effortless. No one observing her and her son in conversation would sense the troubled waters beneath the calm surface.

"He wouldn't be rude to her in front of everyone. I'm sure it means nothing," Nico said.

"Nico, don't defend him. Not to me. It's all right, you shouldn't be concerned about such things. Where is your pretty new girl friend?"

"She's dancing with Spyros. Look at him, his hands all over her. Why do they both have to be such bulls?"

"Nico, I won't have you talking that way about your father, or your uncle either. That's quite enough."

"He promised you he wouldn't see her again, didn't he?"

"It really is none of your business, Nico. What happens between your father and me is none of your business."

"The whole world knows you gave him an ultimatum. If it's not my business, then whose—"

"Good evening, Your Serene Highness. What a lovely gown," Simi said, turning to one of her guests who was passing by.

Nico went to cut in on his girl, who seemed to be enjoying the old-fashioned touch-dancing his uncle favored. They swung into a ragged face-to-face, and soon the other dancers were picking up the tempo and the orchestra took the cue to swing into something really hot and snappy. Suddenly there were many couples on the dance floor, moving as if a signal had been set off by their host's laughter.

Without words, Theo and Sophia glided onto the dance floor together. In the midst of gyrating soloists who moved around and toward and away from each other, never touching, those two were holding each other lightly, drifting slowly in conjoined response to the beat, eyes locked and bodies moving to the rhythm.

Simi Tomasis had her back to the dance floor, and the nondancing guests were too civilized to stare. They murmured about many things, leaving the gossip for first thing in the morning.

When the music ended, Theo released his partner and said, "That's all, Sophia. Now be a good girl, will you?"

"Oh, no. I wouldn't want to bore you," she flashed, but she took the cue and wandered toward two men who greeted her with naked admiration in their eyes. Theo sighed and turned away, his glance skimming the company. In an alcove of the salon, beneath an enormous porthole with one-way glass that looked out on the lights of the harbor, the Cassidys had taken a table, and once more the young senator was deeply engaged in conversation with Robert Keith. His wife seemed to be listening intently. Theo made his way to them.

"And de Gaulle didn't like Pleven," James Cassidy was saying, "he much preferred Daladier."

"Exactly right!" Keith agreed. "Very good. You know your history, Senator."

Theo had guessed right. The two men had much to say to each other. Bringing them together was a good idea. As he neared their table, they looked up at him, nodded in greeting, but went on with their talk. Liz Cassidy also nodded, once, and then concentrated on Keith's words.

"At Tours, just before the collapse . . . de Gaulle and the red wine and the sardines . . . do you know that story, James?"

Theo leaned down and held out his hand to her. She looked up, puzzled.

"Come on," he said. "They're in fine shape, they don't need you. Come on, come on. . . ."

"I've heard several different versions of it," James Cassidy said eagerly to the prime minister. "Could you set it straight for me, finally?"

As Keith launched into the tale, Theo tugged lightly on the slim hand. Liz Cassidy looked at him with her wide brown eyes, but she didn't move.

"Come on. . . ."

"What?" she asked.

"You'll see," Theo said, smiling. "I'll show you. You'll see."

She looked down at their two hands. His grip was strong and gentle, his hand almost square with broad, thick fingers. He held hers calmly, not urging, but waiting.

". . . and there he was, de Gaulle, ready to shout 'à la bataille!' but there wasn't any bloody battle. . . ."

She made up her mind with a nod, and stood up. He still held her hand as she hesitated for an instant, looking down at her husband, who was raptly attentive to the story.

". . . the whole goddamned line was in a shambles, there was no battle at all!"

She took her hand from Theo's and passed it lightly over her husband's shoulder as she rounded his chair. Cassidy looked up at her and nodded quickly, abstractedly, turning his attention immediately back to the prime minister.

"Good God, what did he do then?"

She followed Theo out the near door to the promenade deck, where she stopped to breathe in

63

deeply of the fine sea air. The moon touched her gleaming dark hair with a soft glow that shone through the artificial twinkling of the lights strung forty feet above them.

She knew he was staring at her; the full concentration of his admiring attention was like an electric current in the air and impossible to ignore. She smiled at him, the first real smile she had favored him with. She put one hand on the rail.

"What are you going to show me, Mr. Tomasis?"

"My etching," he said.

Her smile said: how nice. And also: how boring, how unamusing.

He played the game of pretending to think she was interested. She would be, soon.

She stood quietly and turned from him to look out at the sea.

"Come," he said, touching her bare arm. She nodded as if her thoughts were elsewhere—out to sea or perhaps back in the salon—but she followed him. Along the wide promenade deck with its glistening brightwork, past the lighted windows and the music and muted voices, past clusters of guests and couples getting the air, to the doorway amidships which led to the wide marble staircase.

Did she hesitate? Did she falter when he led her down the carpeted corridor and turned into the foyer of the master suite, when he reached into his pocket for the key? No, it was his imagination. Not she, not the chiseled cool American, the senator's wife, the famous beauty of the international society pages. He opened the door and stepped back to let her precede him into the sitting room.

She caught her breath in surprise. Not at the unexpected vastness of the room, or its simple elegance. Not at the vaulted ceiling that reached two decks above to a skylight open to the stars. Not at the white velvet expanse of carpet, the deep red chairs, the enormous tiled fireplace, nor at the expanse of bedroom that opened beyond the arched open doorway. Not even at the indirectly lit paintings—Rouault, Manet, Lautrec, Miro, Dufy, Picasso. She noted them, nodded as if authenticating their origins, but it was the single medium-size etching of the full figure of a man that drew her attention.

He had been right about the senator's wife. She was a thoroughbred, and knew her stuff. She would be difficult, maybe impossible to fool. He would win her confidence, her friendship—and Theo thought no further than that—only by candor, honesty. That was what he had sensed about her in the first moment; he had an instinct for people, and he was rarely wrong. Liz Cassidy was the real thing.

He said nothing, waiting for her to examine the etching carefully and to turn to him for explanation. The artist who had signed the etching was unknown to her.

"My father," he said quietly. "A portrait of a memory, of my father, Plato."

"How it dominates the room," she said. "Even this huge incredible room. This small etching—this man, your father—draws the eye. What happened to him?"

"You want to know? Really?" he asked, almost shy suddenly, caught in a very real emotion in the midst of a game. But he had brought her here as a very special thing; almost no one came into this room, ever, except Simi who shared it with him, and Nico, of course. Why had he brought this American woman here, what was there between them that made his blood race like a boy's . . . more than the simple excitement of the chase. He had no sexual interest in her, she was too thin. And faithful to her husband anyway, he'd bet a tanker on that. Why had he felt an irresistible impulse to bring her here, to show her the portrait? In her eyes, though, he saw that he had been right to do so. She softened now, her eyes frankly interested, intelligent and wanting to know more. She sat on one of the red silk chairs facing the etching, and waited for him to explain as she gazed at it.

"You want to know about my father . . . about this portrait . . . there was one night I remember . . . you want to hear, hah?"

"Yes."

He believed her. And he wanted to tell it. "It was strange," he said, leaning against the wall so he could watch her. She sat with her elbows on her knees, her chin cupped in her fists, listening. "It had been raining for a long time, on this night I remember. Suddenly, this night, when it happened, the moon burst on the town like an explosion of light . . . you know what I mean?"

Her eyes looked from the etching to the man, and she nodded for him to continue.

"The town was lighted up with the moon and filled with shouts and screams . . . and thunder, things blowing up . . . shots. You see, it wasn't the moon alone . . . although I was a little boy then, too little to know what was happening. I thought it was the moon exploding."

Unexpectedly, his face lit with a wide grin as he caught a bit of quicksilver from the complexity of emotions in his memory. He leaned forward to her. "My father . . . you want to know? His name was Plato. Imagine that."

He turned to look at the etching, and they both admired the earthy figure, stepping forward with majestic presence. The man was dressed in Anatolian simplicity and had bristling mustaches. His eyes were fierce, like Theo's own.

"Plato . . ." he repeated.

Liz Cassidy was suddenly uncomfortable, but she couldn't take her eyes from the revelation of raw emotion on Theo's face. It was almost as though he had forgotten that she was there.

She knew other men like this, or thought she did: newly rich, self-made and proud, surrounding themselves with costly works of art to prove that they were sensitive, or at least appreciative, or maybe only able to buy and sell other people's emotions on canvas. But this moment of unabashed sentiment was unaffected, private; she felt almost like an intruder. His forcefulness, his strength were suddenly swept way to reveal some inner nakedness that was totally alien to her experience. She was touched—and curious.

"My father carried me in his arms. He was running. Everybody was running. The church was burning. The Turkish soldiers had set fire to the church."

His voice was unsteady, breaking. She waited.

"The priest . . . I remember the priest . . . he was carrying a big silver cross from the church. They took him, the priest, and put him against a wall in the moonlight . . . against the long white wall . . . and they shot him." He raged inside as he relived the horror, and his face revealed his anger, his hurt. For a moment; then he recovered himself with a little smile. "Ah, the Turks," he said.

"And your father?"

"And my father . . . he put me in a place where they couldn't find me. And later, in the morning . . . from the bridge over the river . . . with others, in a line on both sides of the bridge . . . he was hanging."

Liz was silent. She wanted to reach out, to touch his hand, but she did not. Always controlled, never revealing her own emotions, she watched his handsome, lined face contort and tighten with the memory. She knew that he would continue, and she knew that the story was true.

"My God, I remember," he said. "My mother told me they wanted money not to hang him. But there was no money. That was the day I swore that the Tomasis family would never want for money again."

Liz stood up, uncertain of her own feelings. She took a step toward him, but stopped close to the etching and turned to examine it more closely. Theo watched her.

"He's beautiful," she said simply.

When at last she met his eyes, he knew that he had touched her. Their moment of communion was not long, but it was a kind of sacrament, never to be forgotten by either of them.

Yes, he had brought her here to show her himself, to make her understand that he was human, vulnerable, a man capable of feeling, not the boor he had shown himself to be upstairs in the library. Sure of his strength, he was not afraid to show his weaknesses to anyone; yet no one came here to this room. He had brought her because it was the only way to melt her, to win her to his side. But now that it was done, he too felt something melt inside him, and wondered which of them was, in fact, at the helm.

She looked away from him, back at the etching.

After the silence, he spoke in a lighter voice, the passions of his memory laid to rest. "Actually," he said, "he might have been a very small man, not like that portrait at all. He may have been short and skinny . . . I don't know. To me he was huge and strong. But I was a very small boy.

"Years later, when I was a young man in South America, and there was some money, I went to an artist and told him what I thought . . . what I remembered, in here—" He touched the thick gray hair at his temple. "The way I remember my father. And the etching is my memory of what my father was like."

"You're a very complex man," she said thoughtfully. Her voice was as soft as a child's. "Why did you want me to know about your father?"

Now when their eyes met she saw total candor, as alien in her experience with strangers as the rage and love he had revealed moments before. "So you will know me," he said.

Confused, she pretended not to understand. "Why?"

He smiled. "Because, Lizzie . . . Lizzie is okay?"

She nodded.

"Because if sometime I offend you, you can say to yourself, 'What can you expect, he comes from a peasant. Turks, and Greeks, and little towns. Barbarians. A Levantine. Common.' "

She took her eyes from his, masking her disappointment. Now he was playing a game. She glanced over the enormous suite with its private collection of paintings, its simple, elegant furnishings. "No, you're not common, Theo," she said slowly.

"Sounds fine when you call me Theo."

She shrugged and stood up. "And how could you offend me, Theo?"

He did not touch her, but his voice was like a rough caress, and she almost flinched when he answered, "Oh, I will, Lizzie, I will. Don't rush me."

It was not meant as a joke, and her discomfort deepened. Something stirred inside her, more than compassion or curiosity, a quickening response that she would not name. It was time to go back to the predictable, civilized company that played by the rules she understood. She moved toward the door and he took her arm to lead her from the room. Nothing more was said between them as they moved down the long hallway, but just before they reached the stairs, Theo stopped and indicated the narrower steps going down to the next deck below.

"Will you come with me to see another work of art?" he asked her.

Liz hesitated, and then nodded. She followed him down the stairs to another hall lined with dark paneled doors on either side. They were all closed. Theo signaled to a steward who stood at attention near the stairs, and the young boy quickly took out a large ring of keys and ran ahead to open one of the doors.

Theo strode inside and turned a switch which illuminated only one circle in the small dark room. In the center of the light stood a voluptuous bronze figure of a nude woman holding a sword in one hand, an apple in the other. She was about two feet high, and mounted on a simple square plinth whose patina gleamed darkly. The walls behind and around the statue were stark white, and the concealed ceiling spotlight made her seem the only thing in the room.

Liz Cassidy was impressed, and her response was not entirely due to the breathtaking beauty of the statue. She glanced from the circle of light to the man in semi-darkness at her side. The door behind them was open, the lights from the hallway were at his back, and he seemed to loom very large and silently inscrutable. She looked back at the lovely sculpture and took a step toward it.

"Demeter," Theo said. "The mother-goddess."

He stepped toward the little nude figure and touched it with his thick fingers. He ran his hand slowly along the smooth round shoulder and traced the outline of the statue's upthrust breast.

"She's beautiful, isn't she?" he murmured.

Liz stepped close to him.

"Yes," she agreed softly.

The statue was splendid, a museum piece thousands of years old, delicately cast by the unknown artist. The force of life was represented here, earthy and bountifully created, yet smoothed and controlled through the essential nature of the cold burnished bronze.

But much more than her admiration for the work of art was her wonder and confusion about the man who owned it. His quick changes of mood, from jocular to sad, from sensitive appreciation of such a work to unchecked passion for money and power, caught her by surprise. Fascinated, she watched his strong hands moving sensuously across the gleaming nude figure.

Theo Tomasis was like no man she had ever met.

"The lady of the golden sword," he was saying, "and the glorious fruits. A lady of many mysteries. I love her."

Liz Cassidy tore her eyes away from the mesmerizing sight of his hand caressing the statue. But there was nowhere else to look. Only the circle of light on the statue, reflecting now in his intense face. She hid her disturbing uneasiness in a bantering question.

"A lady of many mysteries," she repeated. "Is that why you love her?"

"Oh, no," Theo said. He took his hand from the statue and half turned back to the flesh and blood woman.

"Then why?" she persisted.

"Because she has great tits," Theo said.

Liz, surprised, threw back her head and laughed.

". . . a very important thing," Theo protested in mock seriousness.

"In a statue?"

"In any woman, in any form. I love all women. Demeter, my wife, you. You understand?"

"I . . . yes, of course. I think we should be getting back now, Theo."

"And I like you, as well. That is also very important," he said as they left the room. The steward, who had been waiting discreetly a few yards down the hall, went to lock the door behind them.

"I like you too, Theo," she said, smiling, conscious that he had deliberately put her at ease again.

"The few sides of me you have seen," he pointed out.

They reached the steps and began the ascent to the upper decks.

He led her back to the salon, where the dancing was continuing more frenzied than ever. The young people had taken the floor; the more sedate guests had dispersed to the dining rooms, the guest suites, the decks. The table where James Cassidy and Robert Keith had been sitting was empty.

The chief steward came up to them with a message.

"Senator Cassidy asked me to tell you he would be waiting in the library," he said.

Alone in the quiet study, the senator was pacing restlessly, glancing at titles of books on the shelves that lined the room. He looked toward the door when they entered and smiled to see them.

"There you are!" he exclaimed.

"Sorry if we took too long, Senator. Your wife is so appreciative of good art, it is a pleasure to show her a few of my favorites."

"I'm sure she enjoyed it very much. It's only that . . . I've had a phone call from the States. I'm afraid we have to leave, right away. I'm sorry."

"A phone call?" Liz echoed. Theo could feel the excitement that vibrated through her as she left his side to put her arm through her husband's. She looked up at him expectantly.

Cassidy nodded, unable to suppress a wide grin. "The National Committee," he said. "There's been a decision, finally."

"Oh, Jim!" she breathed, and he nodded. "I'm so glad," she said with controlled pleasure. They both smiled at Theo, radiant with their news.

"The National Committee?" Theo nodded. He knew what that meant. He understood the politics of many countries besides his own. "That is terrific news, terrific!" he exclaimed.

"There will have to be a formal announcement from the committee, you understand," Cassidy said quickly. "And it is only an endorsement, not the nomination. Nothing official yet, of course."

"Of course, of course! I understand. May I offer my congratulations, Senator?"

He reached out to shake Senator Cassidy's hand, and then opened his hand to Liz. She took it warmly. There were stars in her eyes and a wide smile on her lips that illuminated her face.

"My helicopter will take you back," Theo said, leading the way out onto the deck. "To your house, if you wish, and then to the airport."

"Thank you. Thank you very much," James Cassidy said warmly.

Theo led them to the copter landing and spoke a few words to the waiting pilot. Within moments, the rotors were spinning and the senator and his wife were aboard.

"Theo, thank you for a memorable evening," Liz said, but he could see that her thoughts were already far in the future.

"Any time," he shouted over the hum of the engine. "Have a good trip . . . good luck!"

As the helicopter rose in a vertical arc from the deck, the little crowd that had gathered on the flight deck waved. Then heads turned to look curiously at Theo.

"There goes the next president of the United States," he said, "and the next First Lady."

Voices began to buzz, and some of the people on

the flight deck held glasses high in the air as if to say, "Wait! I didn't get a chance to talk to you yet!" but the helicopter was up and away, heading over the harbor and off into the night.

CHAPTER FOUR

"Is it true, Poppa? Is he really going to be president? How do you know?"

"Ah, Nico. Are you having a good time? Enjoying yourself?"

Theo put his arm around his son and they strolled down to the pool deck, letting the others pass them on the way back through the yacht to the salon and guest suites. Theo stopped at the edge of the pool and looked down at Poseidon, waging his eternal war with the elements.

"It goes, Nico? The thing with the *Selena?*" Theo asked.

"Yes, it's done." Nico was grinning, proudly. "I didn't get a chance to tell you earlier. You were . . . busy. With the guests."

Theo was enormously pleased. "Ah, Nico, Nico!"

He opened his arms to the boy, who hesitated, then submitted to the enthusiastic paternal embrace.

"Tell me, tell me," Theo urged, impatient to hear of his son's triumph. "The details."

"Athens called about an hour ago," Nico said. "Evangelou used his power of attorney and signed the papers. You own the tanker now."

"No! *You* own the tanker, Nico. You see? You see?"

"Oh, Poppa!" Nico's pleasure faded in a sigh. "I wish . . ."

"What, Nico, Nico? What do you wish? Come on, let's walk, and you tell me everything, how you did it, every detail. Such a beautiful night. Come on."

They walked along the promenade, and Nico talked while his father nodded his head, gestured with his hands, roared with delight and alternately hugged and pounded the boy's shoulders.

"I told Evangelou to use the contingency funds out of the Ionian subsidiary," Nico said. "He agreed."

"Nothing escapes you, nothing!" Theo beamed. "How much?"

"About the same as Spyros offered . . . just a little more. The letter in the safe was mentioned—"

Theo interrupted with a shout. "As good as me! By God, Nico, today you did a wonderful thing! You bought a tanker . . . you're going to build an empire! Bigger than me! Bigger!"

The boy was silent, but Theo ignored that in his excited dream for his son. "You see, you see!" he exclaimed, "you go into a deal, go with a loaded gun! That's the way, Nico. Loaded, so you can bring home the meat. Human meat. That's dealing, Nico.

77

That's trade, commerce . . . the whole thing. Believe it, Nico, believe it. It's life, it's drama, it's everything!"

He quieted; the boy's silence seemed to loom as a wall between them. Was it so hard, the first kill? He couldn't remember, but he was sure he'd never had a qualm himself. Ah, but his case was different. There was no Poppa then, helping, pushing, giving him the chance. The boy was still soft, his mother's influence; it was not bad to be soft, but the metal had to be tempered with the fire of real life. He was learning now. He felt burned, perhaps? A little thing, it would heal quickly when the thrill of success washed over him.

"Ah, Nico," he said tenderly, "more than anything . . . listen, more than anything I want in the world . . . you and me. To work together, to understand each other. . . ." His words stopped, dammed for the moment by emotion.

Nico turned a stricken, hurt face to him. His voice was pleading. "Poppa, how can I understand?"

"What?" Theo was confused. How could Nico understand—what? His own father? His lifelong dream that they would be as one?

"Why do you bring her here?" Nico said bitterly.

"Her? Her? Who, Nico?" Theo was thinking of the cool and lovely American who had just left. But Nico was nodding toward a group of guests who stood laughing on the deck ahead of them. Sophia Matalas's laugh rang out, as always, above the rest.

"How can you do it, Poppa? I can't understand you, I never will!"

"Understand what? What is there to under-

78

stand?" Theo said. "Hey son, I am a Greek! Like you! A Levantine!"

To him, that explained everything, the hunger for all of life's moments, the blazing heat of the sun that made the blood simmer and boil over, the lust for knowing all, possessing all, living every moment to its overflowing richness. Petty jealousies and conventions were not for men like him—or his son. Rules of other men did not exist for them. More to the point, the rules that women lived by were bits of gravel to be shaken out of their boots. What was the matter with Nico? Was the boy going to moralize now, to his father? To the man who created him, who gave him life and all the wealth and power he could garner in a lifetime?

Theo forced himself to speak softly, to control his anger.

"I have the right, and you have the right, my son, to live as you decide, as a man. . . ."

"A man, you think a man must be a brute, an animal. I don't understand, I don't want to. Do you know how hurt my mother is, how shamed in front of everyone that you bring your whore here, making an entrance like . . . like . . ." Suddenly Nico broke away and walked quickly toward the rail.

"Nico, Nico," Theo crooned. He touched his son's arm and the boy shrugged it off, averting his head. He moved farther from Theo, toward the music and lights of the party.

"Nico!" Theo bellowed loudly. The guests standing a few yards forward turned to look at him, their laughter dying away. He was dimly conscious of them, and of Sophia, glittering, flashing, watching him.

79

But he didn't give a damn. "Nico!" he shouted in a rage.

Nico half-turned, his face a pale, sad shadow above his white jacket and the dancing lights at his back. For a moment they looked at each other across the gulf of party guests. Then Nico turned and disappeared into the salon.

The fury and hurt that rose in Theo tore at his innards like the claws and teeth of a wild boar. He felt the rage taking over, obliterating the gnawing, almost unbearable pain of his abandonment. The group at the rail was silent, watching him.

His face grim, he strode up to them and reached out for Sophia's white arm. He gripped her flesh tightly and would have yanked her toward him had she offered resistance. Instead, she seemed to anticipate him and moved out of the cluster of people as if tied to Theo by an invisible cord.

They left the people staring, too polite to whisper until they were out of sight. In a moment Theo had reached the gangplank and was taking the boarding steps two at a time, with Matalas half-running to keep up. They stepped onto the tender and Theo signaled the seaman to go full speed ahead, quickly, quickly. The guests watched as the launch sped off. Then they turned to refill their glasses and began murmuring about finding their hostess to say goodnight.

Theo said nothing as the motor launch sped toward the shore. The line of his mouth was set in a grimace that Sophia Matalas knew well. She knew enough to keep her mouth shut, too, but her keen eye picked out the papparazzi waiting for them on the dock. She leaned back against the cushions, took her hand mirror out of her evening bag, and applied a fresh slash of red lipstick for the photographers. Her hair blew freely in the wind, giving her exactly the madcap, just-out-of-bed look the newspapers and magazines loved. As the tender slowed to tie up at the pier, the reporters and photographers ran to meet them, shouting and snapping their bulbs. Theo groaned and swore under his breath. Sophia laughed and posed for an instant, before he pulled her to the dock.

A very young photographer knelt near the steps to grab a closeup. Theo knocked the camera out of his hands; it dangled from the startled young man's neck.

"Out of the way, you son of a bitch!" he snarled.

The photographer fell backward and clutched at his camera, but the others relished the moment and flashbulbs blazed as Theo shoved angrily at them, forcing himself and Sophia through the mob.

Sophia smiled and tried to pretend that her arm was not being yanked painfully. The diamond bracelet cut where he gripped; she was sure there would be a scar. But her teeth sparkled as brightly as the cutting stones as she turned this way and that, laughing. All in a night's fun, her expression said. Ah, la dolce vita! But the loss of her dignity was something Theo would pay for later.

Her sportscar waited at the end of the pier. Another photographer, dark and swarthy, knelt at the door of the Maserati and waited, camera angled upward. Theo let go his hold on Sophia's wrist and took two running steps toward the car. He lifted his foot abruptly and kicked the camera out of the man's hands. He yanked open the door as the photographer fell backward, and shouted at Sophia.

"Get in here!"

But Sophia swung around and threw both arms

around Theo's neck. Flashbulbs went off like the siege of Naples. In the midst of the explosion and glare, Theo dragged her inside the car. He slammed the door, narrowly missing a reporter's clutching fingers.

Theo stormed around to the driver's side, glowering, and climbed into the car. He took a moment to turn to Sophia, who was still smiling and waving through the window as the last pictures were snapped.

"Crazy!" he shouted in her ear. "Crazy bitch!"

She laughed, even when her body was jerked forward and then back by the car's sudden start. Theo thrust his foot on the gas pedal, shifted down and tore out of the marina and onto the street as if he were heading the Mille Miglia race. He turned onto the steep, winding Corniche road behind the pink palace at 115 kilometers per hour, and Sophia leaned back against the yielding kidskin seat to enjoy the ride.

He missed a hairpin curve by less than the width of a hairpin, the Maserati spinning out of control for a split second, skidding with one rear wheel in the air over the sheer precipice. Theo fought the pull of gravity and speed to bring the car under control, while the gravel spun and spat against the windshield a hailstorm like gunshots. Sophia stretched out lazily and laid her arm across the back of Theo's seat. She smiled at him, and when he was able to relax his grip on the wheel, he shrugged, pressed his foot on the accelerator again, and raced away up the narrow winding road. He was playing the odds, betting that there would be no other car on the road. He was lucky.

The sportscar screeched to a careening stop at

Sophia's villa. When he cut the engine, there was utter silence for a moment. The trees all around them were like darkly brooding sentries.

"Eh, Theo," she said, "you are angry at Nico so you want to kill us both."

"What the hell does he want?" Theo shouted. He beat his fist on the leather steering wheel. Then he seemed to become calmer. He turned to Sophia, who waited for his attention with a little smile—sympathetic, knowing.

"Come," she said, touching the back of his head. She opened the door and got out of the car. He sighed and climbed out of his side and came around to take her in his arms. The moonlight skittered through the leaves to highlight Sophia's long mane of windblown hair, her extraordinary breasts pressing against the soft folds of her gown, and her red, red mouth that understood his needs. Together, they went inside the house and up the wide stairs to her bed.

"He interferes in my life," Theo said as he unbuttoned his shirt and loosened his tie. "But he doesn't want me to interfere in his."

"He is becoming a man now, Theo," Sophia said.

She reached out to caress his bare chest with her long tapered fingers. He held her close and felt for the zipper at the back of her dress. In a moment, she was as bare before him as his beloved statue of Demeter. The mother-goddess. He thought briefly of the American woman. Not a woman, really—a First Lady soon. She might be valuable to him, but never a woman of flesh and blood, not for him. Pity. A waste. He held Sophia's warmth against himself and soon forgot every-

83

thing in the overpowering deeps of passion and lust fulfilled.

Much later, they lay side by side, taking pleasure in the familiarity of their bodies together. He lit a cigarette and watched the hazy smoke drift upward in the pale moonlight that angled through the window.

"I can't speak to him, Sophia," he murmured. "I can't talk any sense to him. He means so much to me, and I can't. . . ."

He turned his head on the pillow to look at her. She was softened, relaxed, warmly sleepy now. Sophia's beauty was very precious to him. Only he could subdue her, this torrid bitch of a woman. For him she would do anything; only for him and only sometimes. He had to fight her, to outsmart her, even take insolence from her sometimes, but she was worth the trouble. They were alike, the two of them. There was no distance between them. They came from the same dirt. Her village in Italy, his village in Greece—the same.

She listened to him, her great eyes wide, her mouth pale and a bit swollen from his kisses. She listened, and he talked to her as he could talk to no one else, no one.

"Why can't I talk to him, my own son? You and me, whatever is important, we tell each other. We talk. But with Nico . . . we speak a different language. I don't understand. What does he want? Tell me. Tell me."

Sophia sighed. "Theo, we speak to one another because we're friends. When we need to, we reach out, friends." She touched his cheek with one soft finger, tracing a line that she loved. "Give that to Nico," she said simply. "Stop treating him like a child."

"Child? He's a man. I told him."

"And do you believe it?" she asked quietly.

"Of course! What are you talking about? Sure, he's a man . . . lots of girls . . . every day, falls in love, out of love, makes love . . . what are you talking about!"

He grinned and rolled over on top of her to show her what a man was.

"He's like his poppa," Theo cried lustily. "A Greek! He's got his mind in the right place!" His hand clutched at her and she shrieked loudly, "Jesus Christ!"

Theo fell back on his pillow, grinning sheepishly.

"I'm sore," Sophia groaned.

Theo laughed. "Finally. Good."

She laid her head on his chest. After a few moments, she said, drowsily, "He doesn't like me, does he? Nico."

"No."

She stirred and moved upward. She put her arms around his neck. She murmured low and sensuously against his throat.

"He is afraid that you'll leave Simi," she said. "That we'll get married."

"Married?" He was startled. His eyes stared at her in the fading moonlight that would soon give way to dawn.

Suddenly he shoved her away, hard. She fell from the bed, screaming and clutching at the sheets, at his hair, his hand, scratching and furious.

"I'm married," he said angrily. He looked down at her. She lay naked on the floor, curled like a rattlesnake ready to spring.

"You son of a bitch!"

"You're married too," he pointed out, as if reasoning with a retarded child.

She unwound herself from the tangle of bedclothes and came slowly toward him. "No man is going to kick me out of his bed," she said, threatening.

". . . and the way it is is the only way," he concluded calmly.

"No man gets away with that," she said through clenched teeth. She brought her fist forward to swing at his face. He grabbed her arm and pulled her off-balance so that she fell on top of him. He took her in his arms, talking to gentle her.

"*Glyka mou,*" he said in Greek, and "*cara mia,*" in Italian, soothing, crooning, holding her arms down while his body covered hers and his legs held her in a scissors-grip.

She bit his nose, hard. His hand flew up to touch it, and she wriggled free of his grasp. He laughed and rolled onto her again.

"Let me go . . . you bastard . . . bastard. . . . *Let me go!* I'll kill you, you son of a bitch!" She bit and clawed and struggled violently, murder in her heart.

Theo laughed again, holding her down with his body, liking the angry hot flesh squirming beneath him.

"If we got married," he shouted over her shrieks and screams, "if we got married, hey, you know we . . . come on, Sopheee-a, we would fight, we would yell at each other . . . I would look for a ballet dancer . . . an opera singer! You would be very unhappy, Sopheee-a. . . ."

Suddenly he yowled with pain.

Her hands had worked loose; she held his

testicles in a ruthless grip, squeezing until Theo lay back in helpless agony.

"Jesus Christ . . . oh, my God . . . oh, my God!"

She got on her knees, straddling him, still holding him tightly, the tears drying on her cheeks in her glee at getting back at him.

"It hurts?" she said in mock solicitude, letting her soft hair fall over his contorted face. He managed to nod, groaning with the pain.

"Don't lie," she said calmly. She squeezed harder.

"IT HURTS! IT HURTS!" he roared. "WHAT DO YOU WANT?"

Her grip went slack. She leaned over and kissed him lightly on the lips. He moaned. Still holding him, she smoothed back a strand of unruly hair from his moist forehead with her free hand.

"You don't want to marry me?" she asked.

He opened his eyes, amazed. She still straddled him; their faces were only inches apart.

"Marry you . . . oh, Jesus. . . ." he muttered.

It still hurt. He laughed, a guttural snort of ironic bewilderment mixed with pain.

"You'll make me no good for anything," he moaned.

"I don't care." Her hand closed again, threatening.

"Let me go, Sophia."

He tried to roll over onto his side, to bend his knees to ease the pain. She stared at his face, then moved silently off him. She stretched out next to him, not touching.

He lay curled up, nursing his pain for a few moments, and then raised his head in astonishment to look at her. She was breathing regularly, sweetly, in the peaceful sleep of innocence.

87

CHAPTER FIVE

High in the clouds that choked off the view of Manhattan, the board room in its formal dignity seemed suspended from the mundane cares of the streets below. Three walls were covered in soothing dark raw-silk ocher: the paintings were chosen for their blandness, as a background that would not distract from the important business being discussed around the polished walnut conference table. The wall of glass windows gave a sense of well-being to the gathering, as the silent whiteness brushed lazily past, not yet changed into grime to fall on the streets below.

Theo Tomasis sat in a high-backed leather chair at the head of the long conference table. Next to him, his lawyer, Michael Corey, was reiterating the agreement just reached by the ten distinguished men who sat listening. A few were idly doodling on the thick white pads of paper set before each place. One or two jotted down an occasional note, figures, reminders to themselves. All listened very carefully. They were an impressive group, representing controlling interests in major sources of wealth and power in the United States.

One was a general in the U.S. army; another was a former senator; there was a trustee of the Metropolitan Museum of Art, and the head of a large university. Every man in the room controlled an individual fortune as well as corporate power.

A few discreet feet behind Theo Tomasis, the only woman in the room sat with a stenotype machine on her lap, the keys clacking under her fingers as she recorded every word.

". . . and finally, gentlemen, as laid down in Section 19 of the United States Merchant Marine Act, only American citizens and/or corporations in which such citizens have controlling interests are entitled to buy these surplus tankers. . . ."

The lawyer was the best that money could hire. Only in his late forties, Michael Corey was head of one of the most prestigious law firms in New York. He was tall and lean, good-looking and carefully groomed. His red tartan vest was the only real color in the room; he spoke softly, with the assurance of a man who knew his business and that of others. He deferred with a genial smile as Theo interrupted him.

"I want you to understand, gentlemen," Theo put in, leaning forward in his chair, which tilted with him, "that owning the ships . . ." He opened his hands. "That's your department. They belong to you, to this new corporation of yours formed here this afternoon. I'm only interested in using them. Commerce."

He looked around at the eminent faces. One or two nodded, the others showed no response other than careful, thoughtful attention. He nodded to Corey to continue.

"Now, since the tankers cannot be sold for foreign-flag operations, and we wish everything to be legal, of course, I have drawn up these papers for you to sign," the lawyer said. He motioned to a young man on his right, who stood with a fluster of self-importance and picked up the stack of legal documents neatly piled before him. He began to move around the long table like a well-trained waiter, setting before each man a folder with his name on it.

"You will control fifty-one percent interest in the corporation," Michael Corey continued. "Mr. Tomasis will retain forty-nine percent ownership."

As the men opened their folders and scanned the documents, pens poised to sign, Theo leaned back expansively. "I must say, gentlemen," he remarked, "I have never been honored by such fine associates. It is a great day for me, a peasant—"

"Gentlemen," Corey cut in smoothly, "Mr. Tomasis will be lending the corporate body the funds necessary for the purchase, as we agreed. Four million dollars for each of the twenty tankers . . . the total sum being eighty million dollars. Mr. Tomasis is putting you all in the way, gentlemen, with no risk whatsoever, of making a nice little return. On your signatures only."

He glanced down the table and up the other side. The three men who had not yet signed did so then. Michael Corey smiled, and looked at his watch.

"I think we may all consider this hour well spent. And now, thank you very much."

As the young assistant gathered up the signed papers, the men rose from the table and began to shake hands, to smile and move with accustomed grace from the seriousness of business to the equally important small talk that frames such gatherings. As they snapped shut their briefcases and began to leave the room, Theo held out his hand to each and grinned with unrestrained pleasure.

"Partners," he exclaimed several times, shaking hands and pounding one or two of the men on the back.

When the group had left the board room, Theo caught the smiling lawyer in a bear hug.

"Ah, Michael, it's done!"

"It went smoothly, I think," Corey agreed.

"They seem like smart choices, Michael. All of them seemed fine," Theo said.

Corey nodded. "Good men all, and true."

"Good and true in the pocket?" Theo came back quickly. He released his hold on the younger man and stepped over to look out the window. The drifting cloud was closing in now, leaving warning drops of moisture on the thermal pane.

"You've got nothing to worry about on that score," Corey assured him.

"All legitimate, hah?"

Corey chuckled. "Listen, as long as you've got some clout in the White House now—"

Theo spun around to stare at him. "What clout?" he asked. "Cassidy spent a few hours on the *Belle*

Simone once, before he was even elected. That's no clout."

"Maybe not," Corey smiled ingratiatingly. "Maybe not with Jim Cassidy himself, but . . . he did invite you down there, didn't he? And, if you should happen to meet his brother while you're there . . . a personal relationship with the attorney general can't hurt, Theo."

He closed his briefcase and came around the table to shake Theo's hand warmly. "Give my regards to the president," he said.

Theo was thoughtful as he stood alone in the empty room, gazing out at the blank white cloud as if he could see something out there. A little smile played over his lips, and then he turned to the door leading into his private office, where he would have a sauna and a shower before taking off for Washington.

The White House gala was in the tradition already made famous by the new First Lady. Her taste and charm had captivated not only staid Washington, but the whole world. In the previous administration, artists and poets and exiled musicians from war-riddled countries had been emboldened to refuse invitations to the White House, but now all that was forgotten in the new and exciting reign of the handsome young couple who had taken over from the old guard.

Theo wondered how much she had changed in the year since their private moment on *La Belle Simone*. It didn't occur to him to question whether she remembered; she must. She was pregnant now, and in her rightful place as the symbolic and actual Demeter—the mother-goddess. More than mortal, yet ripening with the source of life inside her belly. How beautiful she was these days—her photograph graced virtually every magazine cover and front page of major newspapers of the world; visiting a hospital, ordering new drapes for the Blue Room, accompanying her handsome husband on a speaking tour, attending parties, greeting famous guests.

"Mr. Tomasis, how very nice to see you again. Your wife could not be with you?" she said, smiling.

"No, but she sends her regards to you," he answered. He held her hand for a brief moment, as the long reception line behind him waited its chance. "It is a great thing, to see you again, like this . . ." he said, acknowledging her condition with a gentle smile. "Time passes."

She was like a rare and delicate flower in blossom as she returned his smile radiantly. She nodded.

"A child born in the White House is a very good thing, very good luck . . . my father used to say that all the time," he joshed.

"I think I remember that you had quite a father," she answered seriously.

The president was standing next to her, watching them, as Theo continued to hold up the line. He grinned with pride and pleasure as he reached out his hand to Theo.

"And listen," Theo continued to both of them, "I want to tell you, the two of you, when you get tired of being president, if you need a rest, come aboard *La Belle Simone*. Any time, anywhere. We'll have a fine cruise."

President Cassidy nodded, smiling. "Thank you.

And please give our regards to your beautiful family."

Theo nodded and moved on into the room where the reception was in full swing.

"I meant it," he said later to the First Lady, when the musical entertainment had concluded and the guests were milling about. "Any time you like . . . a cruise . . . *La Belle Simone* is yours."

"Thank you," she murmured. "Oh, John!" she called to the president's brother, who was standing nearby. "Have you met Mr. Tomasis?"

"Mr. Attorney General," Theo acknowledged. The two men shook hands as the First Lady wandered off to greet another guest, a novelist famous for his feisty public behavior, who now seemed absolutely tamed and enchanted by her presence.

"I'm glad to meet you," Theo said to the attorney general. "I have just invited the president and First Lady for a cruise on my yacht, anytime, perhaps you and your wife would join us?"

John Cassidy nodded genially. "We'd like that very much," he said. "But a vacation . . . I don't see one in the offing, not for quite a while." He laughed.

"Yes, I understand. Business, politics . . . it is all the same when one is devoted to work. I am the same, myself. Still, there must be time for pleasure."

"Absolutely right, Mr. Tomasis."

"Call me Theo."

"Theo."

"And should I call you John, or Mr. Attorney General?"

"John, by all means."

They shook hands warmly and moved to join the

other guests who, at a discreet signal from the chief of protocol, had begun to say goodnight to their host and hostess.

Theo flew back to New York after the party, arriving shortly after one A.M. to find Sophia pacing impatiently back and forth in the living room of her suite. Her face lit up as soon as she heard his key in the lock; she knew better than to show anger or annoyance at being kept waiting, and this time her curiosity was too great to risk a petty peevish scene which would only delay finding out everything she wanted to know.

She held out her arms to him and he grinned, threw his hat on a chair, and embraced her warmly.

"Tell me, tell me," she ordered, leading him to one of the deep sofas. "Who was there? What was she wearing, the First Lady? Who else? Any big stars? Important people, hah?"

Theo resisted her urging and motioned to her negligee. "Hey, hey, ready for bed? What's the matter, you tired? Let's go out, let's have some fun! Get dressed."

"Wonderful!" she exclaimed. She planted a huge wet kiss on his cheek and turned to the bedroom. "But come in with me, tell me everything about the White House. Was it terrible? Stuffy, eh?"

He followed her, still wearing his topcoat, and stood leaning against the open door while she changed. "No, no, not stuffy at all. Very . . . civilized."

"Humph," she grunted from inside the folds of the evening gown she was pulling over her head. "Sounds stuffy."

"Well, the White House in Washington is not

exactly the Folies Bergère in Paris, Sophia. Very distinguished people, I met the attorney general, some ambassadors . . . and of course, the president and Mrs. Cassidy were very nice. I think they were happy to see me again."

"What was she wearing?" Sophia sat down at her dressing table to begin the careful application of makeup. Her eyes did not leave her image until she was satisfied that her public mask was perfect.

"A blue dress, long, simple. She's very beautiful, very sad, I think. . . ." He saw Sophia's quick frown in the mirror, and added, ". . . she's too skinny."

They dropped in at the best-known of the modish discos, piano bars, nightclubs, and key clubs that the restlessly chic all-night people had taken up that particular year. The car waited for them outside the dazzling members-only billiard room and bandstand in the east fifties, where Theo became an instant member with the presentation of three hundred-dollar bills; the best table was immediately theirs, of course, as it was in every place they visited. They laughed and danced and drank great quantities, managed to devour a couple of exquisitely broiled steaks, and everywhere they were greeted by people who knew them, or thought they did. By the time they decided to head downtown to an underground cavern where an about-to-be-discovered singer was packing them in, they had picked up an entourage of six other people, and a bevy of cars carrying photographers and gossip columnists was in their wake as they traveled through the deserted avenues of the sleeping city.

Sophia was in her element, and Theo found the night on the town a delicious relief after the "civilized" Washington evening. He was a man who had to blow off steam, and watching Sophia posing for the photographers, listening to her witty and bold comments—not always kind, usually barbed toward some other woman—made him feel back in touch with the coarse and bawdy strain in his own nature, without his actually having to be involved. He could sit back and listen, claiming no kinship to this woman and loving her for the side of himself that she represented. And he loved, too, the publicity-seekers, the hangers-on who wanted to be near them, to be mentioned in the columns the next day as having been in Theo Tomasis' party. He threw money everywhere, astonishing the headwaiters with his generosity, folding hundred-dollar bills in tight little squares to slip into the pockets of the elegant piano players who sang obscure Cole Porter songs. The biggest, brightest, maddest city in the world belonged to him tonight, why not? Everything belonged to him—everything! In one club, a pretty girl who couldn't have been more than seventeen threw herself into his arms, asking to be taken; her eyes were veiled with heavy drugs. Sophia glared, and then took off in a wondrously frolicsome dance with the girl.

The morning rush hour had begun when they finally called it a night and pulled up in front of the Pierre again. People were scurrying to work along Fifth Avenue, and the heavy iron gates in front of the jewelry stores and boutiques were being laboriously pushed open to greet the day.

A gossip columnist was sound asleep in a corner of the limousine's wide seat, snoring quietly. Theo stepped from the car, handed Sophia out onto the sidewalk, and peered back at the sleeping journalist.

"You'd better take him home," he told the chauffeur.

"Yes, sir," the driver said. "Do you know where that is, sir?"

"He looks like he'll crumble into dust if the daylight hits him," Sophia commented. It was true; the pasty-white complexion of the night-crawling gossiper had never seen the sunlight. "Better hurry," she laughed. "I wouldn't want that to happen before he gets a chance to write his column about us."

"Take him round to one of the clubs," Theo said to the chauffeur, "and ask the doorman. I'm sure this happens to him every night. I'm sure they all know where he lives."

"Yes, sir," the driver said.

"And when he wakes up," Sophia called over her shoulder, "tell him to make sure he spells my name right!"

Laughing, they entered the hotel. The plush dark-maroon and gold lobby was populated only by a couple of businessmen from out of town, having their first cigars of the day behind the financial pages of the *Times* and *Wall Street Journal*.

Mario, the hotel's manager, was waiting for them, and when they came in he leaped up from his desk in great agitation. Risking his dignity, he half-ran across the lobby to meet them.

"Mr. Tomasis! Oh, Mr. Tomasis! Thank God you are here, at last! I tried to call you . . . everywhere . . . even the White House . . . the clubs . . . terrible, terrible. I am so sorry."

"Hey, Mario, what is it? Hah?"

Theo took the message from the manager's trembling hand and read it quickly. His face paled. "Get my car back here, call the airport, I want my plane ready at once," he ordered. The manager, not accustomed to such tasks, found himself rushing to the desk to comply.

Theo strode through the lobby with Sophia behind him. "What is it, Theo? What?" she asked.

Passing the switchboard alcove on the way to the elevator, Theo threw back his head to roar, "Get my wife on the phone for me!" in the general direction of the operator, who in her panic pulled out four plugs on trans-Atlantic calls and six locals.

"It's Nico," he said curtly to Sophia as the elevator whisked them upward. "He's had an accident. I'm going back. I'll call you later."

"Theo," she murmured. Her huge black eyes, rimmed with smudged mascara, filled with instant sympathy.

At her floor she stepped off the elevator, nodded to him and moved down the corridor. Theo went on up to his penthouse apartment where he paced relentlessly, waiting for the call to come through.

"Where is his wife?" moaned the switchboard operator over her shoulder to the manager.

"She called from *La Belle Simone*, didn't she? You have the number, idiot. Put me back on to his car, at once."

The switchboard was lighting up with red and yellow lights blinking in a furious fusillade. The operator, in tears, started to plug the calls in at random, just to get the lights out for a moment. She was crying softly to herself and swearing under her breath as she ran her fingers down the list of telephone numbers for Theo Tomasis. She found the number for the yacht, and plugged herself in to the overseas operator.

On the other side of the high partition, the hotel's guests had no hint of the confusion that reigned. Everything stopped for Theo Tomasis. In a few moments, the telephone in his suite buzzed and he was speaking with Simi.

"How is Nico? How is he?"

"They don't know yet. The doctor is with him. It's bad, Theo."

Theo trembled. His whole body shook. At the edges of his vision, darkness threatened to close in. He grabbed the edge of the table and gripped it until the beveled wood cut painfully into his flesh.

"Simi . . . is Nico going to be all right? He's not going to . . . Simi?" His voice was terrified, pitiful, small.

"Come home, Theo," she said from far away.

"Right now," he shouted, and would have thrown down the telephone, but caught himself. He spoke again, more calmly, "And you . . . are you all right, Simi?"

Her voice was cold. She too was frightened. "Yes," she said, and waited for him to answer.

"Okay. I'm coming right away."

He hung up the phone and stormed out of the hotel suite, still in his evening clothes. He would change on the plane.

From the car en route to the airport, he called his pilot. "What's the fastest craft available?" he asked. "Find out if someone can get a 707 ready to go right away, kick everybody off and start revving it up for me. Call me back right away."

He fidgeted, looking out at the housing projects

of Queens and Nassau, the left-over structures from an old World's Fair that dotted the edges of the Expressway. There was little traffic at this hour of the morning, and the limousine hurtled through Long Island without slowing. The patrol cars that started on its trail caught sight of the special license number and fell back to wait for smaller fish.

The phone buzzed as the car was heading off the Expressway onto the thin stretch of highway that led to the airport.

"Yes?" he barked.

"Sorry, boss . . . the Lear's the fastest way right now. Take too long to get anything else in the air. We can be airborne as soon as you get here, no clearance for heavy stuff possible for another hour."

"Okay. I'll be there in ten minutes. Let's go."

He couldn't sleep on the plane. For six hours he sat in the lounge chair next to his made-up bed, unable to read or think of anything except his son. The boy was careless with his life, as if it didn't matter to him. A daredevil, fearless, so young he didn't even value the precious gift of his own life. How had it happened?

The solitary jet made its way through the sky thirty thousand feet over the Atlantic, with Theo silently willing it to go faster, faster. He drowsed a bit and woke time and time again with the image of Nico fresh in his mind.

The glittering water, in the bright morning. Nico at the wheel of his speedboat, the fastest thing on the whole coast. Two great rocks jutting up from the sea, close together; Nico taking the challenge, heading between them, shooting the passage at a tremendous speed. The narrow boat, skimming the water, barely touching the deceptively smooth surface in its race with death. Twisting in the air, avoiding the rocks on either side by inches. The boy at the wheel, looking straight ahead, never flinching, the wind blowing his blond hair behind him, his eyes keen, laughing at the danger. The boy would circle, the whole Mediterranean his own. Seeing a moored white yacht in his path, he would steer straight for it, swerving at the last possible second, cutting a wake behind him that tossed the sleeping yacht high. And then . . . not seeing the piece of water-logged debris, or perhaps a piece of sharp metal lurking just below the calm, open surface the boy thought belonged only to him on this bright, lonely morning. . . .

The plane droned in the early darkness. Theo stirred fitfully, his whole body reaching out to stop the boy, to take the speedboat's wheel and turn it. Watch out, watch out, Nico, be careful . . . and Theo saw the speedboat hit the object, saw his beautiful slim son tossed high in the air, saw the speedboat racked on its side, saw the boy's fine body falling crippled, unconscious, into the quiet water. Sinking, slowly turning downward—but visible, thank God, to the early-morning fishermen who saw it all and dived for the boy.

Still alive, Simi had said. Or had she? She hadn't lied, had never lied. He had to be still alive.

Theo picked up the intercom and asked the pilot for their position. Hours more to go, a lifetime. He tried to sleep, tried to trick his mind into relaxing, tried to think of the important deal he had made in New York, of the heavyweight contact he had established with the White House, of the loveliness of the warm-blooded woman who had, he knew, been pleased to see him.

For the fifth time, he placed a call to the *La Belle Simone* on the radio. No change. Nico was holding his own. Still alive. The vision of the boy's helpless body being thrown from the speedboat wouldn't leave him. It was an ominous picture, full of portentous doom. He thought of the legends. Always, always, the son lived to succeed his father, often by patricide. Live, Theo swore under his breath, live to kill me, if you must. But don't die, my only son.

La Belle Simone was anchored off Mykonos. The Lear circled over the hills, over the bone-white little buildings that clung to the shoreline, over windmills and grassy pastures. The pilot set the plane down on the short runway with skill, and Theo ran for the helicopter that waited there. In a few moments, they were landing on the yacht's deck.

Theo leaped out. "Simi! How is he?"

Simi's silk dressing gown whipped around her body in the wash of the rotor blades. She shouted to be heard. "He'll be all right, Theo! He's going to be all right!"

He held her closely, the two of them on the wide deck, while the crew scurried around them to secure the lines. For a moment, Theo let himself be warmed by his wife's arms, but she was shy in front of servants. She moved out of his arms to lead him down the steps.

"Nico . . ." He ran to the wide bed where his son lay drowsing from heavy medication.

"I'm sorry, Poppa . . . Poppa, I'm sorry . . . I'm sorry . . ." Nico mumbled.

"He must sleep now," the nurse said firmly.

Theo knelt by the bed, making sure that his son still lived.

"I'm sorry, Poppa . . ."

"Don't say that!" Theo blurted, and then the boy's eyes closed and Theo allowed himself to be led from the stateroom.

Simi was waiting for him in the room they shared. Suddenly, Theo was exhausted. He felt the strain of the past twenty-four hours hit him; after all, he was not a kid any more, to go without sleeping. He yawned and started to undress, pacing back and forth, talking excitedly to his wife as he prepared for a nap.

"You know what he said?" There was excitement in his voice, and a kind of elation. "He said 'I'm sorry, Poppa. Poppa, I'm sorry.' What about that, hah?" He looked at Simi, who was seated on the white chaise lounge, watching him. She nodded wearily.

"Seventeen stitches in his ass . . . Christ! And what does he think about? If he hurt *me!*"

Simi said nothing.

"That goddamned kid . . . crazy!" Theo burst out with an almost gleeful relief. Then he sobered in one of his quicksilver changes of mood. "He could have killed himself, that fast in a goddamned boat. I'm going to tell you something . . . my son with the stitches in his ass . . . no more boats, no more motorcycles, no more airplanes! He's a daredevil, he wants to kill himself! No. No more. You want to worry about Nico? I'm not going to worry about Nico."

He sat down to pull off his shoes. Simi arose from the chaise and stood before him.

104

"I want a divorce, Theo," she said quietly.

His head swiveled to look up at her. "Our son's lying down there almost dead, a narrow escape. What the hell are you talking about?"

Angrily, he threw his shoe aside, and got up without looking at her. Her hand on his arm stayed him.

"I want a divorce," she repeated.

"No," he said. "No." He shook his head and pulled free of her. He went toward the bed.

"I haven't bothered you for a long time, Theo," Simi went on. "I've waited. But nothing has changed. I'm not going to live like this any more."

"Like this?" he exploded. "You live on Mount Olympus, for Christ's sake, you live like a goddess! Everything, you've got everything! Like no other woman in the world! What other woman has a life like yours?"

"You really don't understand, do you?"

Her calmness angered him as much as her words. His legs were aching, he was getting old, he was tired. Couldn't the woman see that? He sat down heavily on the edge of the bed.

"I don't have your love," she said. "I don't have you." She paused, and then added sadly, "I have nothing."

Touched, Theo felt his anger wane. He held out his arms to her. She stood without moving, looking at him, waiting for his words, hoping he would find some magic formula, some way to keep them together. She knew he hated being forced to speak, but there was no other way.

"Listen," he said brokenly, his eyes pleading with her, "listen to me. I love you."

She nodded sadly.

105

"I've loved you, for Christ's sake, since you were seventeen years old. Twenty years, more—twenty-two years, I've loved you." His voice was soft, pleading and touching on the old strings which would bring her back to him as they had so many times before. "Seeeemi . . ." Still he held out his arms, naked and strong, and still she stood apart. "I do, Simi. I love you."

"Yes," she said finally. "Yes, you do. Like a possession? Something like that, Theo?"

"What are you talking? What!" He leaped up in a rage and came to her. Steady as a statue, she stood frozen in her grief. He pushed back the silken robe from her shoulders. He saw the terror in her eyes and knew what it meant. He is an animal, she was thinking. He will demean me, demean us both, by taking my body now. He thinks the act of love will do as a substitute for love.

He understood this, but he could not let her go. He pulled on the robe until her breasts were exposed. Her skin was cool and soft, neither yielding nor refusing. She just stood there, and then she sobbed, "Theo . . . Theo . . ."

"You are my wife," he said, like a hurt child who is trying to reassure himself. "I love you."

"Oh, my God. . . ."

He held her nakedness next to his own, and she let the robe drop to the floor. If he noticed that she did not respond, he pretended not to. It would be all right, it always was. It had to be all right. He knew she hated herself for not rejecting him, but he knew she would surrender because she could not help herself. She was his wife.

"You see . . . you see . . . Simi, there is no reason for a divorce. . . ." He held her passive body close and moved with her to the bed. "No reason. None," he said, enfolding her with the gentleness of his love.

In Washington, it was mid-morning. The president of the United States was in conference with his brother.

"A presidential pardon would look well with labor," the attorney general was saying.

"I don't know, Johnny, maybe not with the rank and file," James Cassidy responded.

"Possibly," John Cassidy said thoughtfully, staring out the window of the Oval Office at the Rose Garden. His wife and some of the other Cabinet wives were having a reception for some womens' clubs. It was supposed to be Liz Cassidy's reception, but she was having a hard time with her pregnancy, her first. He caught a glimpse of his own wife, also pregnant but bounding about the White House lawn as if ready to take on a gang of teamsters in a high-jumping contest. He grinned to himself.

"One of the best things you've done as attorney general was putting him in jail," the president was saying. "He was skimming that pension fund and you proved it. How do *you* feel about a pardon now?"

The private phone rang, and he picked it up. "Yes?"

Then John Cassidy heard his brother gasp. "Oh, Jesus!"

The president put down the phone and motioned for John to come with him as he tore out of the Oval Office and down the corridor to the east door.

Minutes later the black limousine was rushing

through the traffic with motorcycles on either side and a siren car ahead. The limousine reached the hospital in ten minutes flat.

"Why didn't you tell me?" the president pleaded with his wife, leaning over her white hospital bed.

Her dark eyes were full of pain and sorrow. "You were busy . . . it happened so suddenly . . . I didn't think . . . oh, Jim . . . I lost our son. It was a boy. . . ."

"Liz . . . Liz . . . don't blame yourself. The doctor says . . ."

"This was our baby. It was our son. Our son," she sobbed.

"There'll be another," he said softly.

Huge tears coursed down her cheeks, as white as the pillow, framed by her dark rumpled hair. He had never seen her so beautiful, so vulnerable and defenseless.

"Oh, my darling, don't cry. We can have another son."

"Yes . . . oh, yes. . . ." She held out her arms to comfort him. There were tears on his cheeks too.

Nico Tomasis recovered with the resiliency of youth. His father's injunction against boats, planes, fast horses, fast cars had been forgotten by the time the stitches were removed. Nico knew that Theo was proud of him, of his daredevil ways, his bravery. And it was the one way that Nico could excel without comparing himself to his father.

The news from America shook Theo deeply. To lose a son, before he was even born! How dark and terrible this tragic loss; his heart ached for the Cassidys. To be president of a great, rich nation, to be young and gifted and well bred, to have wealth and power, to be idolized by millions of people all over the world, to have it all—and to have nothing because your only son was dead. They were young, they would have other sons, but the irony was like a chorus in a Greek tragedy to Theo, reminding him with its fateful timing that he was the lucky one. His son lived. Nico was alive, bright and handsome and strong.

He telephoned the Cassidys to tell them of his sorrow. They were grateful for his sympathy and understanding; his call was one of thousands.

"Come with me today," Theo said one morning to his son. "I'm going to do a bit of business in the village. Come, you'll learn something."

"In the village?" Nico looked up from his breakfast with a smile. They were still on *La Belle Simone*, and the Greek sun was already burning down on them, although it was early morning. A few hundred yards away, the little fishing boats were putting out, and the houses along the beach glistened whitely.

"Come on. We'll play a little *tavli* with the men in the *kafeneon*. Someone is meeting me there, an Arab."

"Poppa!" Nico was amused. "You get so Greek when we're here. *Kavli? Kafeneon?* If we were anywhere else in the world you would say backgammon, coffeehouse . . . or is it that you want me to remember my roots?"

"Both," Theo admitted, grinning. "A little bit of both."

"Don't worry, Poppa," Nico said. He got up from the table and put his arm around his father's shoulders, a bit tentative, a bit shy. "I'm proud to be Greek," he said, "and proud to be your son."

Theo felt the love rising in him like a physical thing, too large for his heart, crowding his blood. He gripped his son tightly for a moment.

"Ah, Nico . . . Nico. . . ."

"Let's go, Poppa," Nico said. He pulled away gently, but embarrassed, as always, by the show of emotion. But he, too, had felt the fearful brush of his own mortality, and the past three weeks had been a healing time, not only of his own flesh but of the family. He was almost glad for his accident; it seemed to have brought them close again, the three of them. If Theo flew off from time to time, it was business, only business. Simi was quiet, as always, but her deep strain of sadness had seemed at bay in these sunny weeks. Nico allowed himself to believe that all was well between his mother and father, and as the yacht bobbed gently on the blue Aegean, with the islands surrounding them and the cloudless sky overhead, his fears and defiances were set to rest.

And yesterday, he had waterskiied and found himself still lithe, still unafraid and, yes—tough. The pressures of rage and love and all other unexpressed emotions that built in him, his father's son, could still be exorcised in his own way. Nico felt good, ready to try again.

When the huge black Rolls Royce turned into the village square, everyone looked up to stare at it, except Theo Tomasis, who was intent on studying the board. He had just rolled double sixes; the game was almost won. The old man playing opposite him, however, had turned to watch the excitement through the open doorway that led to the dusty street.

The chauffeur-driven car maneuvered a U-turn, throwing up the dry dust under its wheels, barely missing a goat who had wandered into the square, stopping before the coffeehouse. The right fender flew the diplomatic flag of a small, oil-rich country.

The car waited, like a giant Trojan horse bearing unseen invaders. Nothing moved except the children and an old woman or two, circling cautiously near the monster, gaping and peering to see what was inside. But the windows reflected only their own distorted images. Slowly, the dust began to settle again.

"Your move," Theo said to his opponent. The old man stared at the car outside the *kafeneon* door, and then at Theo, and then he shrugged, rolled the dice and knocked two of Theo's disks out of their diamonds.

Outside, the huge black Rolls sat silently, waiting.

Theo rolled. Double fours. He put his disks back on the board and moved them forward to an advantage point.

"You will excuse me for a moment?" he asked his opponent in their native language. The old man nodded, clearly relieved that some attention would be paid to the menacing intruder that blocked the light from the narrow doorway.

"Come, Nico," Theo said. He rose, picked up the attaché case at his feet and went outside, with Nico behind him. As they approached the Rolls, the rear door opened slightly. Theo stepped inside and motioned Nico to join him.

A solitary man, unperturbed by the wait, nodded at them.

"Tahlib, my friend," Theo said. "This is my son, Nico."

Nico reached across his father to shake hands with the round, small man in Arab headdress. Dark sunglasses hid his expression. He nodded, shook hands without warmth, and turned his attention to Theo.

He clutched a small brown leather portfolio, which he handed to Theo unopened.

"His Majesty is interested in your fleet of tankers," he said without preamble. "He has set down certain terms. Study them. If they are satisfactory, let me know."

Theo took the portfolio and nodded. "Tell his Majesty I am sure there will be no problem," he said. "Tell him the arrangement will be a good one for the future, a bad one for those who would exploit the resources of your country."

Tahlib nodded.

"And for your kindnesses, Rashio al Tahlib," Theo went on, "please accept this small unworthy gift."

He opened his attaché case, removed a small envelope and handed it to the Arab. Tahlib's mouth curved in a frown as he held the lightweight packet in his hand. He seemed to be weighing it and finding it wanting.

"If you present it to the Banque Nationale in Zurich," Theo said, "you will be assured of my respect and esteem."

The swarthy features broke into a smile, revealing a solid gold tooth. The two men shook hands. Then Tahlib turned to shake hands with Nico, in

112

a gesture of dismissal. Theo climbed out of the car and waited for his son, who stared for a moment at the smiling Arab, at the envelope he held in his hand, and then followed his father into the blazing sun of the square. The heavy door of the Rolls was slammed and the chauffeur ground the wheels in his haste to be away. Dust and small pebbles flew in their wake.

"More bribing, Poppa?" Nico said.

"I'll explain all about it, son. But first I have to finish my game. I've got old Dmitri right where I want him. Come on."

They reentered the dark coffeehouse, and soon the village was back to normal, with the goats and chickens and children and old men in command of the sleepy square again.

CHAPTER SIX

"Nico and I are going away for a little while to Switzerland, Theo. The waters at Crans-sur-Sierre . . . for his back. He's really not well yet, you know. We . . . we both feel the need to get away."

"Get away! But *La Belle Simone* will take us anywhere you want to go! We'll go to China if you like. What the hell is this, get away? I don't understand you, Simi!"

"For a few weeks, Theo. To get the waters, that's all."

"He needs the waters? Or he needs to get away from his Poppa? And you, Simi, you've been sulking around here for weeks. Do you need parties, people, excitement? Do you need new clothes, a trip? I'll give it to you, whatever! And what the hell's the matter with Nico's back? He swims every day, gets on those goddamned waterskis like he's dying for a chance to kill himself again. You're not happy on *La Belle Simone*, the two of you? Look, we can go on a cruise, anywhere you like. The islands, Corfu . . . Crete . . . Rhodes . . . or Venice, would you like to go to Venice? What the hell do you want, Simi?"

"A few weeks in Switzerland, that's all. It's not such a big thing, Theo."

"How about Tragos, we'll go to Tragos."

Simi sighed.

"All right, all right, goddamn it, go to the damn mountains! You want some snow? The sun bores you, is that it? Maybe I bore you? You wanted to be alone with me, just the three of us, didn't you say that? Now you're bored?"

"Theo, you're not here with us that much. Every day you're off somewhere, days at a time, nights, too. Nico and I just thought . . . stop making such a big thing of it, Theo. We're going."

"All right! All right, go."

My dear Liz,

Please, would you and James join me for a little informal cruise aboard La Belle Simone? *I am thinking of you now that the winter has come to Washington; here it is warm and sunny, and all the tourists have gone home—the islands are waiting for your visit, promised so many months ago.*

The legends say that the gentle winds of the Cyclades are guaranteed to whisper away all the sorrows and cares of mortal life. I can promise you complete privacy and all the comforts that La Belle Simone *can provide. If you agree, I shall invite a few others to join us, for companionship and conversation.*

Even the president of the United States must find respite from his work sometime. It would be such a great honor and personal pleasure for me if you would accept the hospitality of La Belle Simone *and the islands of my beautiful homeland for a little while.*

I will look forward to your answer with the hope that I may begin to plan this little cruise with your pleasure and ease foremost above all.

> *With warmest regards,*
> *Respectfully,*
> *Theo Tomasis*

James Cassidy looked at the handwritten letter that Liz laid before him as she moved to her seat at the family dining table. He read it, and looked up at her with a question in his eyes. He didn't want to be hasty, but his instinct said no.

There was nothing he could pinpoint. Theo Tomasis was pleasant enough, charming without any trace of phoniness, and his wealth and power had been, as far as could be proved, honestly acquired. But there were hints, on the international grapevine, of unsavory dealings, imprudent personal behavior, pressures; of a devastating ambition that would stop at nothing. Only hints. There was no real reason to suspect Tomasis of anything other than being very, very attractive to men and women alike. James Cassidy was not a jealous man; there was no reason to be. His wife was above suspicion, their love was solid and true. He would never make

116

any decisions, no matter how minor or major, based on instinct alone.

Across the candlelight he saw a spark in Liz's eyes as she waited for his answer to the note. She wouldn't have handed it to him if she hadn't wanted to accept. Hundreds of invitations came across her desk every week; usually she dealt with them herself. Now she waited for his answer, with her eyes alight with an interest he hadn't seen there for months.

"I don't know, Liz," he said cautiously. "I can't get away. . . ." He set the blue notepaper down next to his plate and turned to his brother John.

"Tomasis has invited us for a change of scenery. A cruise," he explained.

John's wife, Nancy Cassidy, looked up. "Why not?" she asked her brother-in-law. "Sounds like great fun. I hear that yacht is incredible."

Liz was very quiet at her end of the table. She sat with her back ramrod straight, her smile fixed, waiting for her husband's decision.

"You could use a few days' rest," John Cassidy put in.

"Impossible. Not now," the president answered.

"Tomasis' brother, what's-his-name, Spyros, just had Princess Margaret aboard *his* yacht," Nancy informed them.

"Well, I really don't care much for Tomasis," James said slowly. He watched his wife's reaction out of the corner of his eye as he tried to form his words with tact and accuracy. "The few times he's been here at the White House . . . he assumes, and then you have the feeling he wants to use you."

"Has he used you?" Liz asked quietly.

"No. He hasn't, and he won't," James replied.

"Who doesn't try to use the president, when it gets right down to that?" John asked rhetorically.

"James, I want to go," Liz said in her hushed voice that commanded attention. The others looked at her. "I think it would be good for me," she said.

Nancy Cassidy stepped in as arbiter, a self-assumed role in the family. "There are so many things you can do here," she told her sister-in-law. "The best therapy is to keep occupied. It hasn't been that long since the baby, Liz. You're still depressed, it's natural. But you have to keep busy."

"It will be a year in May. That's long," Liz said.

The four at the table were silent for a moment. John and Nancy had several healthy, robust children; it was difficult for them to keep on urging Liz to cheer up, that she would have another chance soon. Nancy was already pregnant again, and no sign for Liz yet.

The waiter served the chicken, and when he had left the room James said quietly, "When are you thinking of going?"

Liz played with her fork. "I don't know," she answered. "Soon."

"All right," he said, "if you really want to, darling." His voice took on a soothing, urgent tone. "But why don't you wait until after the New Year? The Russian minister is coming, and you know he's very fond of you. And the Japanese premier is bringing his wife—"

"James," she cut in. There was a rasp to her tone now, an edgy quality that had never been there before. The perfectly controlled First Lady had been dashed about on the rocks of public fame and private grief for too long. Every moment of her life was exposed to the world, her every

118

word and mood flashed across the newspapers for comment, often biting and critical. It was always a strain; in the emotional turmoil of losing her baby, her control was stretched thin and on the edge of breaking.

Nancy and John Cassidy stared down at their plates as Liz burst out at her husband. "I'm bored! Politics bore me, ambassadors bore me, people with perfect answers bore me . . . and I want to get away!"

In the silence that followed, Liz tightened her fingers around her damask napkin so tightly that her knuckles turned white.

Nancy Cassidy spoke quickly. "Then you should go, if you feel that way, Liz. God knows you deserve a breather."

"I'm *bored*, Nancy," Liz repeated defiantly. "And I want a holiday."

She stood up, and looked down the table at her sister-in-law, avoiding her husband's hurt eyes.

"I'm bored," she repeated, "and I want a holiday. Look it up in your self-help books, Nancy."

They sat silent and uncomfortable. Such a display of emotion was embarrassing, even shocking. It only infuriated her more to know that they were pitying her, putting it down to her unstable mental state.

"I'm going sailing," she said as calmly as she could. "It's called therapy."

She turned and left the room, still clutching the thick white napkin in her hand.

Nancy's hand went out to comfort the president. "I'm sure it's the best thing for her," she said gently. "She's been under a severe strain, really."

"You'll have to stand in for her with the Japanese

premier's wife." It was all that James could manage to say.

"Sure," Nancy agreed cheerfully. "Be happy to. Though won't she be disappointed meeting me instead of Liz? I'll be in my sixth month, maybe I'll wear a terrific red silk kimono."

As Liz Cassidy stepped off the tender, dethorned roses were dropped from the hovering helicopter onto the deck of *La Belle Simone* all around her. Her smile was pleasant, practiced, and formal as she held out her hand to be welcomed aboard by her jubilant host.

Bouzouki music burst forth joyously from the gaily costumed players at the far side of the reception deck. Below, crewmen were busy handing up the luggage, forty-two pieces of matching beige kidskin. A great roar of laughter came up from the loading platform as one of the giant sailors hefted the largest trunk and a single red rose wafted to his head and settled in his thick curly hair.

The yacht's deck looked like a garden, tubs and pots and vases and urns of flowers everywhere; twining vines of blossoms were strung across the awnings and bright petals were scattered on the teak flooring. There was a long glistening white table set out in the starboard shade, with buckets of icing champagne and covered silver platters of food. Eight people, four men and four women, stylishly dressed and at their ease, stood waiting to be introduced; fellow guests on the cruise. White-jacketed stewards stood ready to serve. Everyone smiled.

Two U.S. Secret Service men boarded the yacht ahead of Liz Cassidy.

"Welcome, welcome . . . welcome!" Theo greeted her, holding out both hands as if to embrace her.

"Thank you," she said politely. She held out her right hand to be shaken.

The helicopter circled low, dropping more roses and stirring up a gentle breeze. The sound of its motor was muffled by the stridently cheerful twangs of the fourteen bouzoukis thrumming out a lively welcome song.

Liz Cassidy's hand went to her hair, where a rose had glanced it, and Theo gestured casually to the pilot above them. Instantly the helicopter circled higher, and the rain of roses ended.

"Let me introduce you to the others, who will be sailing with us," Theo said, guiding her toward the waiting row of guests. Each had been agreed upon in advance, of course, between the White House and the host, with careful checking by the Secret Service and a brief personal dossier submitted to Liz herself. She shook each hand, acknowledging them with her broad smile, famous and lovely—if not, at this moment, heartfelt.

The women were dressed in soft whites and pastels, flowing skirts that showed as much leg as was fashionable. Their jewelry ran to amusing costume pieces, expensive but more valuable for design than intrinsic worth. In her white linen traveling suit, Liz appeared set apart from the others, the new arrival and the main attraction. She knew that her simple costume made the others feel overdressed; she didn't plan such things deliberately, yet she knew inevitably that whatever she wore would have that effect on other women. But this was not a competition, this cruise would be an escape, wasn't that what it was all about? No photographers, no reporters describing every detail of her clothes, her hairstyle, her words. How she looked forward to melting into the easy company of these people, to be accepted by them as just another normal human being, a friend. How she longed for the chance to be herself . . . whatever that was. She seemed to have lost herself somewhere in the headlines and the overcrowded public schedule of being the president's wife. As she looked at each of her traveling companions, she searched their eyes for the assurance that here, at least for a little while, she would not be on public trial.

But the introductions and the warm handshakes were, of course, polite and formal, the smiles told her nothing. They never did. Her own smile, she was well aware, revealed nothing more than gracious, empty charm. How long would it take for her to shake off the terrible isolation that was her ironic fate, isolation that came with the honor of being a public person?

"Lord and Lady Allison," Theo was saying, "Jean-Luc Fournier. I believe you already know his wife, Camille?"

"We've met, yes," Liz murmured, shaking hands politely. Eyes, eyes, all looking, smiling, hands touching.

"Bela Nin . . . and Magda," Theo continued down the line. "Ram Karadj. Jefferson Navarro . . . Angela. Madame Naya."

"Hello . . . how do you do . . . hello . . . hello . . . how do you do . . . hello."

The bouzoukis plucked away at their cheerful melodies beneath the murmuring of the guests. Rose petals fluttered across the gleaming teak deck, and beyond the railings the blue waters of the Aegean Sea danced in the sun.

Next to her, Theo Tomasis stood tall and beaming. His hand touched her arm lightly; the energy that flowed from him was like a magnetic force and she was keenly aware of his touch. His pleasure in her presence was as real as the physical manifestations of it—the flowers, the music, the food and wine, the silver and crystal and white napery, the other people assembled for her company—no more real than the vibrations that she felt reaching out to her from the man at her side.

She was tired, so terribly, terribly tired.

"May I freshen up now?" she asked him, when the introductions were done.

"Sure, sure," he agreed, and led her away from the reception area. He gestured over his shoulder to the guests who still seemed to be waiting. "Eat, drink, my friends, *La Belle Simone* is your home!"

"The name of your suite is the Demeter," he said as he handed her down the wide marble steps to the guest deck. "You remember Demeter?"

"Demeter?" she echoed in answer to Theo's question. She looked up at him blankly.

"My statue . . . the lady with the golden sword, and the fantastic—"

He stopped and used both hands to describe a silhouette in the air, a woman's torso, emphasis on the breasts.

What had she got herself into? And risked Jim's disapproval for? This man was crude and now she was trapped. There was no one in the group she had just met who looked particularly interesting, and now this great dark Greek person seemed to think he could say anything he wanted to, make

123

obscene gestures . . . she was his captive on this vulgar yacht.

Liz smiled automatically, letting him know she was not amused. She remembered the statue, vaguely, and a strange moment alone with Tomasis in a room, watching his hands move against the cold, unyielding flesh of the woman—not flesh, bronze. The statue, yes.

Behind them, the Secret Service man saw Tomasis gesturing, and his hand went instinctively to the flat bulge in his jacket pocket.

At the door of the Demeter suite, Theo knocked, and Clara opened it from inside. Flashing him a brief, already preoccupied smile, Liz slipped in and shut the door.

Theo turned to see the security man leaning casually against the red-brocaded wall of the corridor.

"Your name?" he asked.

"Henry," the man answered laconically.

"Well, Henry, I hope you enjoy the cruise," Theo said, and went up to join the other guests.

La Belle Simone put out on the tide just as the sun was setting, and dinner was served on the tree-lined deck off the main dining salon. Liz Cassidy appeared, finally, in a simple rose-colored gown, with no jewels. She was fragile, smiling, beautiful, with her dark hair and soft wide eyes. Her conversation was polite, and almost entirely restricted to answering direct questions put to her.

Theo was sure that a few days at sea, with the company proving ebullient and no talk of politics (he had forbidden it) would liven up the lovely Liz. Her sorrow was deep and her needs greater than a simple holiday could fill. He longed for a chance to get close to her, to talk as they had on the first evening they had met, so long ago. But a great distance, more than the few months of time, lay between that evening and this. She was world-famous now, and she had lost her only child. She walked among them, smiling and even laughing, swimming in the pool and sunning herself with the others, conversing and yet . . . somehow, she seemed not to be there at all. Theo moved carefully around her, beseeching her to enjoy the things he could offer for her ease and pleasure, but the woman he remembered seemed to have vanished from within this cool, controlled, polite and elegant adornment.

One evening, just before their first landfall, the guests were enjoying the sunset from the salon, its wide doors open onto the view of orange and pink and deep red sky melting into a darkening sea. Liz had not yet made her appearance for the evening. She did not drink cocktails and often took hours to herself between the afternoon's activities and the dinner hour. Theo was talking with Magda Nin and Lady Allison when he saw movement along the lower deck. It was Henry, gray-suited as always, sauntering toward the promenade on the aft deck.

"Excuse me," he said quickly.

The women nodded and continued their conversation. Magda had been telling an ancient Hungarian legend, which bore a fascinating resemblance to one of the myths connected with the Greek island of Cos, visible a mile or so off the yacht's bow.

Theo hurried down to the lower deck and caught his breath at the wonder of her. She was standing at the rail alone. Her immaculate profile was out-lined against the soft pastel glow of the sunset. Her hair, tossed lightly by the evening breeze, made her seem like a living figurehead, the only one he had ever discovered fit to grace his flagship. He passed a few yards from the omnipresent Henry and his colleague, the nameless man in the blue suit who wandered the ship restlessly, searching for God-knew-what threats to his lady's safety. Now both men flanked her, at a discreet distance. She seemed oblivious of both of them, and of Theo too as he approached. She was drinking in the glorious sky and mysterious horizon, dreaming her private dreams.

"Hello," he said softly.

She acknowledged his company with a nod and turned again to the peaceful scene laid out before them.

Theo stood a few feet away, leaning on the rail. He tore his eyes from her and pointed off toward the low-lying mountains on the tiny island on the horizon.

"That's Cos, over there," he said. "A lovely is-land, Lizzie. Time has forgotten her."

"Beautiful," she murmured.

"Let me tell you something," he went on easily, unhurried, in a low voice. "This part of the world, the Aegean, the islands . . . it could change a per-son's life forever."

She gazed out and nodded again, without look-ing at him.

"I believe that," he said solemnly. "Lizzie . . ."

She didn't move.

"Aren't you feeling well, Lizzie?" he asked her.

"Fine," she answered. She turned now, looking

just past him, forward to the last rays of light where the sky met the sea.

"The baby?" he persisted gently. "About the baby?"

"Really, I'm all right," she said.

"The guests . . . they're very nice people," he said. He felt almost desperate, wanting to reach her, to touch her somehow.

"Yes," she agreed in a far-away voice.

"The food?" he asked. "You don't like Greek food?" Hoping it would be as simple as that.

She shook her head, no. It was a little shake, not important, not even caring.

Theo was immensely relieved. Something he could fix! "Hey . . . Liz, Lizzie . . . a very simple thing, the food!" His buoyant spirits rose, irresistibly pulling her out of her loneliness. "You don't like Greek food, what do you like . . . tell me . . . Italian? From Spain? French?"

"Yes. French," she said, smiling a little.

He laughed and spread his hands in a wide-open gesture, as if gathering in all the harvest of the world. "Flown in from Maxim's, no difficulty, every day! What do you say?"

She laughed, a low tremulous sound that encouraged him to take her hand and lead her down the promenade deck, toward the salon.

"Tonight, I am sorry—*avgolemone* and *moussaka* . . . but tomorrow! Fois gras, oysters, steak au poivre, a chef we'll fly here, to cook for us every night. Straight from Maxim's! Someone who can turn the grape leaves into haute cuisine, of course! That's just what's lacking here, why didn't I think of that before!"

But of course he understood it was not that simple.

In the morning, they anchored outside the harbor at Mykonos. The women of the party were up and dressed early, eager to set foot in the shops—they had been away from civilization for three whole days. Liz, too, was ready for the adventure. She was dressed in a simple cotton skirt and blouse, with white sandals on her manicured feet. Her sunglasses covered the upper half of her face, but it was hardly the disguise she had hoped. Crowds met them when the tender docked, and followed them across the little square and into the shop. Henry and his colleague blocked the door of the little jewelry shop, allowing no one entry except the women of their own party.

The crowds didn't object. Although the tourist season was over, somehow there were throngs of strangers who suddenly appeared, their numbers increasing as word got out in the village. Women in black, with long skirts and scarves on their heads, stood chattering and waiting to see the famous wife of the American president and the other fine ladies in their pastel dresses with bare white shoulders and red lipstick on their mouths.

Inside the shop, the women tried on handmade necklaces and bracelets, wrapped shawls around themselves and experimented with the look of combs in their hair. But it was Liz Cassidy who was the center of attention. She nodded or shook her head, when asked to give an opinion on someone's whimsical purchase. She selected a bracelet for herself. When she had paid for it, the others quickly finalized their purchases, and they turned to leave the shop.

"They're coming out . . . here she comes . . . quickly, can you see?" Little children were held up to see them as they filed out into the blazing sunshine. Liz smiled tightly, and the Secret Service men cleared a way for them through the crowd.

"Beautiful, beautiful," ran the murmur through the crowd. In the back reaches, someone spat, but no one noticed.

In a café on the near side of the square, Theo and the men of the party drank coffee and played backgammon. He had many local friends in Mykonos, all of whom were happy to see him again. There was much fast conversation in Greek, and clasps on the back and hand-shaking, and toasting in ouzo, which Theo bought for everyone. It seemed that the entire village was out, the men greeting Tomasis and the women staring as Liz Cassidy led the way to another little shop.

Sweaters, blouses, small rugs, earthenware vases, and pottery were for sale here. The stewards who had accompanied them from the ship were soon loaded up with packages, and the excitement of the crowds outside reached a fever pitch.

"Did you have a good time?" Theo asked as they boarded the launch to return to *La Belle Simone*.

"So many people . . . it's very hot," she answered, not complaining, but her sadness like a weight inside her that had to be acknowledged.

"Ah, Lizzie . . . if you could see the islands as they should be seen," he sighed. "I will try to show you."

"It's hard to get away . . . maybe impossible, for me," she ventured. "But I know you are trying. I appreciate it."

Theo's heart ached for her. He hid his feelings with a jovial interchange with Lord Allison, who had just lost hundreds of drachmas in a cutthroat backgammon contest with the young son of the café owner.

"He is a con man, a hustler," Theo chuckled, "you've been beaten by the best. Even I cannot beat him," he added as an afterthought.

The women dressed in their native Greek clothing that evening at dinner, and Theo thought he detected something thawing a bit beneath Liz Cassidy's courteous good manners. But, as always, she excused herself early and retired to her suite.

Delos was the next port of call, one of Theo's favorite places in the whole world. Surely in such a magnificent setting even Liz Cassidy would be moved by the ancient, untouched beauty. No crowds there, not where he would take her.

So much of the island was in ruins; there was a stillness that caught one's breath. One whispered here, on the site of the legends of thousands of years. Mount Kynthos was only a little mountain, easily climbed. The acropolis at its summit had long ago fallen, now only a few boulders and crumbling pillars remained. On the horizon, a vast expanse of blue sea and sky, with other islands dotted here and there as in a dream landscape.

Seated on a fallen column at the top of the rise, Theo motioned for Liz to join him. The others were wandering about, picking up stones, taking photographs in all directions, examining the ruins. The two Secret Service men stood several yards off. They were still dressed in the blue and gray business suits, with immaculate shirts and neckties. They stood out like elephants at a flea circus; why on earth they were called secret, Theo despaired of ever knowing.

She sat down next to him on the fallen granite column.

"Beautiful," she whispered, looking out over the island at their feet and the blue, blue sea and sky beyond.

Theo nodded. "Yes," he said softly. "Therefore, sad."

"Sad?"

"Yes, sad because nothing beautiful ever remains." He looked at her. "True?" he asked.

"I don't know," she murmured.

He leaned toward her and took her bare shoulders in both his hands. She was startled but acquiescent. He turned her gently so that she was facing the south.

"You see?" he said. His voice was husky with emotion.

She saw the rises on the horizon, low-lying islands against the sky and sea, darker blue with tiny flecks of white catching the sun.

"Islands," she said, confused by his hands on her and the grip of his intense feeling for the beauty that lay before them. "What about them?"

She was wearing a cotton skirt and brief shirt tied at the waist, exposing her midriff to the warm sun. He leaned toward her, placing his finger lightly on the flesh below her ribs.

"Syros . . ." he said.

Liz moved away from him. Her glance swept the ruined acropolis, fell on the Secret Service men. She looked back at Theo, clearly annoyed.

"What are you doing?" she asked icily.

"Hey, I'm showing you where we are," he answered, as if surprised by her reaction.

"On me?"

"Sure. I need a belly-button, or it doesn't work. Come on, come on."

She stared at him, her dark eyes trying to decide whether she was in the clutches of a rapist or simply a harmless madman. Having decided, she moved slowly back to her original perch next to him.

He touched her bare midriff again, with one finger. "Over there is Syros," he repeated. "Here . . ." His finger moved with deliberation, and he seemed to be concentrating quite seriously. "Kithos," he said. "And Seriphos . . . Paros . . . Mykonos. You see Mykonos?"

Liz looked down at her bare flesh and his finger touching it. In spite of herself, she nodded.

"Over there, Tinos," he went on. He touched her navel at the edge of her waistband. "And we are right here. In the middle."

He pulled his hand away, and stood up suddenly. He looked down at her, smiling. "So now you see why Delos is called the navel of the Cyclades."

She looked up at him, startled out of her lassitude enough to grin.

"See why I needed your belly-button?" he asked.

She laughed outright, and Theo felt a surge of pleasure that had nothing to do with the contact of their flesh.

"Come on," he said, offering her his hand. "I'll show you the processional avenue, the rest of the temple."

She went with him along the slope of the mountain, with the two dark-suited men behind.

"There they are—the lions. They're called the Naxian Lions, see how smooth they are. I think their bodies and their muzzles were once jagged and rough, to be scary, you see, but time has worn them smooth."

His hand reached up to touch the foot of one giant crouching lion that lined the processional avenue. "Shall I tell you the legend about Leto . . . she was the mother of Apollo, you know. How she came here to give birth to him?"

Carefully he watched her reaction. But her personal bereavement was hidden away, perhaps finally to fade into memory, and her attention was held now by his talent for story-telling.

"Yes, tell me," she said, keeping stride with him along the sun-filled plateau, stepping over rocks and boulders that were once part of the monumental Temple of Apollo.

They strolled, and he talked. She listened with fascination to the myth that had survived all the centuries.

". . . and the god Zeus said to his sister, 'Hey, Leto, you want to see the sun dance? Watch', he said. So the sun did her a little dance, and she got a big kick out of it. And while the sun was dancing, Zeus took Leto up to a very high cloud and screwed her."

He waited, but she said nothing.

"Do I offend you?" he asked.

Liz surprised him with a wide grin. "Well," she said slowly, "if it didn't offend Leto . . ."

Theo laughed. She was wonderful, this woman, wonderful. Her deep sadness, her defenses against the prying, pushing, public world were lifting now. The hot sun of Greece, the sense of history that made one know how temporary life is, the beauty of this world, the company of himself . . . she was emerging, that warm and feeling woman he had suspected beneath the bronze.

He dived into the story with gusto. "Not Leto," he said, "it didn't offend her a bit. But her sister, Hera. Her jealous sister Hera, Zeus's wife, you know."

Liz nodded. They stopped before an upright pillar, several yards in diameter, to stand in its shade for a moment. She looked up at him, waiting for him to continue.

"So Hera sent a snake, and the snake chased Leto all over the place until she found refuge . . . tell me where, Lizzie."

She smiled and pointed one tapered finger at herself. "In my navel," she said.

"Yes! Right here! On Delos, on this island, Lizzie! Here she gave birth to Apollo, the sun god. And Artemis, of course, his twin sister. Right here, it's true. Fantastic, hah?"

She was caught up completely in his enthusiasm and delight. Their laughter brought the others to them, and then suddenly they were being photographed. A man in jeans and T-shirt ran from the ruins below, snapping pictures wildly, crouching and bending for angles. Magda and Lord Allison and the others tried to surround Liz, to protect her from the intruder, but the mood had been spoiled.

They made their way down the mountain as quickly as they could and climbed into the launch to return to *La Belle Simone*.

A few hours later, the telephone rang in the

Demeter suite. Clara knocked on the door of the bathroom, where Liz was getting dressed for dinner.

"It's the overseas operator, Miz Cassidy. The White House on the line."

"I'll take it in here," Liz said. She picked up the extension on the wall next to the sunken marble tub.

"Hello."

"One moment, please, for the president."

"Liz?"

"Hello, Jim. How are you, darling?"

"Liz . . . I want you to come home."

"But why? I'm having a nice time. I'm just starting to feel relaxed, a little. The sun is shining here, Jim. It's warm, and Greece is—"

"Liz, I want you to come home now! Please."

She waited a long moment before answering him. She lifted one knee out of the scented water. It was tan and smooth with the bath oil.

"I'm not ready to come home," she said quietly.

"Liz . . . do you know what kind of publicity this trip of yours is getting?"

"But I'm in the middle of the ocean, Jim!"

"The papers are covering every move you make, every time you set foot on land . . . they're covering it like it was a mass orgy in Yankee Stadium, for Christ's sake."

"What can I do about that?"

"Come home."

She slid down lower in the warm oiled water. "I'm not ready, Jimmy," she said into the phone. There was silence on his end.

"In a few days, maybe . . . or a week . . . let me enjoy myself a little longer."

"Is it so hard, coming home?"

"Not to you. I miss you, Jim. But the rest of it . . . I'm not ready."

"All right, Liz. All right."

"I know why you said that."

"What do you mean?"

"I'll bet you've got a call waiting on another phone, or three or four. Important calls, right, Jim?"

"What's that supposed to mean?"

"Do you love me?"

"Yes. I do."

"Thanks, Mr. President."

"Liz . . ."

"Mmmmm?"

"Have a good time anyway."

"Thank you, darling."

She hung up the phone, smiling.

CHAPTER SEVEN

"There it is. Tragos," Theo said. He pointed to a little speck on the horizon. Next to it was another speck, even tinier. Nothing but blue sea and sky on all sides for many miles around them.

"Mine," he said proudly. "My island."

The yacht was making time, cutting through the calm sea toward Tragos as if in a hurry to get home. The other guests stood along the starboard rail, too, watching the islands loom larger as they neared. Theo and Liz stood a little apart from the others.

"There was no water on the island," he told her. "Everyone said I was mad. If an island is uninhabited, it must be not habitable. That is the way people reason, and why they stand still while others go forward."

He leaned, as if urging the ship toward its destination. Liz placed her elbow on the rail, watching the raw pride and pleasure light his face as he described the Eden he had created. He was not boastful, but neither was he modest about his accomplishments. Liz found herself drawn to this honesty in a way she had never anticipated. She trusted him, to her great surprise. It was a feeling she could rarely indulge. Now she watched his animated face and felt the glow of his excitement reaching out to her.

"I bring in the water," he said. "Every day, three shiploads of water. And twenty thousand kilos of the finest olive oil in all Greece. And cows for milk, and ponies for the children. Almonds. Pipelines. I carved a road out of solid rock. And now, strawberries grow on Tragos. In a few years, our own olives, and grapes . . ."

"Incredible," she murmured.

"It is important to have a place of one's own . . . to get away . . . for protection against the world," he said.

"To come and go, to come back to," she agreed. "I understand it very well."

La Belle Simone headed for the little islands in a straight line and soon they loomed close enough to see the rocky outlines.

"But there are two islands, not one." She smiled, a knowing, teasing smile, and glanced sidelong to see his reaction.

"Oh, well," he shrugged. The implication was: a trick of nature, one cannot control everything. Of no matter.

But Liz persisted, unable to resist the impulse to poke a bit of fun at him.

"Does she yodel from the top of that hill over there?" She pointed to the smaller island. "Is that how you know she's home?"

Before he could respond, she turned to him, laughing, and imitating his own strong accent, she became the aggressor, poking and probing in his own manner, as he so often did with others. "Hey, Theo," she growled, "your actress, what do you say, hah? She's got her island, too . . . Matalas? Who doesn't know! Sophia! The whole world knows!"

Embarrassed, surprised, sheepish, Theo mumbled, "What are you talking?"

Liz let up a little. She resumed her own voice and leaned back on the rail to watch the islands as they began to take definite shape.

"What are you talking?" she mimicked, but not harshly now, in fact almost sadly.

Theo shrugged again, a gesture that was at once capitulation, confession, and indifference.

"She wanted an island, I got her a good price on an island. A very small island, Lizzie. So?"

"I'm sorry, Theo. It's none of my business, of course. I was only joking."

"I like to see you joking. My life is open to the world, to joke, to laugh, it doesn't matter to me. Only that you like me. That matters to me."

Liz turned to stare with wonder and admiration at Tragos as the yacht slowed for the turn into the embrace of two long curving jetties that had been set into the sea to receive her.

"Are those houses that I see? Why, it looks like an entire village! How many people live in your private fiefdom, Theo?"

The volcanic extrusion which had been thrust

139

up from the bottom thousands of years before, black ash solidified into barren rock, had been lovingly inseminated with living seed by this visionary man at her side. Liz gasped as the details hove into view: the verdant trees and sparkling whitewashed buildings, low and pleasingly conforming to the contours of the wavelike roll of the landscape. The smaller island was behind them now, out of sight, and as the yacht nestled inside her private mooring place, the world outside seemed like a vaguely disturbing dream from which one was just waking.

Faint music could be heard, the bouzoukis again, luring them toward the island like the sirens' song that had enchanted the wandering Odysseus. But there were no rocks here that one might founder on; the way had been blasted clear, and the passengers on this ship had nothing to fear. They could begin to make out the people now, waiting for them on the dock. Tiny figures, men and women and children, waving in welcome, with brightly painted horsecarts and wagons waiting to carry them up the low hill from the harbor.

"Three hundred people," Theo said. "Free citizens of Tragos. They are happy to be here, free to leave if they wish, of course. But no one ever does. There is a school, and shops, and all is provided for them. They work hard, but it is good work. We are all friends here, you will see."

"I'm so sorry Simi can't be here," Liz murmured. "Is she better now?"

"Fine, fine," he shrugged. "This morning on the telephone she sent once again her regrets not to be here to greet you. The snow, she claims, is doing Nico a world of good. Snow, hah!"

Three decks below them, the captain shouted

140

the order to drop anchor, and the great winch on the foredeck began to turn with its slow, grinding sighs.

"Tonight there will be a great party in the *taverna*," Theo said. "Welcoming you to Tragos. You will meet some of my people, and there will be dancing, and drinking, and laughter . . . that doesn't please you?" He frowned at the shadow of withdrawal that crossed her face, an almost imperceptible tightening of her lips, a retreat. "Lizzie? Until you have danced in a *taverna*, with retsina and ouzo flowing, and the wild music and the crashing plates, the cries of '*opa!*' . . . you have never seen dancing at all. You don't like that?"

"I'm sure it will be wonderful, Theo," she said.

He took her hand. "Lizzie, there are no cameras allowed on Tragos. No photographers. You are safe here, you know. No inhibitions are allowed on my island."

She laughed at that, and they turned to descend to the waiting launch.

Horse-drawn carts were the preferred mode of travel on Tragos, and the line of waiting wagons was delightfully decorated in bright blue and yellow and red designs. The horses were beribboned; flowing streams of color danced from their manes and braided tails. As the guests climbed aboard the carts, there was much laughing and shouting.

"Hey, Naya, you need help with your ass?" Theo called out as a burly prince was hauled and pushed up into one of the small square two-wheeled carts.

"I want a horse that doesn't do tricks," his royal guest shouted back. The mare that was hitched to his wagon turned around to look at him dourly, and the other guests roared with laughter.

"Stavros will see you home, eh, Stavros?" Theo answered, and the broadly grinning driver of the prince's cart nodded with pleasure.

Finally, all the luggage was loaded and the guests and servants and Secret Service men were on their way in a pleasant parade up the finely engineered road along the hillside. Little copper bells hanging from the carts jangled a merry, innocent accompaniment as they began the easy climb.

The road had been designed to offer occasional, unexpected vistas of the harbor and the sea as they rounded the most scenic curves. The four-seater carts were padded with soft cushions so that the guests could lean back and allow the island to enfold them with its carefully designed harmonies. Theo and Liz and Henry rode in one cart, ahead of all the rest.

Liz gasped out loud when the house came into view. After a breathtaking vista from the highest point on Tragos, the road wound through a cool green thicket of olive trees, to emerge suddenly on a clearing of emerald-velvet lawn. The house sat back against the blueness of the sky, blindingly white with traditional blue outlines painted around its doors and windows. It seemed like a small, unpretentious cottage at first. Low-lying, essence of Greek peasant architecture, the house had cost three million dollars to build. Its simple façade fooled the eye, lulled the first-time visitor into a mood receptive to the endless surprises that lay within.

The halls were wide, with long windows open to the sun on all sides. Every detail was designed and furnished with a connoisseur's eye, but more than that—there was the absolute mastery of space and light and a sense of rightness in every inch of the vast, rambling house that could only have come from a devotion to beauty and tradition. Dark wooden arches invited the eye through room after room of perfectly aligned angles and curves. The white walls were hung with bright primitive paintings and hand-woven tapestries from the long-dead hands of the ancients; obliquely illumined niches held the sculpted treasures of bronze and marble that had given Greece the greatest glory of the ages.

The house rambled in carefully considered wings, ells, and mazes, down the natural slope of the rocks for nearly a mile. Each guest was led by cheerfully welcoming servants assigned to them, to private suites containing sitting rooms, pantries, balconies with sweeping views of the sea below, and bedrooms where comfort seemed to be a natural consequence rising from the elegant simplicity of the environment. Each guest bedroom had its contained, square hallway open to the view, lined with pots of blossoming flowers, which led to a maid's room and bath.

When the guests had been settled, they met in the central atrium of the house, the enclosed garden built around a deep still pool constantly refilling itself from the cornucopia held by an exquisite marble Persephone. Built on a plan found in an excavated ruin, the atrium was hexagonal in shape; each of its six sides opened into a different area of the house itself. The trees which grew there, carefully pruned for height and breadth, were rooted in the soil brought from Mount Olympus itself. The courtyard was tiled in seemingly random pathways, with minute black and white patterns reconstructed in every millimeter exactly as they had lain beneath the feet of the men and women who had lived on nearby islands two thousand years before. Small groups of comfortable chairs and tables holding refreshments were placed among the trees and flowers, all facing the lovely serenity of the pool and the ever-flowing beneficence of the goddess of fertility and—its inevitable other side—death.

"In order to be immortal," Theo was saying to his guests as Liz joined them, "it is necessary to die, to burn off the mortality. One finds it in every religion. In the Greek mythology, Persephone spent part of every year in the underworld, and part above ground. As the crops do. We Greeks accept death as a part of life; but is that not true in the Christian mythology as well?"

"I wonder if you still believe in the ancient gods, Theo, the way you call them up so often?" Lady Allison asked pleasantly.

"I believe in everything," Theo responded seriously. "Everything."

"How beautiful your house is, Theo," Liz Cassidy said as she settled into a chair. "There is a sense of timelessness here, and peace. Yes, one could believe . . ." she trailed off, not finishing her thought aloud.

Lady Allison smiled at her, thinking she understood.

A servant appeared and spoke quietly to Theo. He shrugged impatiently. "Tell her I am not available at the moment," he said.

The man looked beseechingly at Theo, expressing the insistence of the caller without words. Theo sighed and rose from his chair.

"Will you excuse me for a moment? An urgent phone call," he explained.

"So," Liz laughed, "she doesn't yodel after all."

Theo made a face, then laughed too and followed the manservant out of the atrium through one of the glass double doors.

"Now what was that supposed to mean?" Lady Allison leaned toward Liz for a bit of gossip.

"A private joke," Liz murmured. "What a lovely dress you're wearing. Is it one of Yves'?"

The party moved out to climb aboard the horse carts again as the sun dipped down into the sea and the stars turned on their glitter. The ride down the hillside to the village was carefully timed so that at each curve, a new aspect of the rising moon on the water claimed the admiration of the guests.

They filed into the *taverna* in their beautiful gowns and jewels and were greeted with warm shouts of welcome from the sailors and fishermen and farm-workers and their wives and daughters and girl friends. Many hugs for Theo, who returned the affectionate greetings with gusto and embraces. The music was loud and grew louder as the bouzouki players gulped down their ouzo and stood or sat with their instruments like lovers grasped in their arms. Their hands flew over the strings, and the music was irresistible.

Suddenly a red-cheeked farmer, in black baggy trousers and white shirt, leaped to his feet.

"*Opa!*" he shouted. His eyes were wild with excitement and joy and the spirits he had imbibed. He took up a plate from the table behind him and smashed it onto the wide square of wooden floor in the center of the room. It shattered with a loud, satisfying explosion, the bits of crockery flying in every direction. Before the shards hit the floor, the

145

man was twirling in the antic gyrations of the *syrtaki,* and the bouzoukis were bolstering his movements with a wilder and more insistent beat.

Two other dancers leaped onto the floor, an old man and a stoutish old woman; together they stomped and twirled and shouted with the rhythm of the dance. Sensuous and bold, they seemed to be giving a middle finger to time itself; around and around they went, joyously lost in the pleasure of the moment.

"Opa! Opa!" the villagers shouted. A barrage of plates began to shatter on the floor around the nimble feet of the old couple and the farmer, whose ecstasy was deepening the scarlet flush of his face.

The food was brought in a never-ending array of dishes piled high with *souvlakia, zatziki, domathes, taramosalata.* Bottles of deep red retsina wine, the smoky white ouzo, and beer lined the tables, and stacks of empty plates were placed nearby for the diners to help themselves.

Liz Cassidy sat watching. The music was too loud, blasting her ears, and the spectacle of the peasants leaping about the floor with shards of broken crockery exploding all around them was disgusting, terrifying. She looked across the table at Theo. He was eating ravenously, his plate heaped with all the indescribable mounds of stuffed grape leaves, meat balls, and salads with clots of smelly goat cheese and oozing tomatoes. Everything seemed to have a slime of olive oil over it. The plate in front of her was empty.

He looked away from the dancers for a moment, his mouth filled with food. He chewed slowly, watching her, and then gestured with his fork at her plate.

"Throw it," he said.

"What?"

He picked up a dish from the stack on the table and stood up. He watched the leaping dancers for a moment, and then shouted "*Opa!*" and threw the plate with force to the floor near their feet.

"Like that," he said, grinning. He sat down. "You're not eating, so throw the plate."

She shook her head, trying not to shudder.

Theo shrugged and went back to filling his mouth with oily, fibrous grape leaves and rice.

She watched him for a moment.

"I want a steak," she said.

He looked at her, not smiling. Then he said quietly, "No. No steak. On the *Belle Simone,* French cooking, just for you. Here, there is *souvlakia, zatziki* . . . everything Greek." He looked over the platters, apparently missing something. "Hey, no *galaktoboureko* . . . you want some *galaktoboureko,* hah?"

Liz stared at him. "My God," she said, "what's that?"

Suddenly the music stopped. The assembled villagers and house party guests shouted their approval and applauded the elderly couple, who blushed and seemed to grow older as they sank into their chairs. The farmer grabbed a bottle of ouzo from someone's table and made the rounds of the floor once more, smiling and accepting the huzzahs with panting, red-faced glee, lifting the bottle to his lips to take long, thirsty draughts.

Almost immediately the music began again, this time slower, but still loud and strident. The bouzoukis growled in their lower registers, an unmistakable call to the less boisterous, more sensuous side of Terpsichore.

147

"You want to dance?" Theo asked Liz, gesturing toward the floor with his fork. She shook her head, no. He nodded, not having expected anything else. He looked slowly around the room, and his face brightened. Liz followed his glance to see what had usurped his attention.

A radiantly lovely young woman of about thirty was slowly moving to the music, alone on the floor. Her movements were unabashedly voluptuous, but her attention was inward. She danced for herself, for pure response to the urgency of the reverberating call of the deep-throated instruments. Her face was magnificent in its concentration; one felt an intruder at her solitary pleasure. Her dark hair hung long and straight along her shoulders. The simple white cotton gown she wore hinted explicitly at the full-bodied ripening flesh; the intimate curves of muscles and breasts and thighs and calves undulated slowly, gravely, her body one with the pounding, reverberating music.

Liz looked at Theo, who was watching the peasant woman with undisguised appetite. He put his napkin down slowly and rose to his feet. In a moment he was on the floor, moving sinuously to the music, facing the woman, his back to his own guests. The whole *taverna* held its breath for a moment as the two on the floor locked eyes and their bodies glided slowly, slowly toward each other.

Then cries of *"Opa!"* and cheers rang out, glasses of wine pounded the tables and a plate smashed loudly on the floor beneath Theo's black calfskin shoes. He moved with agility and grace in the ritual dance, oblivious to everyone except the young woman.

Shocked and mesmerized by the unabashed sexuality of it, Liz could not take her eyes from them.

148

Another plate came crashing into flying fragments behind Theo's retreating figure. The woman flushed and lifted her arms straight out from her body, not beckoning to him but balancing herself as if to soar. Suddenly, she knelt, still weaving with the beat, and slowly rose, snapping her fingers, her shoulders thrust forward, now back, forward again. Theo responded, his movements explicitly inviting as he closed in, danced around her, never taking his eyes from hers.

Liz Cassidy sat rigidly, caught in the spell, unable to assemble her thoughts in the fervid display of sensuality before her. The mano-a-mano of the dance was accelerating now, the contest soon to be joined. And then, suddenly, the two solitary figures on the dance floor became as one; their feet following an intricate pattern and their bodies swaying, gyrating, leaping and crouching together.

Plates and saucers came crashing now from all directions, and the shouting became frenetic, encouraging, bawdy, bold.

"Eh, Nadia! Nadia! Eh, Tomasis! *Opa! Opa! Hah!*"

Now they were carried by the manic tempo of the music; their movements became passionate, antic, wild. Most of the patrons of the *taverna* were on their feet, applauding and keeping time with the music, leaving off their hand-smacking only to grab plates and crash them onto the floor in climactic release from the unbearably mounting excitement of the dance.

In a sweeping, graceful arc, Theo bent over the peasant woman and threw his leg over her body, high and straight. She surrendered, her long hair brushing the floor, picking up bright bits of broken crockery in its tangles, her eyes flashing up at him and her wet open mouth laughing now. Then she was up, up, swept in his lifting arms high over his head, and he whirled with her as the music rose to a deafening explosion.

A hand touched Liz's shoulder, and she spun around quickly, close to a scream. Her attention had been so totally absorbed that she had not realized she, too, was standing. And clapping in time to the music. The touch of the farmer's great hand on her bare flesh made her head snap around toward him; she felt faint, for an instant.

He was saying something to her in Greek, a wide smile revealing several missing front teeth. It was the man who had danced alone before. She saw that his tunic had a patch of blood on it, where flying crockery had grazed his arm. He was grinning and gesturing toward the dancers.

"Orea chorevi o Tomasis, hah?"

Not understanding, she smiled and nodded.

"Opa!" the farmer shouted in her ear, and reached for a dish from the stack on her table. He threw it onto the floor and laughed with glee. Plates were smashing all around the quick feet of Theo and Nadia now, and they were laughing too, and leaping to avoid the flying shards.

The farmer gestured to Liz, handed her another plate. She stared at him, then back at the dancers. She took the plate, and threw it, suddenly, onto the floor.

It landed whole, unbroken. The farmer reached for another, and handed it to her with a gesture which obviously meant: let yourself go!

The frenzy of the dance was at its height; the music bore Liz with it; the red-faced peasant man with his bloody sleeve was unbearably close to her. The outrage of being caught in this orgiastic scene and the farmer's insistence, his odorous proximity, filled Liz with a mixture of anger and sensuality and unthinking passion she didn't know she possessed. She grabbed the plate from his hand and threw it onto the floor, aiming at the dancers' feet. It shattered, satisfyingly loudly in a cacophony with the others.

"*Opa,*" she said softly. "*Opa!*"

The two Secret Service men moved closer to the table, skirting the standing, clapping, shouting crowd to keep their path of vision clear to the First Lady. Their faces showed no expression as they watched the astonishing sight.

She was part of them all, part of Theo and Nadia and the farmer at her side, and the other guests and the villagers and the music and the heat and the dance. She cheered and smashed the plates, one after another, shouting encouragement as the dance began to spiral to a slower tempo again.

The farmer handed her a glass of smoky white liquid. She took it, but her wide eyes were questioning. He gestured for her to drink it.

"Ouzo!" he shouted in her ear. Again he gestured, with his hand cupped to his mouth. His fingernails were dirty. He threw his head back in an imitation of drinking. Liz stared at him, laughed and put the little glass to her lips. She downed the fiery liquid in one gulp, and then raised the glass high in the air.

"*Opa!*" she shouted. The farmer nodded, grinning.

She threw the glass onto the dance floor. It smashed with a fine spray of splinters near Nadia's foot. The young woman sidestepped it, in the rhythm of the dance, and never took her eyes from her partner's face.

The woman's face was shining; there was a rosy flush something like satisfaction in her smile now, and her black eyes seemed to flash with a new knowledge, a sense of triumph. Dark ovals of perspiration stained her white dress where it clung damply to her body. Theo, too, was sweating profusely; his immaculate shirt, open at the throat, revealed the glistening gray-black hairs on his broad chest, and the wetness of his flesh came through his undershirt to darken the finely woven linen. The climax of the dance had been reached, evidently; the music was slowing and the dancers' movements once again took on the separate qualities of two, moving apart, slowly, slowly. Theo spun gracefully away from Nadia in a wide arc, his arms open, his head down now, alone. The woman understood, and in her own graceful concentration, she whirled slowly away from him and was enveloped in a group standing at the edge of the floor.

Now it was subsiding, the cheers and smashing of crockery had stopped. Only the solitary dancer, the handsome, broad-shouldered, elegant figure of the man; self-absorbed, moving alone with the private sensations of the liturgical thrumming.

"Hah!" she heard him sigh to himself as his gyrations brought him close to her, then away. "Hah!" softly, to himself.

Without knowing it, she was before him. Her hands were raised above her head, arched with fingers just touching. Her feet moved as his did, describing half-circles, wide and narrow, forcing her body to sway as his did.

Jacqueline Bisset as Liz Cassidy.

Preceding page: Anthony Quinn as Theo Tomasis, The Greek Tycoon.

James Franciscus as President James Cassidy.

Camilla Sparv as Theo's wife, Simi.

Edward Albert as Nico Tomasis.

Marilu Tolo as Theo's mistress, Sophia Matalas.

La Belle Simone, Theo Tomasis' palatial multi-million-dollar yacht.

Theo on the bridge of his super-tanker, the *Hellas*.

Sophia Matalas and Theo are besieged by fans and photographers outside a London theater.

President and Mrs. Cassidy greet Theo at a White House reception.

After the assassination, Theo offers condolences to the widow.

On their wedding night, Liz banishes Theo from her bed.

An agonized moment: Theo learns that his son is dead.

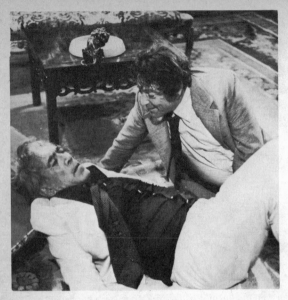

Theo and his brother Spyros (Raf Vallone) fight—and come
to understand each other.

Weary and saddened, Theo is comforted by his young wife.

Their eyes met. There was no surprise in his, only an inevitability, an understanding, an acceptance. Locked together, following some ancient, atavistic tracing, they danced. He held out his hands to her; she took them slowly. They moved together with the teasing, beckoning, passionate rhythm of the music. The crowd was hushed now, watching them.

It was nearly an act of love; the dance encompassed the two of them as if the gods had planned it this way.

Suddenly, Liz Cassidy snapped up her head to look wildly about her. She was overwhelmed by the smoky heat of the *taverna*, the smiling eyes of her fellow house guests, the gap-toothed leer of the farmer with the dirty fingernails, the stares of the peasants, the inexorably sensuous presence of the man in whose arms she moved. Suddenly she broke from Theo and walked rigidly off the floor.

She strode through the people, who backed off instinctively to let her pass. In a moment, she had reached the door and stepped outside into the dark starry night. The security men followed and stood in the doorway, watching her move toward the horse cart. They allowed Theo to pass them, and then quickly followed as he climbed aboard the cart to join her. They commandeered the next wagon and reined in, ready to go.

Theo softly gee'd the horse, and they moved off. Liz sat trembling against the straw-filled pillows. There was no sound now except for the slow clopping of the horse hooves as they turned from the village square up the road carved out of rock.

CHAPTER EIGHT

"I'll talk to you about my son, Nico," he said.

A wave of relief and—disappointment? surely not that—washed through her. She emitted a nervous laugh, unlike herself. But nothing was familiar, not even herself, this night. His words were soothing, and she felt her tumultuous emotions gradually coming under control again, despite the scene she had just been party to, despite the strangeness, despite the starry quiet of the sky and the melting golden full moon that lit the countryside. Despite being alone with him. She listened for the sound of the other horse, behind them, and the easy hoofbeats, at a discreet distance, reassured her.

He wasn't going to talk about the dancing, about the two of them, dancing . . . she felt his nearness more than ever, saw out of the corner of her eye his profile in the soft light of the moon's aura, the outlines of his body with the damp white shirt clinging to him. As he talked, she let herself relax. She leaned back to let the peaceful, quiet countryside and the moonlight envelop her.

"He is a man now, my Nico, and begins to take an interest, a real interest. So a few weeks ago, I let him hire a man for a very important position, very important. 'Nico,' I told him, 'whoever you choose, this is up to you.' He was very serious, very proud."

"And you were very proud of him," she murmured. Thank you, Theo, for talking of mundane things, for letting me get myself together. Tomorrow, I'll think about what has happened here; for now I'll let him soothe me, he understands.

Theo clicked to the horse and nodded as the animal slowed his pace on the uphill climb. "Well, Nico came up with this fellow, a good man. But to test him, you see, I said, 'Son, this man is not a Greek, this man you want to put in such an important job! And, Nico,' I said, 'this man is a Jew. What Jew ever successfully ran a shipping business?' "

Liz smiled. "Noah," she said.

Theo pulled up on the reins, startled. The horse stopped. Theo turned to her and stared, his mouth open in wonder.

"He said 'Noah,' " she repeated, laughing.

"Hey! Hey, Lizzie . . . Noah! Sure! That's exactly what he said! Noah! Of course . . . hey, Lizzie!" He laughed with delight, a roar that echoed in the silence. Behind them, the other horse neighed impatiently.

"I like you very much," he said. He made no

reach to touch her, but sat with the leather reins in his hands, his eyes bright as he held her gaze.

The turmoil of her senses rose again inside Liz with a fervor that made her know the surcease had been only temporary, even a trap. The pulse beat heavily in her temples, her hands shook and she clutched them tightly in her lap.

"I've got to go home," she said quietly.

"What are you talking about?"

"Tonight," she said firmly. "Home. To America. Fly me to Athens, Theo. I'll get a plane for Washington. Now."

"But they don't expect you for two more weeks! No, no, Lizzie, what have I done?"

She was silent. She wouldn't look at him.

He picked up the reins again, and the horse began to move toward the house at the top of the hill. He spoke sadly now, not trying to persuade her, but voicing the simple fact of his feeling.

"Lizzie . . . like no other person, you make me feel alive."

The moon cast a whitish blur over the sloping landscape. Far below, the sea was black, with a sheer glint of gold leaping now and then as the soft moonglow touched the water.

"I can't stay on these islands anymore," she said softly. "Whatever happened . . . it's done. I want to go home."

He didn't answer.

"I have to," she added. "You know, Theo."

He drew in his breath like a sharp pain. "When will you come back?" He kept his eyes forward, on the mane of the laboring horse that pulled them upward.

"Never," she answered.

"Never . . . ah, Lizzie . . ."

Nothing more was said. The cart pulled up at the house, and behind them, the other cart. In silence she went to her quarters to tell Clara to pack.

They kept the Medal of Honor recipients waiting, for just a few minutes, while they stole privacy. Jim Cassidy had his arm around his wife; his hand gripped her shoulder tightly. Her fingers hooked into his belt and her body fit snugly against his side as they walked through the Rose Garden. A few moments alone; a reaffirmation of their closeness, their need for each other, their own life. Together.

"Thank you for coming home early," he said. His fingers caressed her shoulder. "I missed you."

"It wasn't only the publicity?"

"That, too," he admitted, smiling. "But not only."

"I missed you too. But I'm not sorry I went. It . . . it was an interesting experience."

"Feel better now?"

She glanced at him, as if he'd read her thoughts. But he was referring to her sadness, the scene she'd made at dinner before she left Washington. It seemed eons ago.

"Yes, much better," she answered.

"You did need a change. You were right to go, but I'm very glad to have you back."

"I don't want to go away without you again, Jim. Ever," she said. Her hand around his waist tightened.

"That's a funny thing to say," he laughed, "but we'll see if we can arrange it. I've got a speech

157

coming up in Detroit next week, want to come along?"

She wrinkled her nose. "No," she grinned.

"Welcome home, darling."

He would have kissed her, but a White House guard was standing at the end of the path, smiling toward them. They returned his greeting and went back to the Oval Office where the Medal of Honor people were waiting.

The telephone console was lit up with a battery of waiting calls. Theo's knee touched the button on the inside of his desk, and the buzzer sounded as if signaling an urgent call that could not be ignored.

"Excuse me, gentlemen," he frowned apologetically to the two Greek businessmen seated opposite him. He picked up one of the telephones.

"Yes, yes, what is it?" he said. His secretary, outside in an office of her own, recognized the signal and responded with the name of one of the callers who had been waiting on the phone for some time. "All right, I'll talk to him," he said. He hung up and turned again with a shrug to the waiting men: what can you do? He lifted another phone to his ear.

He spoke in French. "My bottom price is as stated in the memo," he said. He waited for an answer, and smiled at the men across the wide desk, who pretended not to be listening. ". . . then I suggest you seek other funding," he said curtly. The voice on the other end of the wire became shrill, pleading. Theo listened, smiling.

"Excellent," he said at last. "I'll be in Paris on Tuesday. Yes. Goodbye."

He hung up the phone and swiveled his enormous chair to his left, where a young man stood waiting to make notes on a large legal pad. "Paris. Tuesday," he said, and the secretary nodded as he jotted down the information.

Theo turned back to the two men. His desk was extraordinarily wide and his own chair slightly raised, so that visitors to his Athens office were required to look slightly up at him, and from a respectful distance.

Theo spoke in Greek. "Gentlemen," he said, "my instructions stand. Offer the Italians a fair price, inform me of their reactions, and we'll take it from there. Good morning."

He reached just a bit less than halfway toward them, across the desk, and the two men leaned far over to shake his hand. They hurried out of the huge room with its austere Empire furnishings, as the telephone rang again.

"Yes?" he said into the secretary's line.

"Nico is calling," she said crisply.

A broad smile lit Theo's face as he took his son's call. "Nico! How are you, son? How does it go?"

"Fine, Poppa, fine. I think they'll do business—"

"Good, good . . . but Nico . . . make those German sharks come to you, hah? Let them see you are not a man to play games with . . . remember what I said, hah?"

"Sure, Poppa. Listen, they've made a decent offer, but I think if we hold out . . . I don't think they have another market just now."

"Good boy, wonderful! Keep them waiting, let them sweat, Nico. I'll see you in Hamburg before the week is out. Okay? Fine, son. Take care, okay? You have some fun, take a little time to enjoy yourself, hah? Don't make the deal yet. I'll see you Thursday, okay, son? Good boy!"

He hung up, beaming, and turned to the young man. "Hamburg . . . Thursday," he said, and the secretary made a note of it.

The buzzer sounded.

"Yes, yes, what is it?"

"Mr. Spyros Tomasis is here to see you."

"Spyros? Here? Okay, okay, let him come in."

Theo settled back in his chair, allowing a grimace to darken his face for a second, then wiping it away with an impatient smile as his brother strode into the room.

"Theo! Hey, hey, it's been too long since I've seen you. Just found out you were in Athens this morning. So I thought I'd take a little ride to see my brother, he won't come to me, what do I care? I'll come to him!"

"Hello, Spyros."

"You're gloomy? What's the matter, Theo?" The burly man settled himself in one of the chairs facing Theo's desk. He reached into the porcelain humidor and helped himself to a Havana cigar, rolling it between his fingers as he leaned back expansively.

"What the hell? I'm a busy man, Spyros. Always glad to see you, of course, but it's a busy morning."

"Sure, sure, I understand. You think I'm not a busy man, too? I'm a very busy man, Theo."

"So?"

Theo glanced at the blazing console, wondering whether he could do the old buzzer trick on Spyros. Take another call instead of wasting time. But there was something important going on here; Spyros never wasted his time, either. The two men faced each other warily. One smiled, sniffed the cigar; the other waited.

Theo turned to the young man at his side. "Go on, I'll call you when I need you."

The secretary nodded and left the room noiselessly.

Spyros waited, and when the door had shut, he turned to his brother.

"Listen, it's a busy day, right? So maybe we can do a little business, you and I."

"What kind of business?"

"Shipping business, Theo! What else?"

"What's on your mind, Spyros?"

The stocky, balding man in the white turtleneck sweater leaned forward, unable to play the cat-and-mouse game any longer.

"A tanker, does that interest you? A tanker, four hundred thousand tons, Theo." He articulated each syllable carefully, watching the man behind the desk for a sign of interest.

"Big," Theo commented, unimpressed.

Spyros was not bothering to hide his excitement now. His eyes glittered, his fist closed around the unlit cigar. He wet his lips and spoke quickly.

"But four hundred thousand dead weight tons . . . bigger than Onassis even, biggest in the whole goddamned world!"

"So?"

"Mine, Theo! Mine! Hey, Theo . . . I'll go to Osaka and sign the contracts next week and—"

"Yesterday."

"What?" Theo's interruption had knocked the wind out of Spyros's sails for an instant. He wasn't sure he had heard right.

"Your agent signed the contracts yesterday," Theo said calmly.

Spyros's astonishment quickly gave way to a deep, rumbling laughter. He nodded and laughed, and nodded, throwing his head back and forth with unrestrained zest for the joke. Theo grinned and then got caught up in the infectious laughter. The two friends, rivals, enemies, brothers—rivals, enemies, but also brothers—roared until their sides ached. Solemn little eyes winked reproachfully from the phone console, important callers still waiting patiently in the hope that Tomasis would deign to speak with them. At the other end of each of the signals: hope, fear; propositions, deals, exchanges to be offered, barters and bargains to be struck; fortunes to be gambled or guaranteed; weighty political decisions to be made, a country's fate hanging in balance, its sea power awaiting the telephone to be picked up.

And Theo laughed with his brother, because the joke was on Spyros. Through his guffaws, he gasped out the further information, "In Tokyo . . . at the Mitsubishi Hotel . . . two-thirty in the afternoon . . . hah!"

He wiped his eyes, and shook his head. "I have spies, you have spies . . ."

"I know, I know!" Spyros answered happily. The cigar was crumbled from the grip of his fist. He threw it in the basket and reached for another. He stopped laughing slowly, a little sheepishly.

"Ah, Theo, it's true. But then . . ." He glanced across the desk at Theo, the laughter over but his eyes dancing merrily. "But then how could I not know about the king?" he asked with feigned innocence.

He was rewarded by the sight of Theo's face, unable to hide the surprise blow. He leaned over

162

the desk, lowered his voice, held out his hands in a display of openness.

"The king of Saudi Arabia," he explained. "How could I not know of your interest in him?" He shrugged. "You have spies . . . I have spies."

The two men stared across the enormous desk at each other, steel meeting steel.

"What do you want, Spyros?"

"A light. For this excellent cigar."

"Don't smoke it in here. They stink up the joint. Hard to get the smell of Cuba out of the silk upholstery."

"Okay, okay. I don't much like cigars anyway. Why do I smoke them, I wonder?"

Spyros turned the cylinder over and over in his stout fingers, staring at it as if his mind were preoccupied with the puzzle. Theo waited him out.

"This company," Spyros said finally, "this corporation you formed . . . with the Americans?"

Theo nodded.

"It's my understanding that you're going to offer the twenty tankers the corporation bought to the Saudi king."

Theo waited for his brother to go on. He showed no emotion now.

"You'll be cutting a lot of throats, Theo. The transport companies, the oil companies."

"Yours," Theo said quietly.

Spyros nodded assent. "And eventually, I think also the American government, my friend," he said. "After all, if the king of Saudi Arabia had his own ships, why should he pay to haul his own oil? Then . . . maybe he'll start thinking, what does he need the oil companies for at all . . . then maybe he'll think . . . who knows what he'll think?"

"So?"

"Are you going to make the deal, Theo? Is it going to work?"

"If I want it to work, it'll work," Theo said shortly. He was beginning to get irritated.

"I want to help you," Spyros said, smiling his most sincere smile.

Theo's grin was wary, thin, sardonic. "You?"

"Why not . . . hey, Theo, why not?" He grinned widely. "For the good of the family, Theo."

"Shit!"

"Sure! The family! Our family: you and me and your Nico. Three men—and no women now that we are both getting divorced."

Theo peered at Spyros, trying to see beneath the constant posing, the game. His eyes were cold. "You're going to divorce Helena?" he asked.

"Who can live with her? Of course! Yes, I'm going to divorce her!"

"That's a terrible thing to do, Spyros."

Spyros laughed, without humor. He waggled his finger at Theo. "You moralizing, Theo? You, too, will have a divorce!"

Theo controlled his anger. There was still something that Spyros wanted, something more to be learned here today. Not to throw away in a moment's rage. He spoke with his jaw set tightly.

"No. Never," he said.

Spyros laughed. "But Simi is going to divorce you, my friend! Oh, yes. My spies—"

"Never!" Theo shouted. His fist came down hard on the white wood desk. Some papers scattered to the floor.

He calmed himself, then reiterated, "No, Spyros. Simi will never do that. Never. Never."

Spyros shrugged.

"*All right!*" At the end of his patience, Theo almost spat the words. "Talk to me!"

Spyros got down to business. "I have ships, you have ships," he said. He nested the fingers of his two hands together in front of him. "Together," he said.

He watched his brother for a reaction, but none was evident. He went on, explaining. "Ah, the power, Theo. Instead of twenty ships, we go to the Saudi king with thirty-five ships. We go to him with fleets of ships . . . we could have an empire, Theo . . . the two of us together."

"Partners," Theo commented.

"Partners."

Theo leaned back in his chair. "Spyros . . ." he said.

Spyros sat with his hands meshed before him, waiting.

"Screw you," Theo finished.

There was a long silence in the room. Some of the lights had gone out on the console board, calls canceled, weary of waiting, other decisions taken.

"You will regret it," Spyros said quietly.

"Regret is for fools," Theo spat. "And I tell you something. If you take up a knife, make sure . . . and guard your throat!"

Spyros got up from the chair. He reached for the porcelain humidor and returned the second cigar to it. He walked toward the door. As he reached for the knob, he turned back.

"And I tell *you* something," he said. "Simi is going to divorce you for sure."

He left the room.

"I'm losing my tan," Liz sighed, stretching her long legs against the sheets. She looked down at herself, and then at James, who reached up to hold her again.

"Some sunshine, that's what you need. What we both need," he said. "How about it? Let's duck out to the beach tomorrow . . . just the two of us."

"Oh, Jim! Can we? Can you get away?"

"What's the good of being president if you can't take your wife to the seashore once in a while? What's the good of having that house empty all this time . . . let's do it."

"Oh, yes!"

"Can't have you losing your tan."

"You could use a little yourself," she murmured. She held her arm against his pale skin. "Look at that."

"Ummm . . . if you keep doing that, I won't be able to reach for the phone to make the arrangements," he grinned.

She leaped up, took the telephone from the bedside table and handed it to him. He stared at her with admiration and love as he spoke to the chief operator.

Early in the morning, they were in the air on their way to the Cape. An all-night flurry of hurried arrangements had kept the key staff in a flutter, but everything had been done, and here they were. Security had flown ahead to check out the house and the beach; the cabinet meeting had been postponed, and the press politely requested not to follow on this briefest of weekends. Just the two of them, alone.

And a single deranged man with a shotgun who

166

stalked the high dune beyond the presidential compound.

Jim and Liz walked along the beach at low tide, their arms around each other, their eyes downcast to watch for bits of beach glass for her collection, odd shells and pebbles washed up by the ever-renewing waves. They enjoyed the wet, hard-packed sand between their bare toes, pointed out the bubbles here and there that revealed hidden clams burrowing down. The sun was warm and the beach was deserted, except for the Secret Service men who had the grace to stay out of sight, and the solitary assassin who had waited unseen for days and weeks, waited for this moment.

"How about a swim?" Liz shouted, breaking away from her husband's arms to run toward the gently breaking surf. She headed into a breaker and was gone from his sight for a moment. Her head emerged atop the wave; she was laughing and tossing her hair and beckoning to him.

He ran to join her. He thrust his body forward into the crash of the oncoming wave. He seemed to shudder and his body fell awkwardly onto the cresting breaker. She saw his arms fly up. There was no sound except that single loud report of a shot. The swirling whitecapped waters began to run crimson. His body floated on the curl, and was overtaken by another wave that carried him onshore where the shouting, running Secret Service men were suddenly closing in.

The horror didn't fill her until much, much later. She walked through the nightmare of days and nights that followed with admirable dignity. She felt nothing. Shock propelled her, shock kept her moving . . . that and the splendid training she had received all her life, to show no feelings, to perform as manners dictated, to smile.

John and Nancy were there; there were others; thousands came to pay their condolences, their respects, to gape at the bereaved widow and murmur words that couldn't reach her dead ears. She shook hands, smiled sadly, nodded, marched in the state procession, received dignitaries and knelt in the church. Like a robot, a well-trained zombie, feeling nothing. Alone in her room in the middle of the night, she sat at her dressing table and stared at nothing, not even alive enough to wonder if she would ever feel anything again.

Now the ceremonies were done, and it was her last night in the White House. Everything was packed, ready to be moved out. A new presidential family was moving in. Only this last night to be got through, and then perhaps the public would forget her, leave her alone in her grief, stop staring and quoting and following her. It was some small thing to look forward to, peace, seclusion, privacy.

She stood in the reception line in her black dress, with no makeup except pale lipstick, her hand as small and cold as a sliver of ice, offering it to be shaken as the heads of state and friends and mourners passed it from one to another.

She heard bits of what they were saying, meaningless.

". . . to convey in the name of my country our extreme regret . . ." ". . . the world grieves, the world is less today . . ."

The languages were many, and the words were sincere.

". . . my country, which is stung by sorrow . . ."
". . . my people mourn, we have lost a friend . . ."
". . . my deepest condolences . . ." ". . . a dolorous
time, we grieve with you . . ."

One hand that took hers was the Greek's—what
was his name? Theo? He looked sad too. Everyone
looked sad. Her eyes met his and fell away, remembering nothing, feeling nothing.

"My dear Lizzie . . . I feel great anguish. If
somehow there could be a way to share your
loss . . ."

"There is no way," John Cassidy cut in, saving
his sister-in-law as much as he could. "Thank you,"
he said, dismissing Theo Tomasis as the rest of the
line pressed forward, offering soft voices and futile
efforts to console.

"It is over," Simi said.

"Not now, Simi, not now. I've barely walked
into the goddamned house. Ah, the tragedy of it
. . . that sad, lonely, terrified woman . . ."

"Yes," Simi murmured. "I am sorry for her. The
whole world is sorry."

"Come upstairs with me," he said heavily. "I
feel old today, old . . ."

But she stood at the foot of the long, curving
staircase, not moving as he began to climb upward.
He looked back in mild surprise.

"Come, Simi?"

"No, Theo. It is over. I am trying to tell you."

"What, what?"

"Our marriage. I am leaving. No more ulti-
matums. No more . . . anything, Theo. Goodbye."

She turned to walk out of the house. He didn't
go after her this time. His heart was too heavy to

169

move. He stood halfway up the stairs and watched her go.

"Over," he repeated in the empty hallway that echoed his voice muffled by priceless tapestries. "Nothing is over!" he roared suddenly, "Nothing!" There were tears in his eyes as he climbed the staircase. If they had threatened to hang him by the thumbs until he told, he couldn't have said who his tears were for.

CHAPTER NINE

He had never been so alone before. The years he had spent as a boy and a young man, wandering the world in search of his fortune, had been filled with people—people to get the better of, women to conquer, men to challenge, people in authority to bend to their knees, men to sip coffee with and to discuss business, politics, money . . . he had never really been alone before.

Now he wandered the empty rooms of the house in Antibes, hearing his own footsteps. He strolled down the sloping lawn where no guests were to be found; it had been Simi who invited them, she who had attracted and entertained—it struck him now that he had been a guest at his own parties.

The days were the same, and the nights, too. Working, traveling, making deals, doing business.

Sleeping in Sophia's arms, in Milan, Athens, Paris. Other women in other places. Another cruise on *La Belle Simone* filled with exciting people and touching at new ports. From everywhere in the world he called Simi, to plead, to cry, to shout, to joke, to call upon their years of marriage as a sacred trust that she, she was violating with her absence. She remained calm and remote. He surprised her at the apartment in Paris, threw himself prone on the carpet to beg her forgiveness. She spoke of lawyers and of a settlement. She would take the house in Antibes, make no claim on *La Belle Simone*. She spoke of Nico and his great unhappiness. Theo didn't understand; what did Nico have to be unhappy about; what was wrong with him, wrong with Simi, wrong with the world?

In Sophia's embrace, he raged at Simi for deserting him. In Nico's company, he grew impatient with the boy's softness, ended up railing at him, until they could talk only about the business. In business, Nico was like himself, getting tougher, learning it all. Nico would be all right, his son. His son would inherit, carry on, be bigger and more powerful than Theo himself even dreamed. Someday. He rarely saw the boy anymore, only for business conferences, on the run. If they dined together, there was strain, silences.

Alone, bereaved, he thought often of the beautiful, wan young widow in America, whose right to solitude was brutally violated every day; photographs appeared on every sleazy magazine from Hollywood to Hong Kong, from Nome to Rio, showing her wide, terrified eyes startled by the flashbulbs that exploded at her from every direction. When she went to the hairdresser, when she dined in a restaurant, lunched with friends, walked on Fifth Avenue, when she went to church to pray, when she attended a horse show or a polo match, if she so much as smiled, the gossips made headlines out of it: "The Merry Widow Laughs Again," or "A New Romance for Liz?" They took it upon themselves to give her public advice: "Time to Stop Wearing Black." They asked in thirty-six-point type across a tabloid cover: "What Now, Lizzie?"

He was appalled and grieved for her, for himself, for such a world. He telephoned her once in a while.

"Are you all right, Lizzie?"

"Yes."

"Let me offer you peace, privacy. *La Belle Simone* waits for you, any time."

"Thank you, Theo. I think not. It's kind of you . . . but I'm all right."

"I'll be in New York tomorrow. May I see you, dinner?"

"I'm sorry, Theo. I have an engagement."

"All day? Lunch, perhaps?"

She was silent. He understood that he was only adding to the pressures on her. But he, too, was lonely.

When he hung up the phone, he punched one of the lighted console buttons at random. Gruffly, he figured out a way to screw the man at the other end of the line, no matter who it was; there was always a way, and the brief stab of pleasure he got from besting someone in a money deal got his juices running again.

"You owe your government $765,000, you need to turn over this shipment. I know, I know, don't

173

ask me how I know. That's my price, take it or leave it . . . be here tomorrow, we'll sign the deal."

Then he could attend to other matters, his head cooled and his emotions channeled once again into pure energy. Nobody would get the better of Theo Tomasis, nobody. Not Simi, not anybody.

"Get Matalas on the phone," he told his operator.

"Eh, Theo! You are coming to my opening tonight? It will be splendid, so exciting. My greatest triumph."

"Sure, sure. Where are you tonight, Sophia?"

"London, you asshole! The Royal Repertory Company. People have been buying tickets for months, I told you. Last night I told you. Everyone will be there. The queen, maybe. Or the prince, at least. You'll be there?"

"Yes, sure. I'll be there. Be wonderful, Sophia. I'll be there."

The splendid new National Theatre complex on the south bank of the Thames was aglitter with jewels, lights, smiles, polished shoes and polished nails, painted faces and shining hairdos, magnificent gowns designed by the famous couturiers for this gala occasion. Sophia Matalas the Italian spitfire, playing Delilah with England's premier repertory company. A she-lion storming the heights of British culture. That's what brought out the rich and curious. Perhaps the drama purists stayed home; but at the last moment there had been a surge for tickets, sending the price of a seat skyhigh; so perhaps even the purists had succumbed to the lure of the Matalas presence.

Matalas was perhaps more notorious for her shocking public behavior, her well-known association with Tomasis, her flamboyant appetite for publicity, than for her acting skill. But it was unfair; she was a serious artist and rarely disappointed her audience, no matter how unlikely the undertaking. And everyone except Matalas and her fellow performers, who knew from rehearsal what she could do, expected the worst.

Theo watched her with some amusement from his seat in the fourth row. She had gusto, and guts, that woman. And she really can act, he thought; look how she holds the entire audience and no one even stirs. Matalas held the rapt attention of the audience like a stunt driver who might or might not make the next perilous turn. And she made it—as she always did. In the front rows, the peers applauded politely, heartily, reserving their critical comments for later—perhaps after they had read the reviews. She was a success, again.

Nothing could bring that voracious glee to her face except the applause itself. Theo watched her bowing, accepting a huge bouquet of flowers, nodding as long stemmed roses were thrown to her feet, smiling with victory and a well-deserved satisfaction of achievement.

"Did you like it, darling?" she shouted to him over the crowd in her dressing room. Flushed and radiant, seated before the huge light-rimmed vanity table, she was reflected over and over in the tricky series of angled mirrors. Everyone stopped their chatter to look at him as he entered the room. Then they greeted him with kisses and handshakes, and in a moment Sophia rose from her little throne to return the attention to herself.

"It was fine, Sophia, fine," he said. She sidled up to put her arm through his. One hand reached behind her, and the little maid hastily took the ermine coat from its padded hanger and handed it over. Dragging it on the floor, Sophia led Theo from the dressing room.

The Rolls was waiting in the alley just outside the stage door, and there was an adoring, screaming crowd in the space between. Sophia laughed and waved to them as they pushed in on all sides, holding forth programs to be signed, hands to be touched. Theo burrowed his way through, using his shoulder as a flying wedge. Sophia, as usual, was reluctant to escape the mob, but he pulled her along and his driver opened the door for them just as they reached the car. Theo handed Sophia inside, picked up her trailing fur (which now had a heavy footprint on its once-white hem) and climbed in beside her. The chauffeur slammed the door and went round to the driver's seat.

Before they could get away, a short, wizened man in a stained gray homburg leaned into the open window. He grinned at Theo, touched his forefinger to the brim of his hat, and handed over a document. Surprised, Theo took it. Then the car moved ahead cautiously through the throng that filled the alley with cheers and shouts in praise of Sophia.

"What a glorious triumph!" Sophia said, leaning back luxuriously. "A night to remember, for all those wonderful people."

Theo reached up to turn on the reading light above him. He turned the document over in his hand.

"What's that?" she asked. She had thought it was another program for her to sign. When she saw the official legal seal and the red type on it, she was only mildly interested.

Theo closed his eyes. He clutched the paper in his hand tightly.

"Theo? What? What is it?"

He didn't seem to hear her. He murmured to himself, rocking slightly with the pain.

"Simi . . . ah, Simi . . ." He opened his eyes again and stared at the paper in his hand. "The divorce," he said.

She shrugged impatiently. "It's about time, isn't it?"

Theo broke open the seal and began to read the document. "For adultery," he said.

Sophia tried to hide her smile. She turned her head to look out at the bright street lamps shining through the fog as they passed. "How could she?" she murmured. The grin played at the corners of her mouth with a life of its own. She couldn't help it, but she had the momentary grace to try to hide it from him.

He read further into the document, and then, to her great surprise, she heard him begin to laugh. A snort, quiet at first, then a rumble and a roar as spasms of mirth overcame him. He leaned back against the upholstery and let the laughter shake his whole body. Sophia stared at him as if he had gone completely mad. She was even a little frightened of him, as one would be in the presence of sudden, inexplicable irrationality.

"What's funny?"

He didn't answer, but when he met her quizzical glance, his merriment seemed to be renewed. She reached for the paper, but the legal language was too dense and she was too impatient to read it.

"What's funny?" she demanded again.

He pointed to some words on the top page of the thick document. At least he had stopped laughing, although his eyes still danced with amusement.

"Adultery," he said, ". . . but not with you!"

He began to laugh again. She grabbed the document tightly in her two hands and her eyes went wildly over the page. Theo leaned forward and put his arm around her shoulders. With the other hand, he pointed to the words.

"Here . . . right here . . . you see? It says, 'did wantonly commit adultery on several occasions on the yacht *La Belle Simone* and in other places with a woman Penelope Scott—'"

"Penny!" Sophia's outrage hit high E-flat and hung on the enclosed air with a piercing vibrato that would have done Aida proud in the second-act curtain scene.

Theo laughed again. "Here . . . read, right there . . ."

But the dark eyes were aflame with the injustice of it. Sophia's vivid red mouth burst open with an explosion of ripe Italian obscenities.

"How did she dare! Everybody knows . . . everybody . . . everybody! . . . that I am the reason for the divorce! Not that pale, nothing Englishwoman . . . not her . . . me! Me! Matalas!"

Theo was enjoying her performance. "Hey, hey, Sophia," he grinned. "It's very funny, hah? Simi has a good sense of humor, hah? Hey, Sophia . . . what do you say?"

Sophia snatched up the document as if to tear it in bits, but it was as thick as a libretto. In her fury, she threw it at the glass partition between themselves and the oblivious driver. She sulked, staring out of the window away from him.

He looked down at the carpet, the twisted petition for the end of his marriage lying at Sophia's feet and his.

"No," he said to himself, "no, it is not funny, after all."

He leaned back again, letting the pain course through him. Never in his life so alone.

They said nothing more until the car stopped at the Connaught. The doorman opened the door and Sophia stepped out, her smile ready in case the papparazzi were waiting. But she, too, was suddenly alone. Wrapping the ermine around her in the chill of the London night, she turned back to the car, waiting for Theo to follow her. Instead, he reached over to pull the door shut, almost in her face. He picked up the phone and said a single word to the driver, and the car pulled away smoothly and silently, leaving Sophia in the doorman's care.

At the Claridge, where he had his apartment, he stopped in the lobby to give instructions to the concierge. He wanted a call put through to Massachusetts at once.

"Yes, sir, immediately, Mr. Tomasis," the man assured him, trying not to bow, nodding his head as if he had a nervous tic. Theo grunted and strode to the elevators.

He paced. He threw off his coat and scarf. He poured a drink, Perrier water and brandy. He sipped at it, loosened his tie, threw it to the floor. He went to the window, pushed aside the heavy drape and looked down at the street for a moment, then closed the curtain again and paced near the desk. He eyed the telephone, waiting. He threw off his jacket and loosened his shoes. He sat down heavily at the desk, finished off the brandy, got up and went to the bar. He poured himself another brandy, neat this time. He glanced at the telephone again, walked over to it, forgetting his drink behind him.

"What do you want . . . come on, come on . . ." he said to the silent instrument.

He went into the bedroom. The telephone next to his bed was as silent as the other. He unbuttoned his shirt, slipped out of the shoes. The phone rang, shrill and jarring.

He leaped onto the bed and grabbed the receiver.

"Hello . . . yes, yes, this is Tomasis . . . yes . . . Lizzie? Lizzie. It's Theo. How are you?"

He sat on the edge of the bed, nervous as a boy, feeling her low, musical voice strike deep resonances within himself.

"I'm well, Theo. I'm fine. I'm at the beach cabana. How are you?"

"Fine, fine . . . I can tell in your voice you're stronger, I'm glad, Lizzie."

"The operator said London. It must be very late there, Theo."

"Yes, I suppose so . . . is it a bad time for you? Too early, too late?"

She laughed. Her laugh was soft, throaty, too brief. "No, neither late nor early. I'm happy to hear from you, Theo. It's nice of you to call."

"Lizzie . . . all evening tonight, a very long evening, I've been thinking . . ." He trailed off, uncertain for once in his life.

"Yes? Are you still there?"

"Oh, yes, I'm here, Lizzie. Listen . . ." He plunged ahead, wondering why this was so important to him, this skinny woman, sad and lonely. "Listen . . . we talk on the phone, but . . . and letters are no good . . . the phone is no good. Lizzie, when are you coming, when do I see you again?"

"It . . . it isn't possible, Theo. People wouldn't understand . . ."

"Screw them!" he raged. "Screw people, all right?"

He was rewarded with a thin, tense murmur which might have been agreement. "What do they think you are, the Statue of Liberty in black clothes? You want people to say, 'Isn't she wonderful, she's still grieving her heart out . . . for over a year, what a wonderful widow, so sad, so fragile' . . . for how much longer, Lizzie?"

Now it was her turn to be silent.

"Lizzie? You're alive, you're young, you're full of joys you haven't touched on yet . . . you can't spend the rest of your life mourning."

"I know," she said quietly. "But the family . . . my brother-in-law is going to run for president, Theo. Did you know that?"

"Well . . . screw him too, Lizzie!" He leaped up from the bed, taking the long cord with him as he began to pace again, talking earnestly, pleading on the telephone. "John Cassidy runs for president, let him! Does that mean you have to isolate yourself? Hey, listen . . . put on something special and go to a party! What's it going to cost him, the state of North Dakota? Huh?"

Now her laughter came easily, he could tell the difference.

181

"Ah, Lizzie, it's good to hear you laugh."

"You're kind of a tonic for me, Theo. You . . . you're so different from most of the people I know. You can usually make me laugh. Thank you for that, Theo."

His pulse was racing; this was important to him, and he knew it was not the usual thing. He wanted nothing of her, nothing, except to make her a little happier, a little less lonely. He thought briefly of the woman he had sensed and—for the briefest moment, touched—who lay hidden and frightened beneath the surface. But it wasn't like that, it wasn't a conquest he was after, not this time. Two lonely people, that was all, friends, maybe.

"Hey . . . hey, come on," he said. "We'll take a little cruise . . . Tragos, hah? It's yours if you want it, Lizzie, my island, for as long as you like . . . what do you say?"

"I . . . I couldn't . . . not now . . . really."

The hesitation, could it even be longing, that he heard in her voice gave him encouragement despite her words.

"Hey, Lizzie," he crooned softly, "do something, for yourself? A favor, for yourself . . . rejoin the world! Hah, Lizzie? Life is waiting for you . . . life!"

He wondered how he could sound so sure when his own life had become bland and deadened. He'd never felt like that before. He spoke out of habit, remembering what it feels like to be fully, wonderfully alive. He was talking as much to himself as to her.

"I'll call you soon, Theo," was all she said. "Soon. I promise."

"Goodbye, Lizzie. Soon."

"Yes. Goodbye."

She hung up the lucite extension phone and reached for her sunglasses. She was never without them any more. They were huge and round and dark and hid most of her face from curious eyes. She laid her head back on the lounge chair again. Flat on her stomach, she felt the sun trying to warm her legs and back and arms. Futile. I'll never be really warm again, she thought. She listened to the surf, breaking with easy laps a few yards away.

"He sure is persistent, I'll give him that," Nancy Cassidy grunted from the other lounge on the sand nearby.

"He's kind," Liz said. Her head was turned away from her sister-in-law. "He means well," she added.

"Oh, sure, sure. I didn't mean to imply that he didn't. What'd he want this time?"

Liz bit her lip to keep from saying what was so often on her tongue these days: leave me alone. Instead, she threw her head up in a listening gesture and turned toward the house far on the other side of the wide dune.

"Was that a child I heard? Crying?" she asked, wide-eyed. She stared through the mask of her sunglasses at Nancy, who reacted instantly.

"I didn't hear anything." But she was sitting up, peering with her hand shading her eyes.

"I'm sure I heard something," Liz mumbled, putting her head back down on the padded cushion. "Sounded like someone crying," she repeated.

"I'd better go see," Nancy said, worriedly. She grabbed at the straps of her swimsuit and got up, gracefully striding across the dry expanse of sand toward the dune. She started calling off the names of her children in no particular order as she went.

Liz closed her eyes again and tried to think. An image danced across her memory, laughing, uninhibited people, whirling and shouting, music that compelled the senses to forget everything else. A tall, handsome man with graying hair and a strong virile body, dancing . . . a feeling of freedom, to be what the moment begged, to forget obligations, responsibilities, duties, sadness. The music of bouzoukis in her head was torn by the faint bark of a dog.

Liz half-turned to look down the beach. John Cassidy and his Labrador were running toward her, little tiny specks at the water's edge, getting nearer. John jogged with taut determination; even from here she could see his elbows at his sides, held firm and rigid, his chin upthrust as he breathed the way he had been instructed. At his side the dog leaped and barked, running toward the water, retreating joyfully with each wave that threatened to douse him.

She sat up. Nancy had gone over the dune, probably all the way to the house to check on the brood, to count their runny noses. Liz reached for her beach robe, shrugged herself into it, waited for John to come panting up. The dog shook itself. Wet sand and salt-water droplets splashed across her robe.

"Any iced tea?" John asked. She nodded and pointed to the canteen. He took a long drink and threw himself down on his wife's recently vacated lounge. His breath came in long, controlled gasps as he settled down for the moment.

"Johnny . . ."

"Yeah, Liz?"

"I'm going to go away, Johnny."

He looked at her, seeing nothing but the soft blowing hair and the huge dark glasses that covered half her face. Her mouth was neither smiling nor inquiring.

"Fine," he said. "A change of scene, why not?"

"I'm going to Greece," she said quietly.

He set the canteen down and gave her his full attention. "Tomasis?" he asked.

"Yes."

Slowly, John Cassidy shook his head. "That would be a very wrong thing to do," he said carefully.

"Wrong? For whom?"

"For you, Liz. For all of us. For the family."

A little smile flickered across her lips. "Ah, yes, the family. I'm thinking very seriously of seceding from the family, Johnny."

His eyebrows went up, but he said nothing. He had caught his breath now, and he sat on the edge of the lounge with his hands clasped between his knees. The dog bounded up with a wet stick in his mouth. John took the stick from him, patted the Labrador's head, and threw the stick. It soared high, landing a few feet beyond the water line. The dog plunged right in after it, oblivious of the wave that pushed him back. He pushed himself forward and grabbed the stick in his mouth to come joyously loping back toward them with it.

"The Cassidy togetherness is becoming a pain in the ass," Liz said.

"That's a sad thing to hear."

"I'm tired, John."

"I know. You've been through hell, Liz, no one

would deny that. But we want to protect you from as much as we can, to help you—"

"I know. I know it, of course I do. Bnt I'm tired, tired of Cassidy politics. I'm tired of having to share my loss with all of you—"

"It's our loss too, Liz."

She went right on as if she hadn't heard him, hadn't heard it all before, a thousand times. "—I'm tired of being the world's greatest widow. I'm young, and I hate my clothes," she finished lamely. She had almost quoted Theo Tomasis, when what she really wanted was to find herself again, her own self, not someone else's image of what she was or should be.

"Liz . . . okay. You're absolutely right. But to go off with that Greek—"

"And ruin the Cassidy image? Oh, God!"

John looked serious now, really worried. "Yes," he said. The dog bounded up, ignored now, with the sopping stick in his mouth. "I believe it, Liz," John said solemnly. "If you hurt the family, you hurt the country."

Slowly Liz removed her sunglasses. She stared at him for a long time before she answered.

"And you want me to continue the deception, playing the tragic widow, because it's best for you? Because you're running for office? Liz Cassidy, the public shrine. Anguish behind a veil. It means a lot of votes, doesn't it? And votes for you are good for the country, yes, I believe that, John, but I'm not willing to give up my whole life to it. Not now, when it's only a pretense!"

He looked at her, shocked and pained. He said nothing, knowing she must get it out. Better say these things to him, now, and then let them be forgotten, than for her to keep her feelings bottled up where they might explode any time.

"God, Johnny, it won't work! Oh, I'm a widow, all right, but the pain is not that sharp any more. The dead are dead, and I don't weep that easily any more. I choose not to."

He put his head down, hidden in his hands. The dog cocked his ears, whined a kind of question, and then dropped the stick to sit down, awaiting his master's whim.

"Ah, John," Liz went on sadly, "would you want me to wear widow's weeds until a national plebiscite tells me I've grieved long enough?"

She waited, but he said nothing.

"Well," she said, standing up, wrapping the robe closely around her thin body, "today is that day."

She turned away from him and headed toward the house.

CHAPTER TEN

"Please . . . no flowers this time, no orchestra?
I'd like very much to come aboard as an ordinary
guest, quietly."

"Yes, yes, I understand. But ordinary you will
never be."

"The others sound like wonderful company."

"Old friends. Always the best."

"Just six others, no more . . . okay, Theo?"

"Hey, hey, you are not intending to hide this
time? This is your coming-out party!"

"I want to pretend . . . that I'm a normal person.
Taking a little trip, on my well-earned vacation.
Is that possible, do you think? With all your in-
fluence, Theo, can you arrange for that?"

"I promise. You will be here on Thursday,
then? My plane will take you directly from New

York to Piraeus, and I will personally meet you there. *La Belle Simone* will be waiting."

"Yes, Thursday."

"*Yia*, Lizzie."

"What's that?"

"*Yia* . . . it means . . . *ciao. A bientôt.* Till I see you."

"*Yia*, Theo."

He hung up the phone and began quietly to give orders to the young male secretary. The first-class area of the 707 to be cleared of all passengers except one; the plane to leave at her convenience, damn the schedule, the commission that regulated such things could be dealt with later. The other guests to be contacted, personally, by Theo himself. Tragos to be made ready. All business appointments to be postponed.

"But the meeting with the Panamanians," the young man reminded him.

Theo sighed and swiveled his chair to gaze out of the window. In the distance, the Acropolis gleamed in the afternoon sun like a *memento mori,* that aspect of mortality to remind all men that their time on this earth is brief and inconsequential, except for the monuments they leave behind them.

"Tell the Panamanians . . ." It was a seven-million-dollar deal. "Oh, shit. All right, see if you can move the meeting up a week. One week, is all. I'll have a little cruise and then, if necessary, I can take off an afternoon or a day to meet the Panamanians." He leaned forward and picked up the telephone to speak to his operator.

"Get my son on the phone, please." He turned back to the young man who was standing poised

for more orders. The chef—what was his name?—
again to be brought aboard *La Belle Simone* from
Paris. Several cases of the Chateau Mouton Roth-
schild '59 to be stowed in the wine cellar section
of the hold; have the chief engineer check the
area again, there had been slight trouble with the
mechanism that was supposed to hold the bottles
steady in the sway of the ship, make sure the
temperature was right for the wine. Call the tailor
in London about getting the fourteen pairs of
slacks here tomorrow morning without fail. Have
the secretary in Paris pick up some nice baubles
as gifts for the women guests, nothing gaudy,
something appropriate for the season.

When the buzzer sounded to indicate that Nico
was on the private line, Theo was smiling to himself. Ordinary person, indeed!

"Hey, Nico! How does it go?"

"Fine, Poppa. I had a hard time convincing the
Panamanians but they've all agreed at last. They'll
meet with you on Friday."

"Okay, good. But it has to be changed. Don't
worry about it, you did well to set it up. I'll have
Christos switch them around. Listen, Nico . . .
how about taking a little time off, hah? Join me
on *La Belle Simone* next week. A little cruise. Nice
people, just a few friends. You can use a rest, how
about it?"

Nico didn't answer right away. Then he said,
stuttering a bit, "I . . . I've got to fly to New York,
Poppa. There might be some trouble with the
Americans."

"Trouble? What kind of trouble?"

"Michael Corey's washed his hands of us . . ."

"Of course he has! Of course! He had to, Nico;

don't you know he's the new attorney general of the United States? It's the law or some goddamned thing there. He had to give up all his private clients, even me."

"Yes, but . . ."

"Nico, you worry too much. So we'll get a new lawyer, the best money can buy. Not to worry, Nico. Come along for a cruise. *La Belle Simone*, hah?"

"Poppa, you go. Enjoy. I'd feel better if I went to New York, just to check it out, you know."

"Ah, Nico, Nico, what a man you have become! Better than me! Better! Good boy, Nico, you take care of the business while your Poppa plays with his boat, hah?"

"Sure, Poppa."

"You call me from New York, tell me what's happening."

"Right."

"Good boy, Nico."

"Goodbye, Poppa."

"*Yia*, Nico . . . oh, hey, Nico?"

"Yes?"

"How is your mama?"

Now there was a long pause on the other end of the wire. Theo waited. Finally, Nico answered him, in a small, fading voice.

"She's fine, Poppa. Just fine. Is that all?"

"Sure, Nico. That's all. *Yia*, Nico."

"Goodbye, Poppa."

"And don't worry so much!" Theo shouted into the phone, but the line only hummed mechanically.

"You're different," Theo said, "more . . . relaxed.

191

More beautiful than ever. Too skinny, maybe, but that we can take care of."

Liz laughed over her shoulder as she stepped up to board the helicopter. Settled inside, seat belts fastened, the whirr of the rotors postponed the need for conversation. In a moment they were angling above the airstrip and heading out over the water. *La Belle Simone* was visible from here: proud and glistening white, sitting gracefully in the water with her lines as carefully designed as sculpture. She was anchored out beyond the harbor, alone and regal. Below them, sailboats vied with the busy steamships, transports, tankers and freighters of commercial traffic, but in only moments more they were beyond the port and setting gently down onto the gleaming teak of *La Belle Simone*'s afterdeck.

"Hello, Liz, how wonderful to see you again."

"Darling . . . welcome. How I'm looking forward to this peaceful little cruise. Isn't Theo a darling to have us along? Oh, Liz, it's lovely to see you."

"Mrs. Cassidy, a great pleasure indeed."

Liz accepted the greetings warmly, an informal gathering of friends. Some of the guests were in their own quarters, or sunning themselves at the pool; how absolutely perfect, no one made a fuss. Her smile widened and grew deeper as she felt the warmth begin to overtake her.

"You see? No orchestra, no flowers."

"Thank you, Theo. I feel wonderful."

"It was difficult for you to get away from your family?"

A slight frown crossed her face, but Theo didn't see it. They were entering the interior stairway, heading down the corridor toward the guest suites.

"No, it wasn't so difficult."

"Good. Here is your suite. Demeter. Come on deck when you wish; you see? All is calm, as you requested."

"Well . . . I hope it's not going to be too calm," she grinned mischievously, and slipped inside the door.

The ship weighed anchor and began to move out almost immediately. From her huge portholes, and from the secluded little deck outside her sitting room, Liz watched the world slip farther away, hoping as countless other seagoers before her through the ages that the cares of the earth were being left far, far behind.

She dressed carefully. She had brought nothing black, only pastels and bright colors, lots of white. At dinner that evening, she wore a pale watered silk, cut with almost nunlike simplicity. Thin straps held it to her shoulders and the straight lines glided along her narrow body just to her ankles. She wore a single gold chain and her wedding ring, no other jewelry.

Looking at her across his table, Theo felt the old pride rising in him, a sense of his own manhood which somehow had lately become elusive. Simi's divorce, Sophia's demands . . . but here, at his table, was a real lady. Flesh and blood, as lovely as Aphrodite herself. Watching her smile and nod in earnest conversation with her dinner partner, he knew himself to be, once more and always, a man capable of greatness. She was the most famous woman in the world, and she was his friend, his guest . . . no more than that, he promised himself. No matter what. Don't be a goat, Tomasis.

"Do you know what Tragos means?" he asked

suddenly of the woman on his right. "It is the name of my island, you know."

"Yes . . . what does it mean, Theo?"

"It means . . ." his eyes twinkled. The whole company was listening now, their attention on the host. "It means goat," he laughed. "Goat. From this word comes tragedy, the word meaning goat-song . . . it is very complicated. There is no tragedy allowed on Tragos, of course. The name refers to me!"

"To you, Theo?"

"In my younger days, I was called a goat, by one or two women I knew."

Everyone laughed delightedly, and the conversation became general, jovial. After dinner, Theo and Liz strolled out on the promenade deck, under the stars.

"You know that my wife has divorced me?" he said.

"Yes. I heard that. I'm sorry," she responded.

"Naturally I gave her the divorce. How could I cross swords with the mother of my son?"

Liz stared out at the dark sky. "Do you miss her?" she asked softly.

The sky was vast, limitless, with stars so distant and separate in their courses that loneliness seemed to be the condition of nature, inevitable, universal.

"I love her," he answered. "I've loved her for a very long time. And she is no longer a part of my life."

"Yes," Liz murmured. She understood. Suddenly, a part of one's life is cut away . . . a star falls out of the sky and the light is gone, an empty place remains.

"It's very difficult," Theo said. "Yes, I miss her."

194

"I'm sorry," she whispered.

"But my loss is nothing compared with yours. I am being selfish, to ask your sympathy."

"It's not as if she . . . were dead," Liz said.

"Oh, Liz, Lizzie . . . now I'm the one who's sorry. I've been damned thoughtless, talking this way."

"No, Theo. No. It's important . . . to talk. It's necessary, and . . ."

". . . and you understand what it is to lose someone."

"Yes."

"You are very nice, Lizzie, very, very nice."

"It's getting a bit chilly on deck. Shall we go in? I think I'd like a brandy. And a movie! What have you got for a movie, Theo?"

"Something cheerful, lively, sexy, hah?"

She laughed. "Why not!"

La Belle Simone lazed through the azure sea, stopping at little islands here and there. The guests shopped and took coffee in the villages, climbed hillsides on donkey backs for the view, browsed through ancient ruins lying scattered about half-buried temple sites, sunned themselves on the beaches and danced in the *tavernas* to the delight of the local citizenry. They spent money everywhere, and listened to legends that had grown out of each bit of island earth for centuries. They laughed and talked and strolled and became tan from the never-failing sun of the islands. It was a week of peace and adventure and slowly ripening closeness to each other.

"You want to dance?" Theo shouted to her one evening, across the table. They had stopped at a *taverna* in a seaside village. The music was loud and insistent, and many dancers were on the floor. Theo sat with his guests, enjoying the music and exchanging jovial greetings in Greek with the villagers, but not, himself, joining in the dance.

Liz shook her head no. "I think I'd like to take a walk outside," she answered. "Would that be all right?"

"Fine, lovely," he agreed.

They excused themselves from the rest of their party and made their way out into the quiet, moon-lit square. He took her hand to help her across the dusty plaza, and they strolled down a little street toward the waterfront. The white houses shone in the rays of the moon; the night was clear and studded with stars.

"Tell me, Lizzie, about your life since I saw you. It has not been easy, hah?"

"Oh, everyone envies me, or did, you know. Isn't that strange, I don't remember much enjoying it. There was James, of course, but so little of him. We hardly ever saw each other alone. There were always the people . . . kings and comics and dying poets . . . and men of God and presidents and jockeys and . . . and I had to meet them all. And smile. My famous smile."

She made a face in the moonlight. He laughed. Her hand was slim and cool in his. The little white houses of the village were silent and shuttered. No one was about. A dog barked once and was silent.

"I smiled and smiled . . . by the calendar. By the clock! God, it was exhausting . . . it was wonderful, exhilarating, but demanding . . . exhausting. Never to be allowed to stop smiling . . ."

"Never to be allowed to burp!" he laughed.

She laughed too, a low ghostly chuckle that echoed up the deserted street.

"Never," she agreed. "It demanded . . . what? A certain uniqueness." She thought about this, never having put it in words before, and then she added, "And I am not unique. I'm just not, Theo, truly."

"*Skata!*" he said loudly. Their footsteps stopped and she pulled back to look at him quizzically.

"What?" she asked.

"*Skata!* Bullshit! You say you are not unique . . . ah, Lizzie!" He spoke as one might to a naive child, patiently explaining an obvious fact. "Because I am Tomasis . . . and you are here with me now . . . and I would want no other woman in the world to be part of this time. So what does that make you, Lizzie?"

Their eyes met, and she saw that he was serious.

After a beat, she smiled and gave the required answer. "It makes me unique," she said.

"You bet your ass."

Their laughter rang across the sleeping houses as he pulled her, running, toward the tree-lined beach that fronted the town. They found a bench that faced the sea and sat to catch their breath and to admire the moonlight on the water, *La Belle Simone* anchored offshore, her lights blinking at them like the omnipresent goddess of the sea. The fishing boats pulled onshore had nets spread over them, drying in the night air. He held her hand; she felt no tension, no need to pull away. They sat that way, not talking, until the voices of their friends began to ricochet from across the village square and soon they were joined by the others. They all walked along the little beach to

197

the landing dock and climbed aboard the tender to return to the yacht.

"I have to leave you today, for a few hours," Theo said the next morning at breakfast. "Business."

The Panama deal would not wait another day. Phone calls from Athens had become urgent. And there was a disconcerting noise from Nico in New York . . . this Theo preferred not to think about until he was away from the yacht. Never could he allow his American dealings to be complicated by his friendship with Liz Cassidy. Her influence, her connections, her family had nothing to do with him. He would not use this, never. No matter what. But it was something he would have to think hard about. He needed to get way from the illusionary peace of the yacht and the look of contentment on Liz Cassidy's face. He had never hesitated to use anyone before in his life; this time he would be treading on ground more dangerous than he even admitted to himself. He'd think about that later, on the way to Athens.

The Panamanian deal went off well. It was done. He had still not thought about how he would keep his Cassidy connection separate from what looked like mounting troubles in America. Oh, damn, Nico worried too much. Probably nothing to it, nothing that couldn't be fixed. The boy was young, eager to show he could be responsible. Worry belonged to the young. He'd talk to Nico tomorrow, straighten it out. There was nothing that couldn't be fixed.

He returned to *La Belle Simone*.

"Welcome back, Theo, we missed you!" It was not Liz, but one of the other guests who said it.

But the same welcome was there in Liz's eyes, and it was enough. The dinner that night was special—Greek food instead of French. He said nothing but watched her taste each dish with a hearty appetite, and it was enough.

"Tomorrow, a special treat," he told his guests. "A deserted island. Not a soul on it. One of the most beautiful beaches in all Greece. Tomorrow, it is ours."

"Heaven!" sighed one of the women.

"Any treasure there?" her husband asked Theo.

"Why not?" he gestured expansively. "You can look all you like. Whatever you find, of course, belongs to the Greek government. Half. Half to the government, half to Tomasis. That is the law."

The launch went out to the island first, with the servants carrying beach chairs, picnic supplies, towels and portable tents with wide awnings for shade. The second tender brought the guests, almost all in the briefest of bikinis. In a moment, the bodies stretched out on the sand made it look like the site of a failed invasion. Oiled and lotioned legs and backs and arms and shoulders sprawled to roast in the sun.

Liz plunged into the lapping surf and swam with strong, easy strokes the hundred yards or so to the anchored launch. She pulled herself up to its side, laughing, shaking the water from her eyes.

"Theo! Hey, Theoooo . . . !"

He had not joined the others on the beach, but stayed on the tender to work, keeping an eye on the festivities. He had been completely absorbed in the legal papers he was reading, and looked up at her in surprise. Only her head and one arm were visible, bobbing at the side of the gunnels.

He was wearing reading glasses. Quickly, he whipped them from his face and smiled at her.

"A mermaid!" he exclaimed. He got up from the little table and moved to the side where she clung, laughing.

"Get your clothes off, Theo! The sun is wonderful, the island is wonderful, the water is divine ... come on!"

He gestured with the papers in his hand.

"Later ..." he said. "Work ..."

The face she made clearly said, "Party-pooper, you're no fun at all," and in a moment she was away, kicking off from the tender with a delicate movement that cut gracefully through the water. She had an incredible body, after all; in the little strings that passed for a bathing bikini, she was like a shimmering fish beneath the water, but warm-blooded and soft and saucy—like a woman.

He was falling in love with her.

He turned away, settled his reading glasses back on his nose, and sat down to concentrate on the documents awaiting his signature. Impossible, he growled under his breath. Fool.

"Hey ... Theooooooo!"

She was calling from halfway back to shore, waving one long slim arm out of the water to him. He stood up, waved and felt his heart turn over in his chest.

She was doing tricks, water tricks, for him. To make him laugh. She splashed, one leg rose from the water at a comic angle, the toes waggled. Her fingers grabbed her foot and over she went, down beneath the wave. He held his breath, as she was holding hers, until she surfaced again. Now she stuck her tongue out at him, and her great wide eyes blinked and laughed at him.

"Come on, Theo . . . I dare you!"

He laughed.

She's free, feeling free now, he thought. I have given her that, at least. It's a very great thing to give.

He saw her rise from the sea to saunter onto the beach, shake out her hair and drop on a waiting beach towel, near the others. Even from a hundred yards away, soaking wet and mingled with other women with better bodies than hers, she was special.

The launch phone hummed. He picked it up impatiently. "Yes, what is it?"

"Your son, sir, calling from New York."

"All right, connect me."

"Poppa?"

"Yes, yes, Nico, what is it?"

"There's trouble here, Poppa. Might be real trouble. The government is threatening to impound all the ships of the corporation. I think you'd better come—it's serious, Poppa."

"What about that idiot lawyer we hired? Can't he stop them?"

"The deadline is tomorrow, at noon. We've got eight ships in American ports, no way of moving them out before then."

"No way? Hell, Nico! How can you say no way . . . all right, I'll get there as soon as I can. Don't worry, Nico, all right?"

"Don't worry, Poppa! Jesus, how can you say that? I tell you, they're going to impound eight of our ships!"

"Okay. Okay, Nico. I'm coming. I'll be there in

201

a few hours . . ." As he spoke, he looked out at the frolicking picnickers on the beach. They were shouting and waving for him to join them. The captain of the tender was waiting for his nod. Theo could see the smoke rising from the barbecue grill; the French chef was doing something incredible with little guinea hens; he could smell them from here.

He hung up the telephone and crooked his finger at the captain, who hurried over for his orders.

"Drop me on the beach, then get back to the yacht and tell my valet to lay out some New York clothes for me, get the copter ready and tell the pilot to call ahead for me to fly to New York, tonight."

"Yes, sir."

He joined the others under the awning of the dining tent, pretending to have nothing on his mind but their enjoyment for another hour.

He took Liz aside when the five-course picnic was finished. She had abandoned the huge dark sunglasses; sipping on her iced cappuccino, she smiled lazily when he told her that he would be leaving for an urgent business trip to New York.

"Three days, that's all. I have to attend a hearing, settle things with some government sharks . . . but that's nothing for you to know about, not important. The American government and I are the best of friends."

"Of course," she murmured. She was smiling, a teasing smile, bantering to hide any real feelings she had about his leaving. If she had any . . . "Of course you're being an outrageous host, stranding me five thousand miles from home," she laughed. "On a desert island."

"If you play your cards right, I might be able to see that you get back to *La Belle Simone* all right," he teased back. "And the ship is yours, go where you will, for three days only . . . you won't know I'm not there."

"Oh, yes, I will!"

He searched her face for meaning, but found only the sun-touched flush of contentment there.

"Three days only," he said. "Go back to Mykonos, if you like . . . or Patmos, for the rugs, jewelry . . . hah? Whatever you like."

"Maybe Athens," she mused.

"Yes, sure. Put in at Piraeus, my car will take you wherever you wish. I'll fix those American sharks—" he caught himself. "I'll be back. Three days, that's all."

They boarded the launch and headed back to the yacht. While the servants and crew carried their picnic supplies and tents and towels from the island and tidied up the beach to its pristine condition for other explorers to find, the guests aboard the yacht showered and rested before dressing for dinner.

He tapped on the door of the Demeter suite just as Liz was stepping into her dressing gown. Clara answered the door and Liz motioned for him to come in.

"I'm leaving," he said, "just wanted to say goodbye. Have a good time, see you on Friday, okay? On Tragos, Friday."

"You look very nice in your proper business suit, Theo," she said, still teasing.

"Liz . . ."

"Yes, Theo?"

203

"I want you to know . . . my dealings with the American authorities, the government . . ."

She looked at him in surprise. In her eyes, he saw the filter of control and caution—distrust—slide like an invisible wall between them. He cursed himself for an ass, for having mentioned it at all. It was not in her nature to suspect ulterior motives. Why had he felt it necessary to even hint. . . ? Because he was, for once in his life, determined to play it straight, for her sake, and he needed her to know that.

"It has nothing, nothing to do with you. With our friendship," he stated boldly. "I only want you to know that, to believe it. It is important to me."

"Of course I believe it, Theo. Anyway, I have no influence any more. You know that. Don't you?"

Her voice had gone so quiet he could hardly hear it. He stepped close to her, lifted her chin with his hand, looked into her eyes for the contact he craved. She smiled back at him, and he knew no more than she wanted him to.

"I would never hurt you," he said softly.

"Call John and Nancy for me, will you?" she asked him, still smiling.

"Of course. Shall I tell them you are having a wonderful time?"

"By all means!" she laughed. She moved slightly away from him. He dropped his hand to his side.

"Friday on Tragos, okay?"

"Yes."

"Goodbye, then . . . for three days only."

"Goodbye . . . goodbye, Theo."

He stepped toward her, leaned forward to kiss her cheek, without touching her with his hands.

Then he left the room and the steward outside in the corridor shut the door quietly.

From the deck of her sitting room, Liz watched the helicopter circle up from the aft deck and glide away into the sunset.

"Goodbye, Theo," she murmured, and went inside to dress for dinner.

Nothing attracted her tonight, nothing in her closet looked worth bothering to get into. Suddenly she felt weary from the afternoon's exertion in the sun and water.

"Clara!" she called, and the maid came quickly from the bedroom. "Clara, would you phone the dining steward and ask him to serve dinner in my room tonight? And tell the other guests I won't be joining them . . . I think I'd like to dine alone tonight, on the deck here."

"Yes, ma'am."

The dining steward arrived in a few moments, pad of paper and pencil in hand.

"Is there anything special you would enjoy for your dinner, Madame?" he asked.

"Yes," she smiled, "I'm very hungry. I would like *moussaka*."

"*Moussaka*, yes," he repeated, writing.

"And a small salad . . . with feta cheese. A lot of it."

"Yes, ma'am. And for dessert?"

She thought for a moment, struggling for a memory buried casually away, months before. "Can the chef make a . . . *galaktobour*—" She stopped, laughing, looked up at the steward for help.

"A *galaktoboureko*, yes, I'm sure he can," he said smoothly, writing it down.

"Thank you," she said.

She looked out at the sky, where the chopper had disappeared and the stars were beginning to glow. She took a step toward the open glass doors onto the deck and then turned to speak to the dining steward, who was at the door about to leave.

"And, steward . . ." she called.

"Yes, ma'am?"

She grinned, a private joke. "Some wine, please. Retsina."

"Yes, ma'am. Will that be all?"

She nodded. He let himself out, and she turned back to the last rays of the fading light. The little desert island was dark, a single rock in the middle of the sea. In a moment, the darkness settled over it and she felt the engines of *La Belle Simone* begin to turn again as the yacht made ready to sail away.

"Hah!" she murmured to herself, and then, louder, she sent a solitary salute to the horizon: "Hah!"

CHAPTER ELEVEN

"Nico, I'll be arriving at midnight, New York time. Let's go out somewhere together, have some fun, what do you say? Bring your girl, Nico . . . you have a girl there, hah?"

"Yes," Nico admitted, "but won't you want to get some sleep, Poppa? It's six hours later for you, don't you think you ought to get some rest before the hearing?"

"Rest is for dead people," Theo shouted into the phone. "I'll sleep a little here, on the plane. What's your girl's name, Nico?"

"Aggie."

"Aggie? What kind of name? Oh, well, I'll bet she's beautiful, hah, Nico?"

"Sure she is. But we have to talk, we have to prepare for the hearing, Poppa, for God's sake."

"Oh, Nico, Nico, when will you learn . . . there is much that can be said over a table, in the company of beautiful women, with a bit of wine, with music . . . sometimes it's better that way, talking."

He could hear Nico's sigh of resignation on the other end of the radio phone.

"Come on, Nico. Tell me the name of a good club, a happy place, lots of people, where you can take your Aggie to meet your Poppa, hah? I'll see you there, midnight."

"All right. How about the Studio Eight? It's on Fifty-seventh Street."

"Fine, fine. I'll see you there. Don't worry so much, son."

"Bye, Poppa."

"*Yia.*"

Theo slept soundly as the plane crossed the Atlantic, and was awakened by the little light above his bed that signaled a quarter-hour to landing. He saw the lights of New York below, the most beautiful man-made sight in the world, exciting, challenging, every light a window into someone's whole life. The concentration of energy and wealth and emotions packed into that city always acted like a battery charging a man; he felt filled with anticipation for the challenge of this visit. Impound his ships, would they? He had a trick or two up his sleeve. Those lights below were shining because Theo Tomasis made it possible to ship the power they needed; he'd have to remind them of that. As he knotted his tie, the plane taxied to a stop at the private hangar of his corner of JFK airport. The customs man came aboard, to be greeted as an old friend. The helicopter took him to the midtown landing dock, and his car met him there to whisk him to the Studio Eight through the lagging late-night traffic.

The club was cheerful, gaudy with abstractions of flashing, ever-moving lights in every color of the rainbow. The music was loud and pounding, and Theo found himself dancing in the American style, as if he'd been born in Detroit, Michigan no more than twenty years ago. His partner was a woman he'd never seen before; she had been moving across the crowded dance floor by herself—he didn't know whether she had been dancing solo or making her way to another part of the club—when he'd caught her hand, whirled her acquiescent, liquid body with the beat of the music. They didn't touch, but somehow they were together; and she laughed as she danced, throwing her head back, showing lustrous teeth that flashed in the strobe lights like some wild, magnificent, animal. He loved her, for that moment, loved it all. When the music stopped, he took her hand and she led him to a table where a thin, unsmiling man sat alone.

"My husband," she said, sliding into her chair.

"Thank you for your wife," Theo said. The man eyed him suspiciously, then seemed to recognize, up through the fog of his glazed waking dream, a face he had seen—where? Newspapers, magazines, somewhere. He nodded happily, reached up to pat Theo's arm. Theo patted him back, made a bowing gesture to the lovely woman who nodded carelessly. Her eyes were already searching the room for something, someone, some elusive fantasy of her own.

Theo made his way to the table where Nico and Aggie were sitting and dropped heavily into his chair.

"Beautiful, beautiful," he murmured. He nodded in the direction of his recent dancing partner, and then turned his attention to the two young people. His hand reached out almost of its own volition, to touch Nico's cheek.

"Magnificent, the mustache," he nodded, giving his approval to the harvest of carefully tended growth under his son's nose. "It suits you, makes you look mature, handsome. Greek," he smiled. "Good."

Nico sat back in his chair, out of reach of his father's outstretched hand. Around their table the waiters seemed to be hovering, ignoring the calls of other patrons, waiting for a chance to serve Tomasis.

"Vodka," he said over his shoulder. "Cold, and neat. For you? Anything?"

Aggie shook her long, straight blond hair, no. She was sipping at a drink that looked sweet and kind of thick. Nico was drinking Mexican beer.

Theo leaned over, to speak in a confidential tone to Aggie, but loud enough for Nico to hear. "My son worries . . . is that what he does all the time, worries? Every time I see him . . . is he that way with you?"

Aggie's smile was angelic. She couldn't have been more than eighteen at the most; her smile was ingenuous and her teeth even and small. She was a beautiful young girl, with a virginal quality that would turn hard, cynical, smart-ass in a year or so. No lipstick, the pink lips needed none. Nico sure could pick them. Why did he shy away from Theo . . . they were the same, the same underneath, the same man, he and his son.

"He doesn't worry when he's with me," Aggie drawled easily, with her innocent smile.

"Poppa..."

Theo turned from the girl's fresh face to his grown-up son. "She's a very pretty girl, Nico."

"Poppa, they've impounded eight of our ships. Tonight. They didn't wait for the deadline. They've taken eight ships!"

"And?" Theo asked.

"And the *Saudi Star* goes into Norfolk tomorrow. They'll impound it too. What the hell are we doing here?"

"Listen ... don't worry so much. What can you do in the middle of the night about ships, governments? Nothing. So why don't you dance a little bit, Nico. Take this pretty Aggie in your arms and dance, relax. Tomorrow ..."

Nico stared across the tiny table at his father, and then shook his head angrily. He turned his face away.

"Nico . . ." Theo relented. He reached across and put his hand on his son's clenched fist. He spoke in a low, reassuring, serious tone, as serious as the boy's. "Nico, tomorrow I'll call Washington. Michael Corey is the attorney general, for Christ's sake. He was my lawyer, my personal friend. I'll fix everything! Not to worry now, all right?" He grinned, trying to seduce a response from his son, who merely sighed again loudly and picked up his glass to drain the beer in one long gulp.

"Hey, Nico, where do you find such girls, such beautiful girls?" Theo teased. "Aggie, she's lovely."

Nico dawdled with the empty beer glass, not looking at either of them.

"Jesus Christ!" Theo burst in a sigh of bewildered resignation. "Talk to her! Dance . . . something!"

Nico's elbow hit the table and he put his face in his open palm, staring at his father.

"Okay, come on, Aggie, come dance with Nico's poppa?"

Aggie nodded, still with the innocent smile of a happy child, and stood up.

"Some poppa," she giggled, as Theo led her onto the floor.

"He's a good boy, hah?" Theo shouted to her as they bounced face to face in time with the beat.

"Beautiful," Aggie agreed.

"Beautiful," he repeated. "All grown up. Settled. A very serious young man."

Aggie threw back her head and laughed. "For sure!" she shouted.

"You like him, hah?"

Aggie's cherubic little face lit up with her smile, wider and more innocent than ever. "I adore him!" she agreed. Still bouncing with the pulse of the music, she was staring over Theo's shoulder with wide eyes. He turned to look.

At their table, Nico was talking with two men in topcoats. They were standing over him. They were not smiling. One was older, with nearly white hair and a deeply creased, weary face. The other was young, as young as Nico. He also had a mustache, with curled-up handlebars. Both men kept their hands in their pockets. In the melee of smartly-dressed disco patrons, the two looked ominously out of place.

Theo left Aggie standing there, still jiggling in time to the music. He reached the table in several strides, ignoring the dancers who ignored him as well.

". . . and I'm telling you, behave!" the older man was saying to Nico. He was waving a forefinger under Nico's nose.

"What the hell is this!" Theo asked quietly as he came up to them.

The younger man turned to him. "Mr. Tomasis?" he asked politely.

"What the hell is going on here? Nico?" Theo looked to his son for an explanation. The boy was sitting there, staring up at the man in the cheap black topcoat who seemed to be using threatening gestures to him.

"Poppa, they're F.B.I." Nico said.

The older man reached into his pocket and flipped an identification card for Theo to see: Norman DiBlassio, Federal Bureau of Investigation, agent. The younger man showed his plastic-coated card: Robert Becker, also F.B.I., also an agent.

Becker was holding another piece of paper in his hand behind the card case. He indicated it with a wave.

"Federal warrant, Mr. Tomasis. You're under arrest."

Theo felt the eyes of nearby patrons on him, and the eyes of his son. He pushed at the paper Becker was holding, flicked it with his fingers.

"A joke," he said, dismissing the young idiot.

"Violation of the United States Merchant Marine Act, Section Nineteen," Becker said formally. He leaned over to tuck the warrant into Theo's jacket pocket.

At his touch, Theo's rage broke over him like a

213

tidal wave. He pushed Becker away. "*Some kind of goddamned joke!*" he shouted.

"Come along, Mr. Tomasis," Becker said, taking Theo's arm firmly.

At that, Nico leaped from his chair, pushing the older agent out of his way to reach his father's side. "Take your goddamned hands off my father—" he shouted, reaching out to them with angry fists.

DiBlassio stepped in between them. He flattened his open hand against Nico's chest, pushing him against the wall behind the table.

"Did you hear what I told you, I told you to behave!" he snarled.

Theo shoved Becker out of his way. The young man lost his balance and would have fallen, but grabbed the back of a chair and steadied himself. By now the people at all the tables around them were alternately cheering and hissing, staring at the scene as if it were street theater being staged for their amusement.

A flashbulb went off in Theo's face as he reached out to grab DiBlassio from behind. With one practiced kick Theo brought the camera up out of the photographer's hands and sent it flying to shatter against the wall. With both hands he spun the older agent around. Their eyes were inches apart.

"If you ever touch my son again I'll break your ass!" he spat into DiBlassio's face.

But the younger agent was right behind him. He grabbed Theo's arm, twisted it up along his back, and snapped a handcuff on his wrist.

In disbelief, Theo dropped his assault on DiBlassio and turned his body around to ease the pain in his arm. He stared down at the handcuff, with its partner dangling in cold glittering threat against his side.

"Want the other cuff?" Becker asked him, a sardonic smile crossing his face. "Going to give us trouble, Mr. Tomasis?"

"Fuck yourself," Theo muttered. Becker grabbed Theo's other hand and twisted the handcuff on it, while everyone including Theo himself watched incredulously.

Nico was standing next to him, disheveled, looking like a little boy despite the handsome mustache.

"Poppa?"

Theo managed a smile. It was, in fact, pretty goddamned funny. Theo Tomasis in a nightclub brawl, handcuffed and led to prison, probably in a goddamned Ford. Hah!

"Pay the check," he said to Nico. He started to lift his hand instinctively, in a kind of wave of farewell, but the hands were locked together and it became a pathetic gesture.

He didn't spend the night in prison, of course. Released on his own recognizance, he caught a couple of hours sleep before heading for Washington.

In a huge conference room at the Department of Justice, he confronted Michael Corey.

"Handcuffed! In a nightclub, for Christ's sake. A goddamned discotheque . . . fingerprinted like some kind of goddamned common criminal! Was John Cassidy behind this? Hah, Michael, my friend, my pal! Hah?"

"John's not in government anymore, Theo. He had nothing to do with it."

"Who, then? Who's out to humiliate me, to get

215

my picture in the papers like a goddamned pick-pocket junkie in handcuffs? You?"

"It was my play, Theo, but that's not why. You should know better than that."

Theo sat down for the first time since entering the enormous conference room. It was a room calculated to impress, to remind its occupants that this was Government. Serious, important. Nothing frivolous took place here, no jokes. The conference table was as slick as glass, the chairs along its length were tall, their black leather rubbed soft through years of constant use.

Theo was not impressed.

"Ah, Michael, Michael, you are beautiful!" he said. He smiled down the length of the table at the attorney general. "A very important man now, very. Beautiful! You suit the office well, Michael, you really do. But what happened, Michael? Back there, when you were just a New York lawyer . . . my lawyer . . . didn't you tell me nothing could go wrong? It was completely legal, hah?"

Corey winced at the accusation he knew had to come. But he stood his ground. Sadly, solemnly, he explained his position.

"But we're not on the same side now," he said. "And what you're doing is inimical to the interests of the government of the United States."

"And you're a prick!" Theo shouted, pounding the table with his fist. "*Arhithi . . .*" His English failed him. He forced himself to calm down, to stay on top of this situation. "I waived conflict of interest for you," he said. "I had trust in you, Michael. Faith. Christ! What are you talking to me about government! Talk to me oil companies, I'll know what you're talking about!"

"All right," Corey said quietly. He leaned forward, his hands open before him on the table, as if to show he had nothing devious to hide, nothing up his sleeve now. "My government feels that the Saudis would never have agreed to their own merchant fleet . . . the fleet that you supplied them, Theo . . . unless they were thinking about eventual expropriation of the oil companies . . ."

The light went on for Theo. "Spyros!" he muttered. "Son of a bitch . . ."

Michael paid no attention to the interruption. He had worked this out beforehand. Knowing it would be difficult to face Theo with it, intent on keeping the enemy clearly in his sights, he explained the reasoning which had led to Theo's arrest.

". . . eventually throwing the oil companies out of the country . . ."

"That son of a bitch brother of mine! He got to you . . . he told me the same goddamned thing! He got to you! You and the oil companies. . . !"

Michael Corey stared at him, waiting for Theo to sort it all out, to catch up.

"Spyros put the same words in your brain and scared the shit out of all of you, didn't he? Spyros . . . ah, Spyros . . ." He ground his teeth together, his fists knotted. He could have killed, at this moment. He glared at the attorney general.

"Michael . . . arresting me is a show of force to the Arabs, hah?"

Corey was evasive. "Well . . . suppose they all got together and decided they could control their own oil. My God!"

"We're two old warriors, Michael . . . tell me, what's the ransom going to be?"

Corey nodded. Now they were through with emotions, histrionics, time to get down to business.

"You'll lose those twenty ships, and a lot of money . . . and my guess is, Theo, it'll take a miracle to keep you out of jail."

CHAPTER TWELVE

She was waiting for him on Tragos.

Long before the chopper came close enough for figures to be made out, he was peering anxiously down through the plexiglas bubble to see if she was waiting. The island, with its tiny satellite nearby, rose from the blue misty horizon at last. As he neared it, its familiar, reassuring outlines took shape.

The sloping rock, green because he had made it so, the white-edged beach, *La Belle Simone* resting in her private cove. And nestled in the high bosom of the hillside, the long, low rambling house, white against the imported forest that secluded it; the thin ribbon of road, winding down to the village; the cluster of white houses, the square, the landing strip . . . yes . . . she was there.

The beach buggy was half-hidden in the low shrubs by a clearing, waiting. The canvas cover, jaunty pink and white stripes, hid the occupants of the customized jeep from his view, but moments ago he had spoken to her from Athens and she had said she would be there, and there she was. The wind from the helicopter rotors set the fringe of the buggy's awning dancing as the chopper eased down onto the painted white circle of rock.

Theo climbed down, waving to her. She was wearing dark glasses, sitting quietly in the rear of the buggy. The driver returned the wave. She sat motionless, smiling beneath the wide mask of the sunglasses.

"I hurried . . . to come home. I was away too long," he said, taking her hand. He didn't get into the buggy, but stood looking up at her, paying homage.

"Yes, you were," she said. "I missed you."

He tugged gently at her hand. "Let's walk, okay?"

She nodded and let him help her down from the buggy. Theo dismissed the driver, who drove off ahead of them on the road to the house.

"I thought, coming home, I thought of how much I *wanted* to be coming home," Theo said quietly as he and Liz walked away from the clearing. He spoke simply, with complete sincerity. "This is the best arrival I ever had."

She glanced sidelong at him, a little half-smile on her lips. Her long legs, tanned and bare, matched his stride easily. In the warm morning sun, the quiet island seemed quite enchanted to him; perhaps to her as well, he thought.

"Because of you, Lizzie," he said.

They had reached one of the ridges where the road curved and the green plantings opened to reveal the sweep of the sea below. He stopped walking, and she stood silently, looking away from him at the blue water. He reached out, touching her bare arm tentatively. Now she turned her face to him. Gently, he removed the dark glasses from her face. He looked into her wide eyes; they revealed nothing of her true feelings.

"Lizzie . . . let's get married."

Now her eyes were those of a startled doe, gauging whether to run, to hide.

"Theo . . ."

He waited. She said nothing more, but looked away from him with a troubled expression. He held her arm tenderly, made no move to press her, trying to be patient, trying to reach the woman he knew throbbed inside this perfect shell. Her arm was cool to his touch.

"What do you think?" he asked, almost in a whisper. "Marry me, eh?"

She looked out at the horizon, as if to find the answer there. In a small voice, she answered. "Theo . . . I don't think it's such a good idea."

He dropped his hand, stood facing her, willing her to look at him, to see the longing, the need in him. The love.

"Why not?" he asked. "Because I'm older? Because I'll die first? You'll live a long time without me?"

A look of pain crossed her face. "That . . . that makes me very sad," she said.

"Lizzie, Lizzie . . . you know why?" He was grinning, almost shouting now with joy. "Jesus Christ! You love me! Yes, absolutely, you do!"

221

She shook her head, hard. "No . . ."

"Yes!" he shouted. "Yes, it makes you sad! Desire and pity . . . the whole essence of love, Lizzie! It's true! *Pothos Ke Iktos* . . . desire and pity! The essence." He turned her shoulders gently, to make her face him. "From an old Greek," he said, smiling.

"What old Greek?"

"Me."

Her smile seemed to get the better of her. But she was not convinced. "Oh, Theo!" she sighed, "It's true, I'd rather be with you than any man I know . . . but another marriage . . . to be controlled again . . . it doesn't make any sense. Not yet, not now."

"You want to wait? You want to marry me, but to wait?"

"I . . . I don't know . . . no. No, it just doesn't make any sense at all, Theo."

Stung, he moved away from her, almost spitting out his words.

"What doesn't make sense? That I'm not like the Cassidys? It's a different universe, hah? I'm a peasant, a pirate?"

She shook her head in protest, but he went on bitterly.

"A shark, is that why? Who'd marry you to stay out of jail. Is that what you think?"

"No," she said. "No."

"But you know, hah? You know that I am in trouble with the U.S. government, and I might go to jail? But if you married me, I would be safe. Is that what you mean? You think that's why . . ."

"No, Theo!" she cut in. "I don't think that."

"Or the Widow Cassidy gets married and shocks

222

the whole world, is that it? That bothers you, eh?"

She sank down on a large, flat rock. "Yes, that bothers me. Some," she admitted.

He knelt before her. It was somehow not incongruous; in any other man it would have been, but Theo's natural grace and his overwhelming sincerity made the gesture moving rather than absurd. She reached out to touch his soft gray curls.

"Oh, Theo . . ."

"Lizzie, why not, hah? What makes sense, what do you want, what?" he asked in a husky stammer.

"What do I want?" she repeated, dangerously close to crying. "What do I want . . . to be allowed . . . to be free, Theo. To be allowed . . . anything. I want to start again, to be permitted the world! Freedom to come and go, to do what I want to, anything, without . . . handcuffs . . . obligations, duties, an image to live up to . . ."

It was as close to the surface as her emotions ever rose; he was encouraged by her tremulous show of passion. Such a small thing to want; he could give her freedom. It was a small thing, he thought.

He sat beside her on the warm rock and put his arm around her cool, bare shoulders. "What I'm telling you," he said, "I can give you this . . . But you must take it, Lizzie . . . you must demand, not ask. Demand! You must laugh and take . . . and get up and shake your shoulders, and be rude, and stand on your head . . . do you know what I am saying?"

"I . . . I think so. Yes."

"Then what is the problem? Lizzie . . . I am Tomasis."

She stared at him, inches away from his bursting energy that could reach out and encompass them both. He could feel her breath, warm and sweet, close to his own face. He waited, felt her pulse quicken and saw the slow comprehension dawning in her eyes.

"Yes . . ." she murmured. "It's true . . . it is possible for you to let me be free . . . isn't it? Yes . . ."

"Yes," he repeated. He held his breath.

She was thinking, hard, about what he was offering. Not a gift, not permission or new rules, but freedom for herself—to be free, to be what she wanted, be as he had always been, as she could be with him. His eyes were kind, the deep creases in his face beckoned to her as a safe harbor, a place to hide . . . no, a strong rock to stand on, freely, herself.

"You know what?" she whispered. Her face lit up with a shy, just-beginning joy. "I *can* do that, Theo. I can stand on my head."

He kissed her then, a tender, almost tentative touching of their mouths, exploring this incredible possibility of their joining. Her lips opened to his with long hunger, and her arms went around him to hold him close. The sun beat down on them; Theo felt the heat deep in the marrow of his body, and she, too, felt warmed again, and safe.

The other guests left Tragos, went back to their responsibilities and obligations. Liz stayed on, feeling each day more at home here, not wanting to leave even to shop in Athens or Paris or London.

"I should order a trousseau," she said one evening. "At least a wedding dress."

"We'll send for the designer, he can come here, no need for you to go anywhere. Who would you like, my darling? Anyone, we'll get him here."

"Oh, lovely," she said. "I'll make a few calls tomorrow morning. Theo . . ."

"Yes?"

"Do we have to do it in such a rush? I mean . . . there are so many plans to make, things to be done . . . people to invite, and details . . ."

"Details can be handled by other people. Just say what you'd like, and it's done. Quickly. The sooner we are legal, the easier it will be on you, Lizzie, you know that. All those phone calls from the Cassidys . . ."

"Yes, I suppose you're right. But still . . ."

"You're right, too, so many details. Not just the dress, or the guest list, the arrangements for the wedding. The marriage itself should be set down in writing."

"What?"

"Yes, a good idea. What you must do, what I must do. How much for what, under which circumstances, what happens if you run away—"

"Theo!"

". . . if I run away . . . all the possibilities should be covered. An agreement, yes."

"Do you think you'll run away, then?"

He reached across the table for her hand. "Never," he said solemnly.

"That really sounds terrible," she said. "Everything written down, ugh."

"But practical."

"A marriage document? A contract?"

"Listen, Lizzie. It's part of Greek culture. I'm telling you. Greek orthodox law tells us that marriage contracts are the way it should be. To protect you, Lizzie . . . hey, Lizzie, it's right!"

"But marriage should be based on trust . . ."

"Of course! Of course, Lizzie. The marriage, yes. But the details . . . when there is so much to anticipate, it is only wise and, in my country, a tradition. Details, that's all."

"Money, you mean," she murmured.

"Yes, but not only that. Not only that. Listen . . . you don't want a child, no child, we'll put it down. A separate bedroom, okay, you want that, fine." He smiled at her startled reaction. "But you would like to come and go," he continued seriously. "You said that, yes? Would I deny that . . . ah, Lizzie!"

She stared at him, warm lights dancing in her eyes. "Thank you, Theo," she said quietly. She understood now, the depths of his goodness, his concern for her, his wisdom and his love.

"Ten nights together a month, okay? At least," he went on.

"Theo!" she exclaimed, shocked and mildly amused.

"I've thought about it, Lizzie. I know what I'm talking about, okay? If you agree, fine. If not, tell me. We'll have it all in writing."

She toyed with her coffee spoon, listening with full attention now.

"Fifty thousand dollars a month, Lizzie . . . throw it away, hairdressers, tips, dresses, I don't know . . . whatever. I don't even want to know what you do with it. Okay?"

She nodded.

"You like to travel, another thousand a day for expenses. Charge accounts, unlimited."

The footman refilled their coffee cups, and Theo

waited until he was out of the room before going on.

"If the marriage is no good, if either of us says the hell with the marriage, okay . . . you get ten million dollars for every year we stayed together."

Her eyes grew round and enormous. Her fingers trembled around the delicate bone china cup. She said nothing.

"Plus two hundred thousand dollars a year, which you will get for as long as you live, no matter what. And if we are still married when I die . . . a hundred million dollars."

The cup dropped from her hand, spilling the dark café filtre across the pale linen cloth. Luckily, the cup didn't break. It was part of a priceless and irreplaceable set that had belonged to a queen who had been beheaded by her husband, in another country, three hundred years before.

"Malakas! Gerouni! Bastard!" she screamed.

Theo laughed. "Sophia! You've been learning Greek, who's been teaching you such lovely words in my language? And your English is improving too."

"I learned them from you, pig! How can you do this to me, how can you marry that stick of a woman, she's nothing, nothing, a picture in the newspapers, she'll make you miserable, you'll see!"

He lay back against the pillows, smiling at her explosive gestures, her flare of passion rising so soon after she had sighed with exhaustion from their lovemaking. She was a fireball, this one, delicious, unquenchable. He had told her the news in a tender whisper, and she had risen from the bed like all the Furies in one, hurling the lamp against the wall with all the wrath of Alecto, Tisiphone and Megaera brandishing their scourges to punish, without mercy, all who violated. . . . What? What were the unforgivable crimes, he thought, as she ranted and raved over him. Violating natural family relationships—that didn't apply here, did it? Excessive arrogance . . . well, maybe.

"Hey, Sophia . . . nothing will change. I swear it."

"You are a pig, Tomasis."

"Yes . . . and so are you. The two of us, Sophia, together. Come back to bed."

"I will come to your wedding, Theo."

"I'll kill you if you do."

"Hah!"

The ceremony took place in the tiny white chapel on Tragos. There was room inside only for the priest, the bride and groom, immediate family, and a few very close friends. Liz Cassidy's stylish mother was there, crying quietly. Nico stood as his father's best man, and Nancy Cassidy served her sister-in-law as matron of honor. John Cassidy stood behind them. If anyone disapproved, they were too well bred to show it. The occasion was solemn, simple, orthodox, and brief.

Outside the chapel, throngs of reporters and photographers mingled with the guests waiting for the ceremony to be over. It had been decided that this once, the official press and unofficial papparazzi would be welcome to Tragos—a special occasion, an announcement to the world that the happy couple wished to share their happiness, had nothing to hide. The villagers and servants who made up the population of Theo's private island were dressed in their Sunday-best clothes and stood proudly with the elegant and titled visitors who had been flown in from Asia, Africa, America, Australia, and all over in Europe.

They had glimpsed the bride as she had descended from the flower-bedecked wagon that bore her and her brother-in-law down from the house. A sigh had gone up from the assembled guests when Liz Cassidy stepped from the carriage to enter the chapel. She was more beautiful than ever, radiant with a special glow after the long months of mourning. The world thought of her as a sad and lonely figure, facing bravely out through a black veil, swathed in black clothes, black stockings, black shoes. Here in the beautiful fairy-tale setting of a private island, surrounded by clear skies and the calm wide sea all around her, protected by the love of the wealthiest and most charming man in the world, she stepped forth from a bower of moving flowers into the sun, and she was luminous with joy and promise. She wore a pale beige dress (the Italian designer stood outside the chapel in the crowd, red-eyed from having been up all the night before with his crew, working on the dress; he also felt a little weepy with excitement about all the publicity he was getting), a two-piece skirt and tunic made mostly of lace and chiffon. The skirt was knee-length, her stockings and simple low-heeled pumps matched exactly. A tiny veil, held to the crown of her head with a row of delicate white flowerbuds, did nothing to hide her shining eyes. She carried a small bouquet of the same rare blossoms that haloed her gleaming hair.

Theo was dressed in a dark double-breasted business suit, with a dark tie and white handkerchief barely visible in his pocket. He found, to his surprise, that his hand was shaking when he held it out to her at the little altar. John Cassidy escorted Liz the few steps down the aisle toward Theo, and in the symbolic gesture of transferring her care from himself to her new husband, John took her hand from his own arm and placed it in Theo's. Then the bridal couple turned together to face the aged priest, who blessed them.

They knelt, and the priest said the wedding prayer in Latin and again in Greek. He presented them with a silver chalice from which they drank, Liz first, then Theo. The priest placed wreaths of white flowers on their heads; they matched the single row already in place on Liz's head, and completed the total costume. At the priest's signal, the couple exchanged rings.

The priest motioned for them to rise, and in his glittering, flowing gold robes, he led them three times around the altar. Then he blessed them again and pronounced them man and wife.

Theo kissed her.

"Welcome to my life," he whispered.

"And to mine," Liz answered softly.

She heard a stifled sob from behind her, and turned to kiss her mother. The little group then hugged and laughed to share the moment. Theo threw his arms around Nico, who said, "Congratulations, Poppa." His own arms were stiffly at his sides.

"Nico?" Liz said shyly.

"I hope you will be very happy," he said solemnly.

She nodded, smiling, and hesitated, as if expecting to be kissed. Theo stepped between them to claim his bride, and they turned to leave the chapel, with the others behind them.

Outside, in the bright sun, the guests threw white rose petals over them and the photographers scrambled for their pictures. Everyone smiled and posed and kissed and shook hands, and slowly the couple made their way to the waiting carriage. The procession to the water was a grand parade of flower-decked wagons and carts, drawn by high-stepping beribboned horses. There were outbursts of laughter and spontaneous songs from an elderly local tenor who had begun the celebration early in the day. The photographers ran alongside to get shots of the glorious bride, who smiled for them and waved, clinging to her new husband.

The launches ferried the guests to *La Belle Simone*. The press were escorted to another yacht, especially outfitted by Theo for their three-hour journey back to Athens. They would have their own party aboard, with free-flowing drinks and a bountiful feast served by charming Greek girls, even their own bouzouki orchestra for dancing if they wished. But the wedding reception on *La Belle Simone* would be strictly private: only two hundred invited guests.

Three orchestras: the twelve best bouzouki players in all Greece playing joyful music in the main salon; a versatile group for rock and nostalgia out on the pool deck where the teak cover had been set into place for dancing atop the water; and a brilliant chamber group brought in from New York to entertain in the library with Mozart and Bach and Haydn.

After dark, there would be a two-hour display of fireworks; six Japanese experts were at work on the intricate pyrotechnical designs even now in the suite given over to them for a laboratory. *La Belle Simone* would light up the sky then, sparkling in patterns especially designed for this night. But now it was high noon, and the celebration was only beginning.

They were in the salon, surrounded by friends, and Theo was teaching his bride the words of a popular Greek song. There was much laughter as she attempted the intricate rhymes, and her voice rang out happily as she tasted the complex syllables and found them impossible. But she kept trying, and so did the others around them, and the musicians obligingly repeated the chorus several times until Liz was exhausted and waved her hand for them to go on to another tune.

The music was played at a lively pace, and the murmuring of the guests, occasional laughter and glasses raised in frequent toasts rang out, but suddenly Liz was aware of a subtle change in the vibrations around her. The focus of attention in the salon had shifted from the bridal couple, slightly, like a daft summer breeze skittered off in an unpredictable direction. She looked up to see her new husband's ex-wife entering the salon on the arm of a stocky, grinning man.

Theo's eyes followed the direction of her glance, and she heard him gasp under his breath.

"Spyros . . . the son of a bitch . . ."

They were heading toward Theo and Liz, bright smiles on their faces, sweeping through the other celebrants who made way for them and tried not to stare.

"Theo!" Simi called out sweetly. She opened her hands to clasp his, and the smile on her face was warm and unrevealing. She embraced him; he stood motionless next to Liz, who kept her bright smile for everyone to see.

"Theo!" Simi repeated, her arms going around his neck. "Are you angry with me?"

"No," he answered shortly. He looked gloweringly over Simi's head to the beaming Spyros who stood close to them. Simi turned to include Liz in her smile, but her words were addressed to Spyros.

"You see, how could Theo be angry?" Simi's grace and poise matched Liz's own, and Liz admired the lovely blonde woman despite her misgivings at the scene that was taking place. The other guests had politely turned away, but their murmuring was low and there was a sense of listening throughout the room, of waiting.

"It was for my sake, wasn't it," Simi went on, to Theo, "that you didn't invite us to your wedding party. You were afraid I might be hurt?"

Theo nodded. He seemed not to even know that he was scowling.

"But I'm happy for you, Theo. Truly I am. Happy!" She leaned up to kiss him fully on the mouth. He stood without moving, without responding.

Simi turned to Liz with her warm smile and a handclasp. "Have a happy marriage," she said, "a wonderful marriage."

"Thank you," Liz murmured.

"Of course! Be happy!" Spyros Tomasis burst out jovially. "Why not!"

Now Theo seemed to recover himself. His anger shrugged away, he put his arm around Liz and

233

faced Spyros and Simi with his genial-host smile. "Have a drink," he said. "Waiter!"

The waiter was at his side, and the new arrivals lifted their glasses in a toast to Liz and Theo. Then Simi and Spyros slipped into the crowd around them, and others came up to drink with the newly married couple.

"Theo . . . perhaps we should move about, see how our guests are doing . . . I'd like to have a dance on the pool deck, with you. All right?" Liz said.

They excused themselves from the salon and wandered through the festive crowds along the promenade. On the aft deck, the pool had been covered with a dance floor and its enormous expanse was reverberating happily to the beat of a Beatles song. The awning had been expanded to cover the dancing area, and all around were tables where guests ate and sipped wine and talked. Everyone greeted the bride and groom with happy enthusiasm.

Nico was seated at one of the tables, with two beautiful young women. He was paying no attention to them, but looking glumly off somewhere at the horizon, thinking his own thoughts.

"Hey, Nico!" Theo brought Liz over to him. "Having a good time at your poppa's wedding?"

Nico got to his feet. "May I present my friends, Paula Smith and Jodie . . . uh . . ."

"DeLeon," the girl volunteered lazily.

"How do you do?" Liz said.

"Hope you'll be real happy, Mrs. Tomasis," the girl smiled up at her.

"Thank you."

Theo had been drinking a great deal of wine and matching toast for toast with the lethal ouzo. He swayed a little as he leaned toward Nico.

"Hey . . . what's the matter . . . your poppa's new wife . . . no kisses? The most famous woman in the world . . . hug her, for Christ's sake . . . you didn't even say hello . . ."

Liz smiled tentatively, hiding her embarrassment.

"Hello, Mother," Nico said icily.

"Hey . . ." Theo was annoyed, and hurt.

Liz cut in, still smiling at Nico. "I plan on our being friends," she said quietly.

Nico looked down, and then his eyes shot up at her again. "I hope you have a terrific time being a Tomasis," he said. "Excuse me."

He walked away, leaving the two girls at the table, and disappeared among the people along the rail.

Theo turned to Liz and took her hands in his. "Please . . . forgive him . . . smart-assed kid . . . goddamned rude . . ."

"Would you care to join us, Mrs. Tomasis?" one of the young women asked, as Theo hurried after his son.

"Thank you," Liz murmured, shaking her head. She walked toward a small group of people whom she knew from Washington, two senators and their wives who had been special friends of Jim's.

Nico stood alone at the rail, gazing down along the steep white hull of *La Belle Simone* to the water far below. His father strode up to him.

"What kind of way is that to act to my wife!" Theo said sternly. He clamped his hand on Nico's elbow and forced the boy to turn to face him. "My wife!" he repeated.

They stared at each other. Nico spat out his words.

"The most famous woman in the world . . . is that how you think of her . . . is that why you married her?"

"My *wife!*" Theo shouted furiously. He shook Nico's arm, gripping it tightly in his barely-controlled rage.

"You said that, the most famous woman in the world . . . Jesus Christ! You married her for that, didn't you . . . oh, my God!" He pulled away from his father and put his head in both hands, leaning on the rail.

Theo spoke quietly, but his voice was angry, threatening.

"She is my wife! You will treat her with honor, do you hear? Honor! And respect and regard! Your father's wife!"

"Bullshit!" Nico groaned wildly. "Bullshit! *Skata!*"

Theo yanked the boy around and slapped him hard.

Instantly, his hand went out again to touch Nico's face where it had begun to flame from the blow. "Oh, Nico . . ." he whispered, shocked and sorry.

Nico pushed the hand aside. He refused to meet his father's eyes.

"Nico . . . it's such a simple thing, a little kindness, a little thinking of others . . . of me, your poppa, the lovely woman who has married me . . . please, please . . ."

He touched Nico's cheek again, but still the boy refused to look at him.

"It was stupid . . . forgive me, Nico. I didn't mean to. Okay?"

Nico nodded, near tears.

"Tell me," Theo said. "What, Nico? What makes you so angry, so sad? Tell me, talk to me."

Nico was silent.

"Ah, Nico . . . be friends with her. She's a child, so vulnerable . . . a woman . . . a joy for both of us! Try to be friends, Nico?"

Nico muttered something, so low that Theo couldn't hear. He moved closer, put his arm around his son and asked him to repeat it.

"I said . . . yes, I'm sorry. I'm sorry for her, Poppa, I . . . don't you know how I feel? It's not Liz . . . it's Spyros, Poppa. Spyros."

Totally caught off guard, Theo pulled away. "Spyros? What the hell has he got to do with anything?"

"Poppa . . . you don't know?"

"Know what! What, Nico?"

"She said she was going to find you and tell you."

"Who, who? What?"

"Momma. I guess she was drinking, and she forgot to tell you. Forgot to mention that she's going to marry Spyros, Poppa."

Theo stared at him.

Nico turned to him, and nodded. "Spyros and Momma. That's right. You going to be friends with him, Poppa . . . how does it make you feel?"

Theo couldn't, wouldn't believe it. He gripped the smooth teak rail with both hands, knuckles turned white. "It's a fucking lie," he said quietly.

Nico shook his head. "No, it's not a lie. She told me today."

"My beautiful Simi?" Theo whispered hoarsely. "And that dirty . . ." His voice rose. People nearby glanced at them, looked away again. "*Spyros?*" Theo's head was shaking as if to deny the words, the facts.

"Yes," Nico said sadly.

"A joke?"

"On you." Nico nodded his head. "To spite you, Poppa! To hurt you and humiliate you . . . like you did her. And Poppa, can you blame her?"

Theo's face seemed to crumble in helpless despair. "Your momma left me, Nico. It wasn't my doing. It was hers, hers. She wanted it, not me."

"It was your fault," Nico said bitterly.

"But she wanted it, not me!"

"She would have stayed, if . . . she stayed all those years, with you and your other women . . . with Sophia . . . do you think it was easy for her, for me. . . ?"

"Bah!" He waved his hand to dismiss all that nonsense. "She wanted me to change, to be another kind of man . . . to be faithful, like a puppy dog . . . no! That's not who she married in the first place. She knows me, she knew me, your momma . . . then she decides it's enough. It was her idea, not mine!"

"Oh, Poppa!"

"So I married a woman, beautiful, famous . . . yes, famous . . . is that why . . ."

"Sure. You'll have your famous woman, and Momma will have your brother." Nico stared at him. The tears now stood in his eyes, ready to spill out. His voice cracked. "What are we doing to each other, Poppa?"

"Nico . . . Nico . . ."

"We're all crazy, Poppa! We are." Nico turned from his father; his tears could no longer be controlled.

Theo watched him walk away.

"Crazy . . ." he mumbled to himself. He glanced over the crowd of chic, important, elegant people. He needed another drink. He shook his head and tightened the line of his mouth, and went to find his wife.

The pool deck was filled mostly with young people. Theo made his way forward, along the promenade and into the grand salon. It was crowded; people were dancing, listening to the Greek music, laughing, eating, but . . . Where was she? He touched a passing steward's white-coated arm.

"Where is she?" he asked.

"Sir?"

"Mrs. Tomasis . . . where is she?"

The steward gestured toward a table near one of the open glass doors at the far side of the room, where Liz sat surrounded by friends.

"No, no," Theo shook his head impatiently. "The other Mrs. Tomasis," he said. "My first wife."

The steward's face remained unperturbed. "I think she's below, sir. In the Diana suite."

Theo nodded, then caught the man's eye. "Alone?" he asked.

"No, I don't think so, sir."

He nodded again, and turned back toward the deck. He strode through the people until he reached the stairway going down to the guest deck, and turned down the corridor.

He gestured to the room steward to leave the area, and strode to the door of the Diana suite to pound loudly on the door.

"Open up, you son of a bitch!" he shouted in Greek.

He heard movement inside, but the door stayed solidly shut. He continued to pound with his clenched fist. *"Anixe, xythithi, anixe!"*

The door opened. Spyros Tomasis, in stocking feet and wearing no shirt, opened the door with a wide smile.

"Theo! An unexpected pleas—"

Theo shoved him aside and strode into the room. Clothing lay about on the carpet and chairs of the sitting room. The door to the bedroom was open. Simi lay naked on the rumpled satin sheets of the bed.

"My honeymoon . . . my ship . . . and you're screwing my wife!" Theo roared. He turned on Spyros and punched him, sending the shorter man reeling against a table, which fell with him, breaking the lamp with a massive shudder of shattering glass.

Spyros got to his feet, rubbing his chin. "You crazy?" he shouted. "Your wife? Hah! You got married today, you dumb son of a bitch!"

Theo strode into the bedroom, where Simi lay on her stomach, her back and buttocks and long fine legs sprawled. Her head was turned on the pillow and she watched him through glazed and uncaring eyes.

Behind him, Spyros was righteously explaining the situation, not that he gave a damn for Theo's fury. "She got sick," he said, "all over herself. I cleaned her up. And me, too . . ."

He gestured toward the bathroom, where Simi's dress was crumpled in a heap on the Roman-tiled floor.

Theo went to the bed and pulled the satin coverlet over Simi's nakedness to cover her.

"You're a crazy man, you know that, Theo?" Spyros mumbled behind him.

His jaw was swelling, Theo noted to his satisfaction. "What's this crap I hear about you and Simi?"

Spyros grinned. Shirtless, his body looked like that of a bear. His chest was covered with ugly, matted hair. Now he lifted his hands high above his head in the gesture of a *syrtaki* dancer, snapped his fingers, and laughed.

"*Opa*," he said quietly.

Wanting to retch, Theo stared at him, and then turned back to the bed and the drowsing Simi. He leaned down tenderly to shake her bare shoulder above the coverlet.

"Hey. Hey, Simi . . . Simi . . ."

Her eyes rolled upward and tried to focus on him. She worked her hand up out of the silken sheets to reach out for him. He sat down heavily. Her hand rested on his knee.

"You okay?"

She nodded, still unfocused.

He looked at her, not touching her now. "You going to marry Spyros, huh?"

Simi blinked her eyes and then began to struggle to sit up. Her hand left him and swept the unpinned hair from her face as she began to gather her strength for the battle.

"Spyro?" she mumbled. "Spyro?"

Spyros came close to the bed to sit on the op-

241

posite side from Theo. They glared across her at each other.

"I'm right here, Simi," he said.

Simi pushed herself up, away from Theo. She fell against Spyros, holding him closely.

"Come to bed, my darling . . . my God, how I want you!"

"Why don't you go to your wife, Theo, I'm sure she must be looking for you," Spyros laughed over his shoulder as he held the lovely Simi's nakedness against his own gross body.

Theo tore out of the Diana suite and burst into the room next door, where he just made it to the commode in time to lose his dinner, lunch, and a great deal of the finest champagne money could buy.

CHAPTER THIRTEEN

The party was winding down. Night had come
and with it came the fireworks and the final feast-
ing at the long tables in the petit salon. Guests
were beginning to take their leave now, although
the party would go on until the sun was high in
the sky again. They left by tender and launch, by
helicopter and by the smaller yachts that pulled
alongside to take them to other islands or to the
mainland. Many would stay the night; there were
plenty of accommodations.

At last, Theo and Liz stepped off *La Belle
Simone* onto the launch, which had been newly
dressed in fresh flowers and sparkling lights. The
orchestra played them off and the guests waved
from the forward rail. Liz tossed her little bouquet
upward into the hands of one of the young Amer-

ican girls. As the tender pulled away from *La Belle Simone*, Theo stepped aft and looked back at the receding yacht with something like longing in his eyes.

Liz moved close to him and laid her cheek against his back. "Theo?" she murmured.

He reached out his arm for her to cuddle into. But his eyes never left *La Belle Simone* until the launch made the turn into the cove and she was out of sight.

The house was quietly lit in welcome, silent except for the maid who had waited to help Liz undress. Theo disappeared into his dressing room and Liz to hers, where Clara began drawing her bath, adding the scented oils to it, smoothing out the exquisite nightgown and peignoir that hung on a silken hanger.

Liz entered the bedroom slowly and stood for a moment with the light from the dressing room behind her, framing her like an aura. She was lovely, and she knew it. It was her gift to him.

Theo stood by the long open window on the far side of the room. He had been looking out, over the trees to the water where *La Belle Simone* lay, still brightly lit, beckoning to him from far out at sea. But now he turned his complete attention to his bride.

"Lizzie . . ." he gasped. "Lizzie . . . a miracle. You are a miracle . . . you bring beauty to . . . my God, you are an angel . . . lovely." His worship of beauty was total, genuine, adoring.

He crossed the room to her, his arms outstretched. He wore white undershorts; his powerful body would have looked ridiculous in pajamas.

She stood in the doorway watching him, her responsive heart opening to him.

The telephone rang, jangling, intrusive.

"Bastards!" Theo shouted. "I told them. . . ." Angrily he reached for the telephone on the desk. "I told you no telephones, I don't care what," he growled.

Liz's ecru peignoir was tied at her throat with a silken ribbon, and the long sheer softness flowed over the subtly shaded nightgown. She waited for him to hang up the phone.

"What?" he was saying. His anger was gone and she could see that he was pleased now, and it had nothing to do with her.

"Oh, sure, sure . . ." Theo said into the phone. He glanced up at her, smiling. In a moment the connection was made. His voice was soft and affectionate to the person on the other end.

"Hey . . ." he said. Then he spoke in Greek, and Liz couldn't understand a word. He was almost crooning into the telephone, and at one point he turned his back on Liz so she couldn't see his face. When he hung up, he was smiling. He turned to her and gestured helplessly toward the phone.

"Matalas," he explained.

He reached up to untie the ribbon at her throat. Liz stood frozen, staring at him, unbelieving.

"Matalas?" she repeated.

"Yes. She wishes us well. She apologizes she couldn't be with us."

"Where is she now?" Liz asked. She was standing stiffly, unresponsive, but he didn't seem to notice.

He gestured toward the window. "On her is-

245

land," he answered. The peignoir fell to the floor in a heap around her bare feet.

"She's sorry she missed the reception," he murmured against her hair. "I said I'll see her tomorrow. You're so lovely, Liz, so lovely . . ."

"Tomorrow!"

He slid his hand down her back, felt her flesh tense and cool beneath the fine silk of her nightgown.

"Umhum," he said, "sure. Matalas says she wants to see me, then there is no question. *Ine fili mou* . . . my friend. My best friend."

He fondled her buttocks, feeling the firmness, touching her with deep pleasure. "Apples . . ." he muttered. "Your ass is like apples . . . delicious . . . mmmmm . . . apple ass . . ."

She broke from him and half-ran across the room. She sat down in a deep velvet chair, her legs tightly wound under her. She was tense and angry, but her voice was cool, controlled.

"Theo . . ."

"Hey, come on . . . what?"

"Theo, why did you marry me?"

He was annoyed. "What kind of question?" he asked. He stood where she had left him.

"Why?" she insisted quietly.

"Our honeymoon night, for Christ's sake . . . what do you want?"

"Tell me."

He sighed and moved out of the light to stand before her, his hands opened in a gesture that indicated his bewilderment, and his patience.

"Okay . . . Lizzie . . . you, that's why. No other woman like you in the world. You make me feel fantastic . . ."

He reached down to take her hand and pulled her to her feet. She felt lifeless, inert. She found herself wondering what she was doing here, in this room, with this stranger, so far from home . . . and yet his nearness was important to her. She stood close to him, wanting to be taken in his arms, to be told that she alone was important to him, that there had been no phone call, no strangeness in his manner for the past several hours. Even back on *La Belle Simone*, during the reception, she had felt him somehow distant, preoccupied, even in-attentive. She had put it down to the intense emotional excitement of the long day, the religious ceremony that bound them together, the awesome fact of being married again—to her. But here, in their private intimacy, she knew that something had been left unsaid.

"I feel more alive with you," he said, holding her closely. " Lizzie . . . I told you, I told you a million times . . ."

She pulled away slightly, still letting him hold her, but not responding physically. Something was off, wrong. She felt cold and frightened.

"And love? What about love, Theo?"

A beat, before he answered. "What love?" he asked, as if she were a petulant child demanding too much. "Sure! I told you."

She felt his closeness, the physical fact of him, but in the quiet semi-darkness of the huge empty room she knew she did not have his whole heart.

"Yes, you have mentioned it," she said softly.

"Hey . . . what?" He cupped her chin in his hand, making her look at him. "You've got a thorn in your ass, hah? What are we talking about, like kids? How many times have you mentioned it to me . . . love? Hah?"

"Not often," she whispered.

"So what do you want . . . what's the difference . . . you want to hear it said? Is that what makes the difference?"

"I don't know," she whispered miserably. She didn't know, it wasn't the words alone, it couldn't be . . . but he had touched her feelings, had opened her to feeling after such a 'long, dead time, and now . . . she was in desperate need of the words, yes.

"You want to hear it said? Okay, I love you." He held her loosely, his hands on both her bare arms. She felt nothing.

"Now you mention it," he said, "and everything is wonderful, okay?"

She was frightened. "Oh, Theo . . ."

She turned away from him and moved like a solitary ghost in her transparent gown into a dark corner near the bed.

"What? What do you want?" he shouted angrily at her.

She whispered in a small, terrified voice, "I don't know, Theo. I don't know."

He stalked the few feet to the bed and sat down. He reached out for her, and when his hand touched her arm, she almost jumped. She looked down at him, his eyes shining with a hunger of their own.

Soothingly now, he tried to mollify her. "Jesus Christ, our honeymoon night, Lizzie. What are we talking about?"

He pulled her gently and she moved toward

him, standing at the bedside, her thighs grazing his knees.

"What do we need to talk?" he said. He patted the bed beside him. "Here we get all the questions and answers. Hah?" He smiled and nodded to himself, and released her hand to lie back on the bed.

After a moment, she sat down beside him.

"Tomorrow is plenty time to talk." He reached for her, but she edged away. Tomorrow.

"Before you go, or after you get back?" she heard herself say coldly.

He propped himself up on his elbows, staring at her, his welcoming smile frozen by what she had said.

"Tomorrow," she said.

"Hey, Lizzie . . ." he said grimly.

"What?"

"You want me to lie to you about Matalas? I won't do that."

She leaned over him again, tantalizingly close to his face. Her perfume was delicate, rare. She breathed the words so that he felt the warm sweetness of her.

"I know," she said. Still close, hovering just above him, resisting the arms that would pull her down, she asked, "Will you go to bed with her?"

He frowned, annoyed. "It's possible. Sure!"

"Why keep her waiting?" Liz whispered. Her hair fell forward, brushing his cheek.

"Lizzie . . ."

He pulled her toward him, knowing what she needed, what she was begging for, but she drew back. She stood and moved a few feet away from the bed. She looked at him.

Her voice was pleasant, distant, cool. "I'm not going to sleep with you tonight, Theo."

He sat up, staring at her.

"It's your honeymoon night, you ought to screw *somebody*. Screw a friend," she said softly.

"For Christ's sake. Lizzie . . . what the hell . . ."

"Go to her. Now. Go on. Get out!"

She crossed the room to stand by the window, watching as he sat up in the dark alcove of the bed, only his dim outline visible as he rubbed his head and muttered.

". . . from the marriage bed . . . it's unthinkable . . ."

"Yes," she answered coolly. "Well, I've just thought about it, and it works out fine. Get out, Theo."

He got out of bed and started toward her. She moved away, not afraid of him, but dead inside.

"You're my wife . . ."

"I think that means something I didn't quite get straight before, Theo. But I'm beginning to. Ten nights a month, Theo . . . wasn't that the contract you wanted? Well . . . tonight's not one of the nights. I want you to go."

He stared across the room at her. There was no mistaking the tone of her voice, the strength of that goddess-like statue. This was not a woman of flesh and blood, after all. After a long moment, she said again, "I want you to go."

She waited. He nodded.

It crossed her mind, after he had left the room and she had bolted the door and climbed into the big bed alone, that she could get an annulment. The marriage was unconsummated, a mistake. She could leave early in the morning for New York, and the lawyers would take care of everything quickly and . . . no! Tomorrow morning the newspapers everywhere in the world would be filled with photographs of her, smiling, happy, on his arm, of the wedding, so touching, in the little Greek chapel—the party was still going on out there.

Liz got up and went to the window to look out into the vast silent darkness, at *La Belle Simone,* anchored far offshore, her lights still ablaze to celebrate the wedding night. She closed the drapes and glanced across the room toward the far windows, closed against the view of the other, smaller island. She supposed he was there now. She didn't care.

The whole world would snicker and gossip and laugh at her if she admitted that she had made a mistake. Not her, not the perfect First Lady, the tragic widow, the beautiful one copied and idolized by so many people. There were many, so many, who would love to see her take a public pratfall, become the object of sniggering and dirty jokes, speculations—no, she couldn't bear it. She was stuck now, stuck forever, with that . . . that *goat,* who had charmed her and seduced her into believing that she was safe in his world . . . He was old, in his sixties. A sob rose in Liz's throat, surprising her. She had thought she was in love . . .

She wandered about the room, her feet cold on the deep carpet, touching things, letting the tears come, thinking they would be the last she would ever shed for him, for anyone. At the desk she stopped and stared at the telephone. There were people she could call, people who would help her, get her out of this . . . no. No. It wasn't possible.

They wouldn't have a chance to laugh at her, never.

She opened the desk drawer into which she had carelessly tossed the copy of their agreement. She withdrew the red-leather-bound document and placed it before her, and began to read it carefully.

Her light was the only one that burned all night long in the center of that private island, that world Theo Tomasis had built for himself.

Liz did not leave her suite for four days. And then she sent word to Theo that she would join him for lunch on the terrace that overlooked the garden.

"I won't divorce you, Theo," she said.

"Of course not! Who wants a divorce? A little misunderstanding, that's all."

"You won't give up Matalas?"

"No. I told you, she is my friend. My best friend. Would I ask you to give up your best friend?"

"I don't screw my best friend, Theo."

"I don't like to hear you talk like that. You're not crude like that. It's not for you, such language."

"I see. Would you like some quiche?" She passed the dish to him and he helped himself to a portion.

"Hey, there's nothing in this. I thought it was spinach pie . . . what's this, truffles?"

"Yes. I've asked Pierre to stay on as our permanent chef."

"Lizzie . . . hey, Lizzie . . . we'll be all right. I care for you, it's true, I do. I had too much to drink, maybe. It was a very big day, our wedding, and . . . it'll be all right, Lizzie? The two of us?"

"Yes. All right."

He got up from the chair to come around and kiss her. She averted her head and his lips grazed her hair, warm from the sun. His hands lingered on her shoulders. "My wife," he said. "You will be my wife?"

She nodded. "Yes," she said. "I will stick to my part of the bargain."

"Good." He frowned, but took his seat again and helped himself to salad. "No feta cheese?" he commented, picking through the Bib lettuce.

"No," she answered.

He sighed, and smiled to show it was fine with him. "I have to go to Washington this morning," he said. "But only for a day or two, if things work out as I plan. Maybe I could meet you in Rome on the way back? Maybe when I come back, we could have a real honeymoon..."

"That would be nice," she said politely. "Call me."

"Every day, Lizzie. I'll call you tonight, and tomorrow when my business is finished."

"If you're not in jail," she agreed pleasantly.

"What!"

"Did you think I didn't know? I figured it all out, Theo, why you married me. It's all right. I don't mind any more."

"Lizzie! I love you, Lizzie!"

"Yes," she replied calmly. "I know that, too."

CHAPTER
FOURTEEN

Theo's new lawyers were nervous. But he was glad to see that Nico was calm, on top of things. At their preliminary meeting, Theo had sat back and let Nico do most of the talking. The boy had a good grasp of the situation and dealt with the legal details and business complexities as if the case would be decided on the basis of such things. It was good, a good presence, the boy was smart. Theo sat smiling, nodding and interspersing his own comments only once in a while. The lawyers were worried, but that was their business. It was time to go.

Theo led the way. The five distinguished, middle-aged men in blue suits and similar ties, all wearing troubled expressions and carrying bulging briefcases, followed him and Nico down the Department of Justice corridor like a bevy of quails who could not fly. With his arm around Nico's shoulders, Theo strode purposefully, smiling, toward the hearing room.

Michael Corey was waiting for them in front of the wide double doors. He was frowning, and his expression only deepened as Theo and Nico came toward him, with the senior partners of the most eminent law firm in New York bringing up the rear.

"Hey, Michael!" Theo's voice echoed in the marble-ceilinged hallway.

"Hello, Theo, Nico," the attorney general said with tight, unsmiling lips. No handshake.

"Happy?" Theo asked him, grinning.

"You're a bastard," Corey answered softly.

Nico stared at him angrily. Theo felt his son's muscles tense under his hand, and he patted the boy's shoulder and let his hand drop away. The lawyers formed a half-circle around them, looking uncomfortable.

"Me?" Theo said in mock innocence. "Ah, Michael . . ."

"You figured it all out, didn't you?"

"What?"

"The man who married the widow of our assassinated president . . . how could we possibly send you to jail? How could we do that . . . to her?"

Theo shrugged.

Michael Corey opened the doors to the hearing room and gestured for Theo and Nico to precede him. The room was somber, enlivened only by the red, white, and blue flag that hung limply in a corner by the window. A dark mahogany table, at least twenty feet long and six feet across, was in the center of the large square room, with chairs widely spaced around it. Three men were already seated at the table, papers spread out before them. They looked up and nodded as the others entered.

"Good morning, gentlemen."

"Mr. Tomasis."

"Mr. Corey."

"Mr. Becker."

"Good morning."

"Mr. Stoneham."

Stoneham was the one sitting at the head of the table, peering over his reading glasses. He nodded curtly at each of them and returned to presuing documents.

Corey took a chair near the head of the table, and Theo sat opposite him, with Nico at his side. The lawyers took seats and there was a general snapping open of briefcases and rustling of papers. Then Michael Corey stood up.

"Gentlemen, I think we can wrap this up in a very few minutes," he said formally.

Theo leaned slightly to whisper in Nico's ear. Nico nodded.

"Mr. Tomasis and I . . . that is, Mr. Tomasis' son and his attorneys, and I, have been meeting for the last few days, and I think we've come up with a settlement that we can all live with."

He had the full attention of everyone in the room. Theo leaned back and crossed his arms.

"I will suggest that the government withdraw its charges of violations of Section Nineteen of the United States Merchant Marine Act, under the following conditions," Michael went on. He placed his spectacles on his nose and picked up a sheaf of papers. He read from them dourly.

"Mr. Tomasis will return title to the government of all of the ships purchased from us. The balance of the mortgage payments due, if any, will be canceled. There will be a fine levied of seven point five million dollars."

There was some rustling at this, and Stoneham leaned forward with a shocked expression.

"Mr. Corey! We had been talking in terms of a fine of three million per ship . . . sixty million dollars, I believe."

Nico spoke up. "That would work an impossible hardship on my father, sir. Along with counsel, Mr. Corey and I have had some conversations about that . . ."

Corey interrupted. "Yes," he said. "Let me explain."

"I wish you would, sir," Stoneham said, settling back with a disgruntled look on his face.

"Mr. Tomasis is currently negotiating with German interests to build tankers with something over two million dead weight tonnage," Corey said. "Mr. Tomasis has agreed to break off these negotiations and bring his business here, to the United States." He removed his glasses and toyed with them as he looked toward the men at the head of the table. "I don't have to tell you what a windfall this would be to our ship builders here."

Abruptly, Michael Corey sat down. It was a farce. He knew it, Stoneham knew it, every school-child who could identify a photograph in a newspaper knew it. They couldn't touch Tomasis. The only question was to find a graceful way out. That's what they were here for. He trusted Stoneham wouldn't make it too tough on him. They were all playing the same goddamned game.

One of the gray-haired men from the Justice Department spoke up. "Correct me if I'm wrong," he said. "But isn't Spyros Tomasis negotiating for available facilities in our shipyards?"

A smile crossed Theo's face.

Corey nodded and said briefly, "The other Mr. Tomasis will have to step back in line. As I understand it, Mr. Tomasis is thinking of an immediate expenditure of a quarter-billion dollars. Money spent here, not overseas."

"Correct," Nico cut in. "My father needs considerable moneys to fund such an operation. I'm afraid that a fine of sixty million . . . or anywhere near that figure . . . would knock the whole thing out of the box."

Corey nodded, then looked at Theo. "Seven point five, Mr. Tomasis, that's the figure you'd be able to handle?"

Theo shrugged, smiling. "A hardship, as my son says," he said, "but I'll find a way. It would take Spyros months, months. I could do this quickly, if the fine was a reasonable one . . ."

Corey looked around the table. "Does that satisfy you, gentlemen?"

The men from the Justice Department nodded slowly, thoughtfully, as if they were thinking it over.

"Seems satisfactory," Stoneham spoke for all three.

Theo's lawyers nodded agreement.

"The rest of the stipulations are nitpicks," Corey went on. "I'm sure you'll have no problem with them."

258

Stoneham nodded again. "If you're satisfied, Mr. Attorney General, then I'm satisfied."

"Me too," the man on his right chimed in.

"Well . . . that's it, then," Corey said. "I'll put the papers in work."

He leaned over the wide table, getting halfway to his feet, to reach out for Theo's hand. But Theo had turned to Nico and was embracing him, pounding him on the back.

"My son!" he said proudly. "My son!" He turned to Corey then and accepted the outstretched hand. The lawyers began to pack up their reams of documents and ledgers and memos and statements.

"How is your wife, Theo?" Michael Corey asked.

Theo caught his eye; the man was a good loser, that was all. No hard feelings. No sarcasm. He smiled genially and nodded with the enthusiasm of a happy bridegroom.

"She's fine, fine . . . very happy," he said. He spoke to include all the men in the room. "You must all come to Greece and say hello," he said. "Excuse me now, gentlemen . . . I must go call Mrs. Tomasis."

He shook hands all around, and then, with his arm around Nico and the bevy of lawyers behind them, he strode out of the hearing room.

Alone, Liz wandered about *La Belle Simone*, and the house on Tragos, and along the lovely paths of the island Theo had created out of barren stone. She touched his things—the statues and books, the heavy silver accessories on his desk—and she thought long and hard about the man she had married. She spent an hour sitting before the etching that was his memory of his father, and it surprised her to realize that she was more than just curious.

She had thought, at first, that she was caught in a hideous mistake, that her life from now on would be a series of strained, cold compromises; she would fulfill her part of a bad bargain. But as she moved about here, alone in the world that belonged to him, she began slowly to understand what this marriage really was.

Liz Cassidy Tomasis was honest with herself. Hurt, angry, sorry, she had looked for signs that she had been wronged and betrayed by a barbarian. But everything that surrounded him was true: the taste in art, the purity of materials, the sense of beauty and unabashed love of life was all around her. It struck her then, with force, that Theo, too, was honest. He had been honest about his friendship with Matalas, insisting that she understand, and she had refused to understand.

They were strangers to each other, but here . . . here, she was the alien, not he. The jealousy and hurt she had felt on their wedding night were strange to him, unexpected. As his behavior was to her.

She sat alone in the moonlight, on the terrace outside her bedroom, most of one whole night, and she knew that she missed him very much. It wasn't just loneliness; she was used to that. It was him she missed. Theo.

Perhaps, just possibly, they might learn to know one another. She had insisted on her personal freedom; he had granted it to her—and would have his own, as well. Maybe they weren't so very different from each other, after all.

He was tender, and she was grateful for that. His long experience with women had made him a skilled and gentle lover; his conquest of her body was a triumph for him in more ways than one. She submitted to him like a long-dead mummy; beneath her warm young flesh was a cold, tightly wrapped shroud encasing her pain and aloneness. But her body responded to his caresses nevertheless. He hadn't expected any more of her; it was enough. She was his now, as much as she would ever be. Between them, there was a kind of understanding, a truce, and the marriage began.

They set up their main home in the mansion overlooking Athens, a fine and formal house with lemon groves and grape arbors sloping down from the highest hill of the city. For months Liz busied herself with redecorating. The classic Greek style of the former Mrs. Tomasis suited the house well, but now there was a new influence, and the stark whites and marbles were slowly replaced with warmth in colors and fabrics; plush reds and royal blues filled the rooms with European and American furnishings; antic abstract paintings and hanging sculptures filled the walls and stairwells, and the illusion of a home began to be composed.

They were kind to each other, more than polite. Each lived up to the agreement, and they found pleasure in each other's company without allowing themselves to want more. The times when they were together were rare; Liz shopped the world for the house and her personal whims; she visited friends when there were parties not to be missed, and would jaunt to Hong Kong or Taos for a special vase, a skirt, a piece of jewelry. Theo found himself in Paris, New York, Geneva, Liberia, as he had always done, and their life together took on the quality of a neutral meeting ground where they would touch down, occasionally, together.

The house in Athens had a garden which delighted Liz, and she would often consult with the gardeners on replanting certain shrubs or flowerbeds; she had the olive grove moved a few yards down the slope from the house, so she could see the Choragic Monument of Lysikrates down below. The monument looked well through the archway of grape vines over the luncheon table, looking over the tops of the lush green olive trees. The view gave her a feeling of restfulness. In Washington she had always enjoyed the vista from upstairs at the White House, the straight-lined Mall with its monuments lined up for her to look down on.

Arnold Scaasi came from New York to design the fabrics for the walls and carpets and drapes of the main living room. He and Liz were deep in consultation one morning in the stripped-down chamber, as huge and empty as a railroad station with no trains or people. Samples of fabric were pinned to the walls, yards of flowing color. A team of painters was waiting to mix colors to blend with the different possible choices. The wallpaper artist who had been brought in from London stood on a ladder, his chin resting on one long delicate finger as he pondered the effect of millefleurs on alternating panels against solids.

The doors were open to the sweet fresh scents of the garden. Liz looked up from the swatch of velvet in her hand when a shadow crossed the light.

"Nico! How nice to see you!"

"I'm sorry. I see that I'm interrupting. Is my father here?"

She handed the cloth to the designer and walked over to hold out her hand. "No, he's gone to Tokyo for a few days," she said warmly. "But please, stay and have some tea with me."

"No, no, I see how busy you are."

Her eyes were pleading with him, and her voice was low. "I . . . I really would be so happy to talk to you for a little while, Nico. Won't you stay?"

Nico glanced past her at the shambles that had been his mother's home. He was about to shake his head and flee, but something in Liz's eyes stopped him. She was very thin, and vulnerable, probably lonely . . . everybody was goddamned lonely, he thought.

"Not here," he murmured.

"No, of course. Out in the garden? It's so beautiful there."

"Okay."

She gestured to a maidservant. "Some tea, in the garden, please, Aphrodite, and . . . how about some *peinerli*, Nico? It's really time for lunch, and I know you like it."

"Yes . . . well . . . all right."

They strolled to a table under the grape vines and sat down. Nico was silent, almost sullen.

"Nico . . ." Liz leaned across the table and spoke gently. "I know it disturbs you to see this house being torn apart. But surely you understand . . ."

"Oh, yes, yes. It's your right, after all. No, it doesn't disturb me, why should it? It's your house now."

"I wish you didn't hate me."

263

The word was a stronger one than Nico would have chosen, and to hear it from her lips, spoken softly and without rancor, upset him oddly.

"I don't hate you. I don't. After all, I'm not a child, to be upset by such a little thing as a divorce. I don't blame you, anyway."

"But you blame somebody? Your father?"

Nico squirmed in his chair. Aphrodite brought a tray with tea things on it, and he was saved from having to reply while Liz busied herself pouring, adding lemon, handing him his cup.

"It's nice like this," he said stiffly, "with the olive trees lower down the slope. You can see the whole city now."

"I'm glad you approve. I mean that. Oh Nico, I do wish you and I could be friends. I'm not a bad person, I don't think I am, anyway. It's not easy, you know . . . but your father is not a bad person, either. Circumstance . . ."

"Yes."

"Don't waste your energy in hating, Nico. We are . . . we all are . . . what we are."

"You learned that from him? It sounds like something he would say."

"Maybe I did. I don't know. But it's true."

"Yes."

The *peinerli* was served, and they dug into it with young and hearty appetites. Two hulls of succulent dough shaped like Viking ships, and platters heaped with things to fill them with: cheeses and chopped meats, tomato sauce, chopped hard-boiled egg, slices of ham, crisp fat sausages and fried eggs, pitted salty olives. They scooped up their choices and Nico picked up the soaking, drippy sandwich to eat it Greek style. Liz used a knife and fork on hers.

"I haven't got the hang of it yet," she confessed. "I get it all over me when I try to eat it right."

"Think of it like pizza," Nico advised.

Liz smiled. "I get pizza all over me, too."

Nico laughed with her, and then they talked of the garden, the playground that had been there when Nico was a little boy. They exchanged stories about the schools they had gone to, the friends they had had, the differences between growing up in Greece and America.

"Your father worries about you," Liz said after a while, when they were finished with their *peinerli* and Nico had leaned back with a cigarette. "You are the most important thing in his life, Nico."

"He wants me to be like him. Just like him," Nico said with a tinge of bitterness.

"Is that so terrible?" she asked quietly.

Their eyes met, and he didn't answer.

Liz said, "I think . . . I don't know . . . but I think that all parents want their children to be better than they are. Isn't that what life is all about?"

"It's hard, with such a powerful father, to know what the hell you are," Nico burst out.

"Yes, I can see that. But you can be whatever you like. You're intelligent and charming and handsome and . . . wasn't it your own choice to go into his business, Nico?"

"Yes. I like the business. I think I can be in his business without being him, though. Anyway, I do my own thing."

"You are a daredevil, he says. He worries about that."

Nico's eyes twinkled with private amusement. "There are some things I can do that he can't."

"Don't be reckless, Nico, just to prove that, will you?"

Nico looked into her soft, dark eyes for a long moment, and then he stood up. "No advice, please."

"Not from me, you mean?"

"You're not so much older than I am."

She smiled. "I would never try to be your mother, anyway."

"I have a mother," he said shortly.

Liz stood up, too, and they walked slowly toward the house. "And now you have a friend, too," she said. She reached for his hand and he held her fingers for a brief moment, then let go and strode slightly ahead of her. At the open doors to the living room, he stopped. "I won't go in, if you don't mind. I've got to get back to the office," he said.

"Yes, of course."

"Thank you for the lunch . . . Liz."

"Nico . . . thank you."

"Right," he said brusquely, and turned to go around the house to his car.

Liz watched him for a moment, then rejoined the decorators.

A few weeks later, on a lovely sunny morning, Socrates and Kazakos, two men who worked for Theo, came to breakfast. Liz handled her duties as hostess with her customary grace and warmth. They all gathered around the table in the garden, exclaiming over the incredible view of Athens below.

A small plane was circling the Acropolis, and

266

they watched as it dipped low over Constitution Square. The pilot was a daredevil; now he buzzed down, barely skimming the Lysikrates, then turned upward at a steep angle and headed directly for their hilltop. In a moment, the plane was directly over their heads, swooping dangerously low to salute them. A wing veered close to the lemon trees, and there was a sudden swoosh of leaves trembling in its wake.

"Crazy!" Theo yelled up at the pilot. He shook his fist and shouted. "Stupid!"

The plane buzzed away, waggling its wings in a sassy gesture.

"My son," Theo explained to his guests. "My crazy son, Nico."

They watched as the little plane looped in a wide figure eight, then shot away toward the airfield at the other end of the city.

"He's quite a flyer," said Socrates.

"With *kolokyfhi* for a brain!" Theo muttered angrily.

"I don't know, Theo," Kazakos put in. "That was quite a thing he did for you on the airline deal."

"It's true," Theo sighed. "The thing with the airline was like a genius." He glowered back up at the cloudless sky, in the direction that the little plane had disappeared. "But then he does things like that! Crazy! Ah, Nico . . . Nico . . ."

Liz smiled. She poured coffee for Socrates and Kazakos. "He's beautiful," she said. "A little wild, but beautiful. A nice boy."

Theo shrugged. "Whatever she says." He nodded, not looking at her. "Anyhow, what we were saying . . . politics . . . I disagree with you, Socrates, Kazakos. Both of you. Go look at the figures, the trends. The vast majority of the world's population lives in planned economies."

"I know, I know," Socrates mused. "But there is no simple, unqualified answer, as you suggest." This was an old argument among the three of them. For years they had fallen into the same discussion; it was almost a tradition.

"He's right!" Liz agreed.

Theo turned to her, his eyes wide with surprise. The other men stared at her also.

"Look what's happening in England," she said. "What's finally going to happen there? Another Socialist state?"

Theo was furious. "What the hell do you know?" he shouted. "This is politics! What the hell do you know about politics?"

She sat rigid, turning white, her eyes stunned.

"I'm talking to these gentlemen about something you know nothing about," Theo said, dismissing her. He turned back to Socrates and Kazakos.

Somehow she found the strength in her legs to get up from the table and walk away from them. The men were silent, embarrassed, as they watched her stiff back until she had gone through the little arbor into the dappled shade of the trees.

Making a joke of it, Theo grinned and said, "But money she knows. Oh, yes . . . she can . . ." He trailed off. The other men were concentrating on their breakfasts, Socrates carefully picking the flesh from his trout with the heavy silver fish fork, Kazakos sipping his coffee with his eyes lowered.

Theo looked toward the arbor. Liz stood in the dim cool path between the olive trees with her face buried in her two hands. Then, suddenly, she began to run, away from him, down the slope of the garden.

"Excuse me," Theo said. He threw down his napkin and rose from the table. "A little fight . . . a little love . . . you know how it is."

He strode across to the arbor, but she was still running. She turned at the rose garden and was out of his sight. He walked quickly after her, cursing under his breath.

"Lizzie . . . Liz-zeee!"

She didn't answer. He came to the rose garden. Not there. He glanced toward the tennis court, the lemon grove, the pool. Nowhere.

"Liz-zeee!"

He turned toward the tall trees on the south slope, but there was no answer, no sign of her. Then he saw her, sitting on the wide stone steps of the terrace that flanked the sculpted fountain. The delicate spray of water from the fountain was the only sound.

"Lizzie?"

Her face was still buried in her hands. He sat down on the step beside her.

"I'm sorry," he said in a gentle voice.

She looked up at him. Tears stained her face. He reached out a finger to touch one of the clear drops on her cheek.

"I didn't mean—"

She slapped his hand from her, hard. "Don't touch me, you peasant! Peasant!"

He stood up, glaring down at her with a wonder composed of both fury and amusement. It was the most life she had shown since their wedding night.

She stood too, and faced him with clenched

fists and flaming eyes. "You boor . . . you miserable son of a bitch!"

She had never raised her voice in her whole life, and she didn't now. The soft tremulous pitch and her impeccable diction made her words seem all the more violent.

Theo stared at her in shock and admiration.

"You animal!" she went on. "You . . . insulting me in front of those people . . . *how dare you . . . bastard!*"

Suddenly her fists were swinging into him, pounding him on the chest, arms, face. He raised his hands to ward off the blows.

"Lizzie . . . wait . . . wait . . ."

"Bastard! Bastard! Bastard!" she cried softly. The tears streamed down her cheeks, and she continued to flail at him. He managed to grip her arms.

"Lizzie . . . I want to talk to you . . . wait . . . listen. Lizzie . . . wait . . ."

His strength held her. She was helpless in her frustration and rage. Tears poured from her eyes.

"Are you going to behave?" he asked sternly.

She stared at him wildly, and then he saw the heat go out of her. Her body slumped in acquiescence. She blinked hard.

He waited a moment, then released her from his grasp. "Listen to me," he said calmly.

"You!" she burst out. In a single quick movement, her sandal-clad foot came up sharply to kick him in the crotch. He was too quick for her. He grabbed her ankle and grinned. "Such an emotion!" he said admiringly.

"Put down my leg," she ordered coldly. She put one hand on the fountain pedestal to balance herself. The indignity of her position did not diminish her regal stance. She was a queen—if a peasant oaf had her by the leg, it was nothing to her. Off with his head. Theo had to laugh, it was delicious.

"Are you going to be nice?" he asked.

"I want my leg," she said, glaring at him.

He released her.

"Now I know what I'm married to. A clown and a boor and ..."

"... and common and an animal ... and you're fantastic," he grinned.

"Peasant!" she said in disgust.

"Peasant ... bastard ..." He touched his cheek where her nails had grazed the skin. No blood, but it stung a bit. "Jesus Christ," he said, "what a woman!"

She was startled by the pleasure in his voice. "Bullshit, Theo," she said quietly.

She turned to go back to the house, but he grabbed her arm.

"No, it's true," he protested. "What happened to the Cassidys . . . those nice, proper people, the lady who had no feelings. Who was that woman who tried to kick me in the balls just now? Hey!"

He turned her to face him. "Let's go make love," he said huskily.

She stared at him. The turmoil within her was subsiding now, but the rage and hatred were turning into something equally disturbing, something uncontrolled, terrifying. The admiration in his eyes, the husky invitation, were overwhelmingly tempting. . . .

"You're crazy," she said angrily.

"Lizzie ..."

"Let go of me, Theo."

271

"Lizzie . . . don't throw it away. The first time I ever saw you cry, get angry, ever try to tear my eyes out . . . a whole new Lizzie . . ."

She looked away, not understanding or trusting the whirling eddy of feelings that had been let loose inside her.

"Lizzie, listen . . . what happened . . . I'm sorry. Truly. Never again.

Crickets were singing in the deep grass nearby; the fountain trickled merrily behind them. He meant it, she knew that. His promises were kept.

"Listen to me," he said. She looked at him now, her eyes huge, not trusting, but wanting to. "I love you," he said.

He took her arm and she went with him a few steps toward the house. "Now come on," he murmured, "to the bed with the thing on top, the one you like?"

She stopped in her tracks. "No."

He smiled, a little half-smile, teasing. Almost pleading. "A different bed?"

"No bed," she said flatly.

He said softly, "*To krevati ine tehni.* Do you know what that means?"

Liz shook her head. She wanted a nap, a dark, cool room with the curtains drawn and the shutters closed against the unrelenting heat, the sun, the world. Closed against him, and the dizzying terror of the emotions he roused in her.

"It means, 'The bed is an art,'" Theo said.

She did not smile. "By an old Greek," she said. "You."

"It is an art," he repeated. He put his arms around her, holding her closely. His embrace was like a safe haven—if only she could believe it.

272

"An art," he said. "And we do it so well. And I love you."

She let her head rest on his shoulder. "Oh, Theo ... Theo ..." It was like a sob.

Then she moved away. "No," she said.

"Why not?"

"It's ten o'clock in the morning." She ventured a little smile, and her hand reached up to wipe the dried tears from her cheek.

"I'm an animal." Grinning, he moved toward her, took her in his arms again.

"We have guests," she murmured.

"They're Greeks," he said, "they know. They'll finish their orange juice and go home." He kissed her nose. "Such a beautiful nose. ..."

Their mouths met, sweetly, hungrily. Then they turned and walked arm in arm toward the house.

In the leafy shade of the arbor he kissed her again, and then he said, "In the contract, Lizzie ... how many more times would you have been available to me?"

She smiled. "This month? Let me think ... six, six more times."

"Good," he laughed. "We'll leave a call for Thursday."

CHAPTER FIFTEEN

Slowly, slowly, she was opening to him. For so long, the hidden dark waters of her emotions had lain quiescent, layered away from her own consciousness with socially acceptable manners and thoughts and polite preoccupations. Now she was beginning to learn to trust: him and herself. She had so much love to give, and he needed love—her love—desperately. And she, too, had her needs; he was teaching her that. Despite his occasional crudeness and his unpredictable rages and demands, she was slowly being led by his candor and undisguised lust into a recognition of her darker self. She had begun to understand that the terror of the unknown could be transformed—it seemed a miracle—into a revelation of herself as a woman. Theo lay sleeping now, his head cradled against her breast, and she was thinking not of herself, but of him. How vulnerable he was at this moment, spent, lying sprawled half across her.

She looked up at the satin canopy over the bed and thought: we have a long way to go. Into uncharted territory. Can we make it together? It seemed so, at this moment.

Someone tapped on the bedroom door. Theo stirred in his sleep, moving closer to her, sighing. She listened to the repeated knock, willing the intruder to go away, leave them alone.

The knock came again, more insistent. Carefully, Liz tried to extricate herself from Theo's embrace without waking him. She kissed his shoulder lightly as she slid out from beneath his heavy body. She reached for her robe and went quickly to the door.

"Yes?" she whispered. "Yes, what is it?"

"Please," the muffled voice of a servant murmured on the other side of the door. "Mr. Tomasis. Please."

She glanced behind her and saw him stir fitfully on the bed. She opened the door an inch or so and spoke quickly to the man who stood there.

"He's asleep," she whispered impatiently. "What is it?"

"Lizzie?" Theo called drowsily. He sat up. "What is it?"

The servant was agitated. He spoke so Theo could hear. "*Afentiko* . . ."

Theo reached for his robe and shrugged into it. He came across the room. "What is it, for Christ's sake," he growled through the crack in the door. "What do you want?"

When there was no answer, Theo pulled the

door open wider, and his tone became sharp. "What?" he asked the servant. "What?"

"Nico," the man said, trembling.

"Nico?"

The servant began babbling in Greek. He was terribly upset, wringing his hands as he spoke. Theo stood absolutely still, listening. Liz looked from one to the other, not understanding a word.

"Topethi . . . Chtipise me to aeroplano . . . Nicos . . . Skotothike . . . Skotothike . . ." The servant broke into tears.

"What is it? What's happened?" Liz cried, seeing Theo's face go white. He leaned one hand against the wall to support himself.

"The plane. Nico . . . Nico . . . is dead," he told her blankly.

"Oh, my God!"

Theo slumped suddenly to his knees. His head bent, he wrapped his arms around his body and began to rock slowly in a terrible, solitary agony. Groans thrust up from his throat.

Liz sank to her knees beside him. She reached out to hold him, but he was oblivious to her, to anything but the sorrow that engulfed him. His groans became the wailing of a soul in hell.

"Theo . . . Theo . . ." Liz looked helplessly up at the terrified servant, who stood with tears streaming down his weathered old face.

Theo's tortured body rocked from side to side. Then, with a shriek, he banged his forehead against the carpet and rose slowly to his hands and knees. His howls were a terrible litany: "Nico . . . Nico . . . Nico . . . Nico . . . Nico . . . Aaaiiiiii . . . Nico . . ."

"Oh my God . . . my God!" Liz cried.

The servant came close, but she motioned him away. Again and again she touched Theo's shoulder, his knotted, trembling arm, his head that rocked from side to side. But it was as if she didn't exist; nothing and no one existed for him now.

"Go away," she said to the old man, who nodded and backed away from the awful sight of his master on his hands and knees. To have been the messenger of such tidings. . . . She could hear his wails as he closed the door.

"Theo, Theo . . ." She tried again to hold him in her arms, and after a long while he turned to her. She rocked him, crooning, until his terrible moans subsided at last.

"Theo . . . Theo . . . my love . . . my dear . . ."

He clung to her then, and let the weeping begin.

The blessed anesthesia of shock took over. Numbed, he walked through the funeral rites with Liz at his side. He took Simi in his arms to console her, accepted Spyros' handclasp, bowed his head as the priest guided Nico's dead spirit to eternity. He was grateful to Liz, although he never said so. He didn't have to; she knew. She knew by the way he looked for her if she strayed from his side; she knew by the way he held her tightly in his arms during the long sleepless nights. She, too, knew what it was to suffer deep, irreparable loss. Once again, the photographers flashed on the sad sight of the beautiful, frail, veiled woman in black, clinging to a man's arm. But this time it was she who was the strength. The whole world wept for her again, a little less than before, a little weary of her sadnesses and joys.

Theo was to be awarded a Gold Medal of Industrial Achievement by the government of Norway. He had planned to fly to Oslo to pick it up, after a series of conferences in Geneva, London and Helsinki. But Liz prevailed on him to cancel the business meetings and to take *La Belle Simone*, alone with her, from Piraeus to the Norwegian port. It would be a reprieve for him, a time for the healing to begin.

On the yacht he spent long hours at the rail looking out at the water, deep in his own sad thoughts. She watched, aching for him, knowing from her own experience about the cutting pain of accepting the finality. She knew he must live it through alone, but she was there for him.

One night she woke to find him gone from their bed. She pulled on her robe to go and find him. He was at the railing of the deck outside their sitting room, barefoot, wearing only his white slacks. He was staring out at the calm sea, the dark expanse of moonless sky. She came up behind him quietly and did not speak.

He explained softly, "Sleep is a very difficult thing."

She raised her hand to his back, stroking the taut flesh over his muscles. "Yes, I know," she said. "For me, too."

"Why, Lizzie . . . why?" He spoke without emotion, knowing there was no answer.

"Come to bed," she murmured, "I need to feel you there."

He nodded slowly. "Soon."

She laid her head against his bare shoulder, and they stood together for a long time, not speaking.

At last he sighed, took her in his arms, and led her back to bed.

In the morning, there were papers to be signed; there always were. Theo had them spread out on the deck table before him, but she could tell he wasn't really concentrating. She held a book on her lap, but she had been observing him instead of reading. Their chairs were close together, facing the morning sun, not the fierce hot sun of Greece now, but the cooler rays of the sea to the north.

Theo had grown visibly older in the weeks since Nico's death, Liz thought. Was it the deeper grayness in his hair, new folds of flesh around his eyes. . . ? No, it was a letting down, a retreat that she could sense in his entire posture, a kind of giving up. He had blankets wrapped around his legs, and his face was drawn, bored. Bored? Theo? It was frightening to think of Theo bored with life, this man to whom life was the greatest game of all, this lover of excitement and challenge. He had taught her to live, to feel—now he seemed to be letting life slip from himself. She couldn't bear it.

Theo sighed and closed his eyes.

It's up to me, Liz thought suddenly. I can return the gift he's given me. I can try, anyway. What else is it for?

She got up from her chair, knelt beside him, leaned over and kissed him on the mouth. Startled, he opened his eyes.

"Hey!"

She laid her fingertips along his lips. "I'm not finished," she murmured. She moved her hand

279

away and pressed her mouth to his, lovingly transferring the beat of her own pulse to him.

He stared at her. Papers slid from his lap onto the deck. "What was that for?" he asked. His tentative smile indicated that the transfusion was not in vain.

"Because I wanted to," she said, smiling. "You see?"

He nodded, and Liz noticed that his lower lip had a slight, almost invisible tic that she had never seen before. She stood and moved to the rail. She turned to face him, leaning on her elbows with the sun behind her.

"You're very dear," she said softly. "You are, Theo."

He was deeply touched. After a moment, he brushed the folders from his lap and came to stand close to her. He put his arms around her.

"You too," he said. "You are very, very dear to me, Lizzie."

"Theo . . ." She pulled away. "I'm not happy with you, Theo."

He frowned. "What?"

"How you look," she said.

He gestured with his hand, as if to brush away her fears. "Ahhh . . ."

"There's only so much you can grieve," she said, reaching out to touch his face.

"No." He caught her hand and held it against his mouth, kissing her palm. "You see . . ." He stopped, not knowing what it was he wanted to say. "You see, Nico . . ."

It was the first time he had said his son's name, and saying it seemed to release something in him, as she had hoped it would. Now the words flowed out.

"Nico . . . ah, Lizzie . . . my son Nico was beautiful. He was my life, my eternity. He was headstrong and smart, smarter than me, even . . . and beautiful, yes, beautiful like his mother . . . he was . . ." He broke off, close to tears. The kind of tears, she knew, that would wash and refresh and bring a kind of peace.

"Hey, I'm tired, Lizzie," he said.

She nodded. "Theo . . . see somebody, will you do that? A doctor? Let him look at you . . . tests . . . for my sake, if not for your own?"

"Sure, sure."

"Will you?"

"Sure," he promised. She nodded, and then hugged him tightly, feeling the cold wind of mortality sweeping past them like the breeze from the north.

"Hey, hey, what's this?" he laughed.

She pulled back so he could see her face, and he recognized what he saw there.

"Me, too," he said.

They stood together as the yacht cut through the choppy water like a knife, clean and fast and effortlessly. They would survive; they were survivors to their toes—Theo and Liz and *La Belle Simone*.

"I'm excited about going to Norway, Theo," Liz said. "I'm very proud."

"Yes." He nodded. "Me, too. Proud of you, my wife."

They were greeted in Norway by polite but insistent reporters and photographers who followed them everywhere. Theo smiled when requested, put his arm around his wife, waved, shook hands with the industrialists and shipping magnates who posed with them, accepted the award solemnly and graciously, smiled again and again, and seemed to the world to have recovered from his great loss. The newspapers and magazines marveled at the virility and strength of this remarkable man, at the obvious love between him and his famous, beautiful wife.

During the nights he prowled *La Belle Simone* or the hotel suite, and lay open-eyed for hours with Liz sleeping in his arms. He hardly looked in the mirror any more; he didn't want to see what he knew was there. He refused sleeping pills or medicine of any kind, as he always had. But when they returned to Athens, he let her make an appointment with the doctor, and he kept it.

He sat waiting, after all the tests and X-rays, electrocardiograms and blood samples and urine specimens and poking and prodding, waiting impatiently for the doctor to say what the results were.

The thoracic X-rays were on a viewing bank, lit from behind. As the middle-aged Greek doctor studied them, Theo sat on a straight chair by the doctor's desk, drumming his fingers on the glass top.

"Well?" he said at last. "Come on, come on. What the hell do you see?"

The doctor, refusing to be harassed or hurried, snapped off the lightbox. He swiveled his chair back to face the desk and looked down at the huge pages of electrocardiograph readings spread out there.

"Hah?" Theo burst out, his patience at an end.

The doctor looked up. "Theo . . . why don't you retire?"

Theo snorted. "To what?"

"To an easy life. Why not? You've got everything."

Theo pointed to the EKG readings on the desk. "Explain to me," he demanded.

The doctor leaned back in his chair. "And didn't I read recently that you've won a medal? A gold medal from Norway?"

Theo nodded. "An honor." He jabbed his finger at the charts again. "What?"

Refusing to be bullied, the doctor kept his tone soothing, professionally friendly. "Theo, you have honor and money . . . everything. What else do you want?"

"More," Theo said curtly. Then he, too, leaned back in his chair. He smiled. "Can you keep a secret?" He waited for the medical man's nod. "I want to be president. President of Greece."

The doctor was startled, and showed it.

"A secret, okay?" Theo said, and the doctor nodded. "Now I have a question," Theo went on. "Okay?"

The doctor nodded again. He realized that this was no ordinary patient, not one to be put off by subtle warnings and soothing words.

"Wait," Theo said. "Before the question, another look, if you please." He gestured at the EKG charts. The doctor looked down at them automatically, then back up at his patient, waiting for instructions.

"If I were to become president," Theo said, "if I became the president of Greece . . . who would serve the longest, my vice-president or me?"

The ringing telephone broke in, and the doctor picked up the receiver. Before speaking, he cupped his hand over it and said solemnly, "Your vice-president."

Theo waited, absorbing the stab of shock, not showing anything on his face.

"Yes?" the doctor said into the phone. He handed it to Theo. "For you."

Theo took the receiver. "Tomasis," he said.

As the message was given to him, flashes of a dream he had lived through in his troubled sleep the night before came tumbling across his mind. He had been standing before the Oracle of Delphi, feeling very small in the huge empty temple, and the Oracle had said to him in a resonant, inhuman voice, "Deaths come in threes." Theo had woken to wander the rooms of his house, trying to shake off the dream. Now it came back to him, and the words that came over the telephone wire were no more human, no more real, no more terrible than the dream. His face went white. The doctor leaned forward.

"Mother of God . . ." Theo whispered into the telephone. "When? Where?" He listened, stiffening with the blow of the terrible news. Then he hung up the phone and stared blankly across the desk.

"My wife," he said. "My wife is dead. She killed herself."

The doctor rose from his chair and came around to him, but Theo was already at the door.

"Theo, please . . . excitement, sorrow . . . you've had too much. A sedative . . . I'll give you something."

But when his patient turned back to him, the doctor saw that hard steel had replaced the mortal bone and muscle and tissue. The man who left his office had no need of the puny miracles of science.

The doctor went to the window and watched as Theo strode from the building into the street below and stepped into his black Rolls Royce.

CHAPTER SIXTEEN

Spyros Tomasis's house was on its own hill, in a suburb of Athens. It took the driver nearly twenty minutes to get there. Theo sat alone in the back seat, shaking his head as if to waken from the nightmare, moaning softly to himself, covering his face with his hands as great sobs ripped from his throat. But by the time the car wound into the driveway, his sorrow had turned to rage. He leaped from the car before it came to a full stop and took the steps three at a time. He pounded on the door, which was quickly opened. Theo shoved the butler aside and pushed his way into the reception hall.

"Where is he?" he shouted.

Several servants, weeping, had gathered there, and one pointed to a pair of thick oak doors. Theo strode across the hall and pushed the doors open.

Spyros Tomasis sat at a desk with his head cradled in his arms. The room was dark, the drapes pulled against the sunlight. A dim lamp spread an orange glow from a far corner.

"I'm going to kill you, you son of a bitch!" Theo roared. He closed the doors behind him and snapped the lock. "Like you killed my Simi . . . my wife, my Simi . . ."

Spyros looked up. His eyes were bleary and swollen. "Crazy," he said, "you're crazy! My wife, Theo . . . *my* wife . . . not yours."

"You killed her!" Theo took a step toward the desk, and stopped. His whole body was taut with the need to strike, to revenge his Simi, to destroy this pig of a man who had touched her, killed her.

"She killed herself," Spyros sobbed. He slumped back in his chair. "Get out of here," he said wearily. "Crazy bastard . . . go, get out of here."

Theo strode to the desk and reached out to grab Spyros by the collar of his shirt.

"Why?" he growled. "Why did she do that . . . beautiful Simi . . . killed herself . . . why? What did you do to her, animal, to make her hate life . . . to kill herself? Why? Why?"

Spyros jumped up, knocking Theo's hand away. He, too, was shouting now.

"Why? Who knows what went on in her head? Why? She took pills, she died!"

The disgust in Spyros' voice made Theo's bitter rage spill over. He grabbed for Spyros and shoved him forcefully against the wall. Spyros' head hit the paneling with a thud, and he began to slump to the carpet. He caught himself and came slowly to his feet again. He stood staring at Theo, rubbing his throat.

"She didn't like her life, so she died!" Theo spat at him.

"She had a wonderful life, Theo . . . everything. I loved her. I don't understand . . ."

"You've got shit in your brain, you don't understand! I had her, so you had to have her."

Spyros nodded sadly. He spread his trembling hands wide, in a gesture of helplessness. "Yet I loved her," he said. "Like you, I loved her."

Theo howled with outrage and anguish. "What I do, you try to be me . . ."

"You do the same, Theo," Spyros pointed out. "What I have, you have to spoil if you can . . . we are the same . . ."

Theo's throat constricted and he made a sound as if he would vomit. The bile that rose in him was hate and pain; the man cowering before him was the epitome of all that he hated—yes, in himself too. All, all was gone now. Nico, the beautiful, the only son. Simi, his wife . . . this man had despoiled her, fouled her beauty, her life. She was gone. Only Spyros remained, his brother, his arch-enemy. Only . . . the two of them in this terrible emptiness.

"My wife . . ." Theo wailed. "My wife . . . Simi . . ."

"You're crazy!" Spyros yelled. "Get out of here!"

"Dead! My God! My God. You, Spyros . . . because of you, she's dead. . . !"

"No!" Spyros shouted wildly. "You! You! That crazy head of yours . . . it was because of you, you had to have everything . . . the actress, the skinny American queen . . . Simi wasn't enough for you. . . ."

With an animal roar Theo hurled himself at Spyros, his hands grasping to slash and destroy the leering horror of the stubbled face. He threw himself on his rival, but Spyros fought back. He kneed Theo in the groin, raised his hands to ward off further blows.

They were not young any more. The battle was joined too late for one bull to destroy the other. Their juices spent, their agility gone, they struggled together out of pure hate, but emotion was exhausted now too, and the exertion of tearing at each other brought groans and gasps. A lamp was knocked to the floor, the papers from the desk went flying, the chair fell on its side as the two aging minotaurs locked horns.

The servants began to pound at the library door, crying out. The two men stumbled, swung at each other, missed, connected. A blow to the chest, a kick too low, a wild punch grazing a shoulder. Grunts, shouts, oaths, dry gasping sobs.

Spyros fell to the floor and lay there, gulping for breath. His back and shoulders heaved in a mighty last effort to pull himself up; he failed and slumped back down. Theo was still on his feet, but only barely. His legs buckled under him, and he slid to the floor on his knees.

Theo's mouth hung open, slack. He couldn't catch his breath. He stared at Spyros, stared and stared, and Spyros stared back. In the dim light, the two confronted each other at last, eye to eye, and in each other they saw themselves and accepted the finality of it.

Theo reached his hand toward Spyros. Spyros' hand, impotent on the heavy carpet, opened slightly, the fingers spread upward. Theo touched them with his own. Then Spyros's fingers closed lightly over Theo's.

Theo nodded, and a last low moan escaped his throat. Spyros sat up slowly. Crouched there, they regarded each other and each nodded in turn. It was not a truce, could never be. It was a kind of contract, an understanding for the moment, a passage of rage into shared grief.

"Your whole life," Theo said quietly, "your whole life, you try to be . . . your whole damn life, Spyros, you want to be like me. Why?"

Spyros nodded. "Why?" he repeated. "Like you do, Theo. Without me . . . to do something better than me . . . without that, you would be nothing."

Theo thought this over, and then he said, "With the tanker, with the *Selena* . . . who was better. Tell me, who?"

"One tanker!" Spyros shot back. "And the fleet of tankers, a whole navy of tankers they took back from you, the U.S.? Hey, Theo, why . . . tell me, why did they do that?"

Theo growled deep in his throat, too spent for anger. The two men could have been talking of the weather, for all the emotion that passed between them now.

"Me!" Spyros crooned. "I made it happen, Theo. I fucked you."

Theo shook his head wearily and sighed.

"Sylvie, too." Smirking, Spyros leaned forward, his head almost touching Theo's. The shadowy light in the room made their intimacy, as they sat there together on the floor, almost obscene. "Sylvie, too," Spyros goaded.

"Sylvie?" Theo was puzzled. The name called up no image to him. He thought probably he had done something to the inside of Spyros's head, messed up his brain. The old man was no good for anything any more.

"Sylvie," Spyros said. "The virgin Sylvie, you called her . . . what? Wild . . . sweet . . . and you would kiss her hair, and you would not touch her because she was nineteen and as beautiful as dawn, you would tell her. Remember now, Theo?"

Theo stared at him.

"How do I know?" Spyros gloated. "She would tell me what you said before we made love, after . . . and we would laugh!" He seemed to be getting his strength back; his ugly face had found its customary leer. Theo was not aware that his own face had gone quite haggard.

"Hey, Theo," Spyros went on softly. "Sylvie? With me, there was no end to her passion."

He waited, and then, with enormous contempt, he sneered, "Because I am better, Theo! From the beginning . . . better! Richer! Better! With the women, with the tankers, with the world . . . better than you!"

"You are nothing," Theo said slowly, deliberately. "You are old. Old."

They sat in the fading reaches of the light, and both knew it to be true.

"And you," Spyros said softly. "You too!"

"Yes," Theo agreed. "And now . . . Simi is dead."

"I loved her, Theo, I loved her too. But I was not you. With Simi . . . I was not you."

"Ah, Spyros, Spyros, what foolish old men we are. Now we have no one."

"You have a wife, Theo."

Theo's eyes opened wide. Yes, it was Spyros who was alone now, not he.

With a groan he raised himself to his feet and stood gingerly, feeling his mouth where Spyros had landed a lucky punch. He looked down at the man on the floor. Then, reluctantly, he held out a hand to help his brother to his feet.

"Do you like it?"

In their suite on *La Belle Simone*, she was posing for him, a new gown. A Balenciaga, a new design especially for the prince's ball. Magnificent, sparkling, a dress only she could wear, but it would be copied thousands of times after she was seen in it, and the original would be given away, never to be worn again. She looked splendid, more beautiful than ever. Pirouetting slowly before him, she watched for his reaction.

He smiled, but there was no light in his eyes. There had been none for many months, since Nico died. How she wished she could find a way to make him laugh, a way to bring him back to her.

"It's fantastic," he said.

"You're certain?" she asked, suddenly unsure of herself.

She gestured toward her closet, where another gown hung waiting. "Or I could wear that one. Shall I try on that one for you? I want to look beautiful, so beautiful. I want you to be proud of me, Theo . . ."

He only nodded, a fixed smile on his lips. His thoughts were somewhere else, and she knew few ways of calling him back.

"I'll try on that one, and you decide," she said. "Here, help me with the zipper."

She backed close to him and he reached up from his chair to slide the zipper down her back. His

292

fingers grazed her flesh as the dress opened to reveal her smooth straight back, but he made no move to caress her. She stepped out of the gown and turned to face him. Naked except for brief lacy panties, she hesitated a fraction of a second, looking down at him.

"Hey, Theo," she whispered.

He opened his arms and she cuddled close to him, but when he made no other movement, she sighed and moved away. She threw the Balenciaga across a chair and reached for the other gown, a Sant'Angelo.

"You haven't told me yet, Theo," she said as she pulled it over her head.

"About what?"

"About the doctor. What did he say?"

He shrugged. The dress was on now, and she was adjusting its straps in the mirror. She watched his reflection.

"He said . . . he said," Theo muttered, as if there was no importance to it.

"Said what?" she asked carefully.

"I shouldn't be president of Greece," he answered surprisingly.

Liz turned to face him. "I'd leave you if you were," she laughed. "Why on earth did he say that?"

"I have everything, he told me. Who needs it?"

"Good," she answered. She moved toward him, concentrating on the sweep of the new gown, the feel of it against her body. "You like this one?"

"Fantastic."

"For the prince's party." She glowed with excitement. "Can't you see my entrance? I love it. Do you?"

He nodded.

"Yes, I think this one. Or do you prefer the other?"

"This one," he said, feigning interest.

"Theo . . ."

"Or the other one, they're both fantastic," he said.

"Theo . . . are you going to mind my going to Paris first?"

He shook his head.

"But you'll be alone," she said.

"Only for a week. I'll work here, on the yacht. People will come to see me, business. Only for a week. You go ahead, have a good time."

She grinned at him and turned back to the closet. She took out another dress, a short, daytime one. It was smashing, a soft wool blend of cashmere, in warm beige, her best color.

"And this one for shopping," she said, showing it off to him.

"Shopping, yes. Very pretty."

"Karen's going to meet me at the Georges V, and maybe Nancy and John. They're invited to the prince's party, too, of course, but Theo. . . ?"

He looked at her, the smile still frozen on his face.

"Are you sure?" she asked.

"Lizzie, it's been so long since you've been to Paris, to parties . . . sure, hey . . . both of us, we come and go, that's our life. Go to Paris, what is a week? And we'll meet, how happy I will be to see you again. Meet friends on the Champs and buy things, and laugh . . . do it, Lizzie."

But suddenly, she wasn't quite sure.

"Theo . . ."

"Do it."

His smile widened to show that he meant it, but he had taught her to know the difference between real feeling and merely trying. He was still hurting from the loss of Nico, and she could only wait for him to come back to her, roaring like he used to, raunchy and vulgar and loving.

"But I worry when I'm not with you," she said tenderly.

"Lizzie . . . show me the dress again."

She held it up. "Do you really like it?"

"Fantastic," he said.

She had to be content with that. She ran her hand along the softness of the dress, and decided it would do. She slipped out of the evening gown and stood in her brief panties, her back to him, while she went over the wardrobe she had assembled for her trip. Had she forgotten anything—shoes for each outfit, all the skirts and sweaters—she'd have to make up her mind which ones to take—or take them all, and decide which to wear on the spur of the moment once she was in Paris.

When she turned back to the room, Theo had gone. Her heart ached for him, but she remembered grief and knew that only the passage of time could bring him back to her, to reality. She would be kind and patient and loving, and she would make herself as beautiful and desirable as she could be, so he would see her again and want her. Want her, Liz—not the other.

A shudder went through her as she faced the truth. It was Simi he mourned, his wife. It was suddenly cold in the Demeter suite, and Liz reached hurriedly into the closet for a robe to cover herself. Should she take the six little silk dresses? One never knew. . . . It was several hours before she had made up her mind on everything and was ready to leave the yacht.

"You sure you'll be all right?" she asked Theo. "Not . . . lonely or anything?"

"Of course. Only a week, Lizzie. I'll see you in a week. Now you do plenty of shopping, okay? Spend a lot of money!"

"Oh I can do that, all right!" she laughed.

He helped her down the steps into the launch, and she turned to receive his kiss.

"Take care, Theo . . . take care of yourself."

"Lizzie! It's only for a week, for Christ's sake. I'm fine, fine."

"Yes . . . I know."

"Goodbye, Lizzie. See you in Paris."

She clung to him for a moment, and then, aware of the captain's discreet glance, she let go. Theo stepped back aboard *La Belle Simone,* and the launch revved its motor.

"Take care, Theo, you hear?" she called back at him. He smiled and waved as he watched the launch move off, its lights visible in the dark night off Mykonos like a bright star streaking away from him.

He was jolted suddenly by the ear-splitting shriek of the ship's alarm. He turned quickly. Crewmen and sailors were running across the deck, heading for the corridor behind the dining salon. He followed them and put out his hand to stop one of the officers who was bolting down the steps from the bridge.

"*Fotia sto mihanostasio!*" the officer shouted. Theo ran with him toward the galley.

The huge kitchen was filled with acrid smoke. It

poured out into the corridor in billowy puffs, choking the men who rushed through it. Theo moved with the others into the galley and saw the flames spurting upward from the enormous stainless steel ovens against the interior bulkheading. Two crewmen were spraying the blaze with chemical foam from fire extinguishers, and the fire was already under control.

"Give it to me," Theo told a sailor, and the man handed over his hose and pump. Theo directed the foam into the last traces of fire, which simmered and sputtered, then gave up a final black stench of smoke. It was over.

Theo handed the extinguisher back to the sailor. As the smoke cleared through the ventilator, he looked around at the glum faces of the men standing about the huge galley.

"Hey . . . what?" he exclaimed. "What . . . you're thinking bad luck? A fire on ship . . . nothing! A fable! So, somebody will eat a piece of herring and fix it, hah? So not to worry, okay?"

He grinned, and the men nodded sheepishly back at him.

"Okay," Theo said. He walked out of the galley.

One of the chefs went to the fish locker, opened the wide door, and surveyed the store of smoked salmon, gravlox, lobsters and shrimps, clams and *kalamaraki*. He reached for a crock in the back of the refrigerator, pulled it out, and set it down on the counter nearby. Solemnly, the chef pried open the lid. He reached inside with a long-handled fork and speared a piece of dilled herring. While the others watched, he swallowed a bite of the salty fish, then offered pieces all around.

Theo leaned over the railing, looking out at the

297

night. All was still now, and only the bobbing lights of late-homing fishing boats cut the darkness. He walked through the empty salon and out onto the starboard deck that faced the little village on the island. He stared for a while at the twinkling lights there, then turned his back to them. He walked down the deck and turned onto the promenade. He could hear his own footsteps against the polished teak.

He sat down in a lounge chair. It was so quiet, so still. He thought of Liz . . . of Simi . . . of Nico. He thought of Spyros, old and broken, alone. Suddenly he pulled himself up from the chair and strode back toward the central staircase. He nodded at the steward who stood guard there.

"Tell the captain I want a boat," he said. "I'm going to the island."

A few minutes later, an old wool cap pulled over his ears, he climbed down the steps to the waiting launch. Soon the boat was nearing the lights of the shore. Theo wondered about himself, what he was seeking now. He shook his head. It's true, he thought, I'm old too.

The boat pulled up at the dock and Theo stepped ashore. He walked along the sand where the fishing boats were beached, their nets gleaming wetly in the moonlight. By one boat a boy was squatting, mending his net with a long needle. He looked up as Theo passed, not smiling. He stared until the old man had gone by, then returned to his work.

It was almost *meltemi* time, and the gusts of wind from the north warned of gales to come. As Theo walked along the beach, he hunched his head down into his jacket collar and punched his hands deep into his pockets. The gusts never stopped, in these straits. In summer, the winds were soft; the *bucadura*, the southerly onshore breeze, was the sailor's friend, but in the long winter months the *meltemi* was a menace. Theo felt it in his bones now, and he hurried toward the single light ahead.

He passed a tiny fisherman's café, shuttered against the night. A few yards farther along the quay was a whitewashed building no larger than one of the bathrooms on *La Belle Simone*, a single dim bulb glowing from its window. He knew the place and felt a surge of pleasure at the thought of company, of being out of the bitter wind.

The door was low; he had to bend his head to enter. Inside the *taverna*, the owner dozed in a corner, a mangy dog at his feet. The dog looked up, cocked his scraggly head and watched curiously as Theo took a seat at one of the small tables along the wall. It was silent, except for the sound of the wind rising outside.

"Hey, Stavros," Theo called softly to the old man. The grizzled head stirred, and a pair of bleary eyes peered over at him.

"Retsina," Theo said, "and some herring."

The dog, so lean his ribs stuck out from his sides, rose with the old man and accompanied him listlessly to the bar. In a moment the owner shuffled out again to set a large jar of herring, a flagon of red wine, a glass, fork and plate before Theo.

"How does it go, Stavros?" Theo asked, and the old man grunted in reply. The dog stayed by Theo, watching him, as the owner moved away to resume his nap at the little table at the rear of the damp, lonely room.

Theo reached into the jar, forked out a piece of herring and ate it, for luck. The dog's eyes were enormous in his craven, half-starved head. Theo held out another piece of the fish, and the dog sidled forward to take it from his hand.

Theo poured a glass of retsina and drank it down. The dog licked his chops, then put his head quietly on Theo's knee.

"Another piece of herring?" Theo murmured. "Why not?" He pointed his thumb in the direction of the old man. "A hundred and twenty years old, he and his lucky herring. Maybe it works." He reached for another piece of the fish and gave it to the grateful dog.

"My friend," Theo said to the animal, "I had a ship on fire . . . and you had fleas. Have some herring. For luck. What we need . . . may tonight bring you a friend! A bitch in heat, with lots of fur . . . and a short tail!" He fed the dog one more piece of herring and then got up from the table. He walked over to the proprietor and put some money in the man's apron pocket without disturbing his sleep. When he opened the door of the little *taverna,* the dog hesitated, not sure whether to follow or not. After a moment he made up his mind, and walked out into the silent moonlight with Theo. Then, suddenly, the dog was off by himself, loping contentedly toward his destiny, whatever it might be.

Theo continued along the quay for a few steps and then turned away from the beach toward the lights of the village. His footsteps echoed on the cobblestones, and the *meltemi* whistled briskly in his ears, whipping up the dust in swirls at his feet. There was no one in sight; the village seemed deserted. Here and there, a light burned in one of the neat little white houses. People were indoors at their hearths, in the houses of their fathers with their wives and their children all around them. Theo walked up the street and entered the deserted village square.

The north wind was shrieking now. A piece of old newspaper danced madly, turning and bobbing across the square. Theo walked aimlessly—past the houses, past the *kafeneon*, dark and lonely, past the shops which had taken in their gaudy displays of rugs and shirts meant to tempt the tourists.

The howling whistle of the quirky *meltemi* died for a moment, and Theo heard strains of music—an old folk song, a primitive, wailing song that he knew from long ago. It was sad and happy, a song about the pains and joys of life, telling that life for all its sorrows was good, joyous, a thing to be celebrated.

The wind picked up again, and he could no longer hear the music. But it had come from—where? Ahead of him. He quickened his steps and came to the corner of the square, where the street narrowed to a cobbled pathway. A feeble streak of yellowish light fell across the stones, coming from a door that was slightly ajar. And then Theo heard the music again. A man was singing, an old man with a cracked and sinewy voice, not strong, but true to the melody. And there was a guitar playing, and a drumming; someone was keeping the beat, the pulse of the song about life.

Theo moved down the two stone steps to the doorway and pushed it open. Inside, several very old men were clustered around the musicians, clapping their hands and nodding their heads. A single weak, unshaded light bulb hung over a wooden common table in the center of the little room. Theo stood in the doorway and watched.

The man who beat the rhythm sat hunched over a large painted oil can held between his knees, tapping with gnarled fingers. The guitar player was aged, toothless; he huddled over his instrument, cradling it and crooning to it as his hands moved over the strings. Between them, another old man sat in a chair, singing the words to the song. His face was deeply lined, and his expression was serious, but there was a twinkle in his eyes as he sang the words of joy and sorrow.

In the middle of the little room, several men were dancing the slow ritual movements of the *tsamikos*. Their hands arched over their heads, they moved with ageless grace and dignity around the table, each clutching a corner of the white handkerchiefs they held aloft. They wore old, ill-fitting and stained trousers, fisherman's boots or run-down shoes, white shirts too large for their shriveled bones; they danced solemnly, drawing strength from the music and their companionship. Bottles of cloudy ouzo and half-filled glasses were scattered on the big table. A few of the old men nodded at Theo as he stood there, welcoming him, and one held out his handkerchief in a challenge to join the dance.

Theo moved slowly down the worn steps into the room, remembering the words to the song. It filled him with its bittersweet understanding as he reached out to receive the invitation. Old man, he wanted to say, I am one of you.

He took hold of the handkerchief and began to dance with the others.

THE BEST OF THE BESTSELLERS
FROM WARNER BOOKS!

THE BEST OF THE BESTSELLERS
FROM WARNER BOOKS!